THE HA-HA CASE

J.J. Connington

Spitfire Publishers

CONTENTS

ABOUT 'THE HA-HA CASE'

Johnnie Brandon is found dead while out shooting rabbits with his friends, and the problem is: Accident, Suicide, or Murder? It is all made very complicated by the financial entanglements in which his rapscallion of a father has tied up the estate, and by the fact that a gentlemanly lunatic with large gaps in his memory wanders on to the scene at the crucial moment. Time for the acumen of Chief Constable Sir Clinton Driffield to be brought to bear on the case.

Praise for 'The Ha-Ha Case'

'A remarkably high standard of ingenuity and workmanship'
New York Times

'A sound and interesting plot, very carefully and ingeniously worked out'
The Sunday Times

'A work in every way worthy of J.J. Connington's high reputation as a detective writer'
Dorothy L. Sayers

'The means of the murder are most ingeniously concealed'
Times Literary Supplement

'First-class'
Francis Iles, The Daily Telegraph

CHAPTER 1 THE GIRL
AT THE STATION

As the train glided into the wayside station, Jim Brandon lifted his well-worn suitcase and a shabby leg-of-mutton guncase down from the rack. Through the windows he caught successive glimpses of fresh-painted white palings, trim flower-beds dripping from a recent shower, a girl's figure on a broad sweep of gravelled platform, a tiny station-house, a handful of waiting travellers by the overhead bridge, and a ticket-collector at the gate giving egress into the station yard. Then, with something which sounded like a sigh of relief, the engine came to a standstill, leaving him facing a bank of velvety turf bearing the name AMBLEDOWN picked out in ornamental letters.

He stepped out of his third-class carriage and cast a glance up and down the station, the questing glance of a man who expects a friend to meet him on his arrival. Then a change in his expression betrayed that he had been disappointed.

For a few moments he waited, as though in hope that the truant would even then put in an appearance. Carriage doors slammed; the engine emitted a diffident whistle; behind his back the train gathered way and puffed out on its farther journey. Five or six passengers who had alighted with him filtered past the ticket-collector and vanished. He found himself left on the platform with one porter and the girl in the leather golf-jacket whom he had noticed as the train came in.

Evidently his young brother had let him down, or else his

premonitory telegram had miscarried. Jim Brandon frowned at finding himself in an awkward fix. Ambledown was the station for Edgehill; but, for all he knew, the estate might be miles away. A heavy taxi-fare would bulk over-large in his meagre budget.

He decided to consult the porter. Probably there would be some local motor-bus service which would land him in the neighbourhood of Edgehill, wherever it was. But as he picked up his luggage, the problem was solved for him. The girl came along the platform and, after a momentary doubtful inspection of him, she stepped forward and addressed him.

"Are you Mr Brandon? I'm sorry I didn't recognise you straight away, but you're not in the least like Johnnie. I had to wait till the other passengers cleared out, before I could be sure that it was you."

Then, seeing that he was obviously puzzled, she added a word or two in explanation.

"I'm staying at Edgehill, you know; and when your wire came, I volunteered to meet you with my car. I couldn't bring Johnnie with me. It's only a two-seater and it wouldn't have held three of us on the way back."

Jim Brandon's face cleared. He was there on a delicate mission; and when his brother failed to turn up at the station, he had feared that he was being given the cold shoulder at the very start. It was a relief to find that, after all, Johnnie had not deliberately let him down. A bit off-hand, of course, sending a strange girl along, instead of meeting the train himself. Still, it didn't necessarily prove that Johnnie resented his intrusion. That was all to the good.

"Very kind of you to take so much trouble," he said gratefully. "I was feeling a bit stranded when I found Johnnie hadn't shown up at the station. You see, I haven't a notion where Edgehill is, or how one gets to it from here."

"It isn't a day's run—just a few miles up the road. Will you bring your things along? My car's outside, in the station yard."

Jim Brandon curtly refused the services of the porter, gave up his ticket at the barrier, and followed his guide off the platform.

He had his own reasons for taking an interest in the cost of a girl's clothes, and half-unconsciously he noted the fit of her leather jacket and the cut of her brown tweed skirt. One didn't get that kind of rig-out for nothing, he reflected. One had to pay for that effective simplicity.

A little two-seater, very spick-and-span, was standing at the kerb, and Jim Brandon noted that it was not one of the cheaper models.

"You might strap your things on behind," the girl suggested. "I'm afraid you'll have to nurse my golf-bag. There isn't much room."

He disposed of his luggage and took his place beside her, with the golf-bag between his knees. It was market-day in Ambledown; and the car had to crawl through the little town, avoiding frantic sheep, lethargic cows, and suicidal dogs at every turn. He forbore conversation while she threaded her way amongst the country carts and lorries which crowded the High Street. As they emerged from the town she turned to him with a smile.

"The limit, aren't they? 'Grandpa parked his cart in the High Street, time o' the Crimean War, and what was good enough for Grandpa's good enough for me nowadays.' I like that conservative way of looking at things, though it is a bit of a bore at times, of course."

Jim Brandon nodded agreement. He had admired her coolness and adroitness in meeting the emergencies of that undisciplined traffic. Evidently she was the sort of girl one could rely on in a tight comer. Not the kind to lose her head or get flustered.

"Nice little bus," he said, by way of making conversation. "What can you get out of her?"

"Johnnie and I came up to Edgehill with a lot of luggage at the back, and we were doing fifty-five most of the way."

"Pretty good, that. Johnnie driving?"

The girl at his elbow laughed gently and shook her head.

"Johnnie most distinctly *not* driving. My nerves are fair, Mr Brandon, but they aren't good enough for that, I assure you. Once was enough. I'll never trust him with my car again, after that. I wouldn't even lend him it to meet you at the station today, for fear of what he might do on the road. That's why I came myself."

"Johnnie always was one of the slap-crash brigade," his brother admitted. "Careless young beggar. He'll come to grief one of these days if he doesn't mend his methods. You're quite right to keep him away from the wheel if you value your car, Miss..."

"Menteith."

Jim Brandon made a gesture acknowledging the information. He shifted his position slightly so that he might covertly study the girl beside him. Brown wavy hair, a short clean-cut nose, a firm but rounded chin: any passable-looking girl might have all these. Her mouth puzzled him. She smiled easily, and even in repose the corners of her lips gave the impression that the smile was not far away. And yet there was nothing vapid in her expression. Jim Brandon found in it something indefinable—mockery, cynicism, a touch of the ironic—which gave her a character of her own. He guessed, easily enough, that Miss Menteith could play the fool if she chose, without ever being the fool she pretended to be.

"I suppose you're staying at Edgehill for the partridge-shooting," she said, after a moment or two, without taking her eyes from the road. "It starts on Monday, doesn't it? Johnnie's very keen."

Jim Brandon seemed slightly confused for a moment.

"I only brought my gun down on chance," he admitted abruptly. "I don't expect to be here for the partridges. The fact is, I'm not coming to Edgehill. I ought to have apologised for bringing you to the station on false pretences."

"Not staying at Edgehill? But Johnnie told me you were coming," Miss Menteith protested. "And Mrs Laxford expects you, I'm sure."

Jim Brandon's shoulders twitched in an almost imperceptible shrug.

"A mistake somewhere, evidently. I'm going to put up at an

hotel, if there's one near by. If there isn't, I dare say I can find some cottage where they'll take me in for a night or two."

Miss Menteith momentarily diverted her gaze from the road and darted a curious side-glance at her companion. Her eyebrows arched slightly as though in surprise at his announcement; but something in her expression betrayed that she was not quite so astonished as she pretended.

"I think I'd change my mind, if I were you," she advised coolly.

Then, as though feeling she had gone too far, she added in a reluctant tone:

"There's the Talgarth Arms in the village, of course. You can try it, if you like. It's only a mile or so from the lodge-gates. I'll take you there first of all and you can fix things up: book a room and leave your suitcase. Then we can go on to Edgehill. I was sent to collect you at the train, you know; and I can't very well turn up empty-handed, can I?"

Jim Brandon seemed to consider the alternatives.

"You're sure they expect me at Edgehill?" he demanded, after a moment or two.

"It would look rather queer if you didn't go there, wouldn't it?" she countered, without giving him a direct answer to his question. "You're here to see your brother, aren't you? He expects you to stay at the house. If you go to the Talgarth Arms, he might not like it."

Jim Brandon could not feel certain whether that last sentence was faintly emphasised or not. He sat back and thought hard for a moment or two before replying.

On the one hand, he had come down there with the express intention of putting a spoke in Laxford's wheel. At any cost, he reflected grimly, he meant to upset that man's schemes, in which Johnnie was to be used as the essential tool. That being so, he had planned to avoid Edgehill, to establish himself instead at some independent base—like the Talgarth Arms—so that he would be free from accepting Laxford's hospitality with its technical fetter of bread and salt. Instead of venturing to Edgehill he had intended to summon Johnnie to the inn and to conduct his campaign of persuasion upon neutral territory, outside the Laxford sphere of influence. That, of course, was the chivalrous method.

But, on the other hand, this observance of punctilio might well be a fatal handicap to his mission. Suppose he asked Johnnie to meet him at this inn. The message would put Laxford on the alert; and he might be strong enough to influence Johnnie— even to prevent him from turning up at all. Already there had been this curious substitution of Miss Menteith for his brother at the station; and perhaps Laxford had a hand in that. It might quite possibly have been arranged deliberately to prevent him getting Johnnie to himself at the start. And now, even if Johnnie consented to come to the Talgarth Arms, Laxford would have an opportunity of priming him immediately beforehand, rousing his suspicions, making him impossible to handle. That would be the worst atmosphere for delicate manoeuvres.

At Edgehill, on the contrary, he could choose his opportunity for tackling Johnnie. He could select a moment when his brother was in a propitious mood. And the thing could be done in a casual way which would give it a far better chance of success.

After weighing the arguments on both sides, he decided to revise his plans and fall in with Miss Menteith's proposal.

"Very well," he agreed at last, "if they expect me at Edgehill, I'll go there."

"I think you should," she replied, with no display of triumph at his conversion to her views. "We'll go straight there, then."

"It's very good of you to take all this trouble for a I stranger," he began.

"No trouble at all," she assured him, with a formality which sounded rather strange from her lips.

Then, with a sudden return to naturalness, she added:

"You and Johnnie aren't much alike, Mr Brandon."

"Meaning that I've got a hooked nose and he hasn't? Most people notice that. There's a streak of foreign blood in our family—pretty far back, now, but it crops out on the surface at times. I've got a dash of the old Norman in me; Johnnie favours the Saxon side of the family. At least, so my Governor says."

Miss Menteith had been thinking of mental and moral differences, more important than those between a straight nose and a curved one; but she made no attempt to explain this.

"That would account for it, certainly," she admitted. "And then, of course, you're much older than Johnnie, aren't you? That helps to make the difference between you bigger still."

Jim Brandon shook his head.

"You're on the wrong track there, I'm afraid. Johnnie looks much younger than he is really. He's just on the edge of twenty-one now. In fact, he comes of age tomorrow. There's only a matter of four years between the two of us."

This seemed to surprise Miss Menteith slightly. She glanced aside at him again as though to check her first impressions. Where had she got this false suggestion of a greater seniority? It did not lie in the leanness of the aquiline features, the curve of the predaceous nose, or the hardness of the mouth. These made him different from Johnnie, but not necessarily older-looking. Then she noted the corners of Jim Brandon's lips and the two vertical lines between his brows. That was where the thing lay, perhaps. Johnnie's normal expression spoke of happy-go-lucky cheerfulness. Worry, if he showed it at all, was like a swift-passing cloud. Jim Brandon's face, on the contrary, hinted at a suppressed grudge against a world which had not used him according to his idea of his own merits. That ever-present yet almost invisible trace of bitterness made him look older than his years.

During the slight pause in the conversation, Jim Brandon's thoughts had taken a very different channel. He was puzzled by this girl who had been sent to meet him. She was staying at Edgehill. She was on familiar terms there, since she spoke of "Johnnie" instead of saying "your brother" or "Mr Brandon." Without risking a direct snub, she had coolly assumed the right to advise him, as if she were an old friend instead of a stranger. She had managed to make him alter his plans at the last moment and go to Edgehill instead of to the village inn.

These were the facts about her; but what lay behind them? Was she an ally of Laxford, despatched to the station with the aim of enticing him into staying at Edgehill? That was quite on the cards, he reflected sourly. And a scheme of that sort had the further advantage that it prevented him from getting Johnnie to himself when they met at the train. Once at Edgehill, he might be kept under supervision. Privacy would be hard to secure. Seemingly innocent interruptions might easily be contrived to break into any tête-à-tête between Johnnie and himself. He could foresee endless difficulties already, and he began to curse his foolishness in dropping his original plan so hastily.

However, the blunder had been made—if it was a blunder—and he had to make the best of it. This girl, whoever she was, seemed inclined to talk freely enough; and he determined to utilise the chance. At least he could learn something about the environment into which he was about to plunge. The more information he had about that, the better equipped he would be to meet emergencies.

"Many people staying at Edgehill just now?" he asked in a casual tone, as though merely wishing to keep the conversation alive. "I suppose you've got a crowd on the premises, for the partridge-shooting next week?"

"Unless you call one a crowd, we haven't. I believe some men are coming down soon, but just now there's only one extra."

"Yourself, you mean?"

"No, I'm not a guest. It's a Mr Hay who dropped in unexpectedly yesterday. I think he's really here on business. He made some joke about lumber. I didn't see any point in it. Then Mr Laxford said they meant to fell some timber at Edgehill, so I suppose Mr Hay came in connection with that."

This information relieved Jim Brandon's mind. Laxford, with a solitary guest on his hands, could hardly contrive to keep the two brothers apart for a whole week-end. It would be easy enough to get Johnnie to himself and to talk things over without fear of interruption. Edgehill, after all, was the right place, since it would give him the choice of the best opportunity when Johnnie seemed to be in an amenable mood.

Then his mind went back to the first sentence of the girl's answer. She was staying at Edgehill, and yet by her own account she was not there as an ordinary guest. She must be some relation of Laxford or of Mrs Laxford—a close enough relation to reckon herself as one of the family, apparently. In that case, he would have to be very cautious in what he said to her. No use giving points to the enemy.

Miss Menteith seemed to have the gift of thought-reading. When he made no comment on her remarks she turned to him momentarily with a faintly quizzical expression.

"You're trying to place me, aren't you? Wondering who I am? There's no mystery about it, Mr Brandon. I'm the Laxfords' governess."

"Are you?"

Evidently a trace of surprise crept into his tone, for now she gave a little laugh of pure amusement.

"You seem a bit taken aback," she commented. "Why, may I ask? Don't I look like a governess? Did you expect a poke-bonnet and mittens, or what?"

Jim Brandon looked slightly confused, but he took the bull by the horns:

"I didn't expect to see a governess running a car like this one. You told me it was your own, didn't you?"

Miss Menteith's amusement became even more marked.

"It seems far above my humble station, you mean? Suspicious affair . . . How did she get it? . . . Queer times we live in . . . We all know what the post-war girl's like, h'm! . . . And all that sort of thing. You'll not be too disappointed if I clear my character? Dissipate these dreadful suspicions and what not? I love telling people the story of my life."

Jim Brandon glanced sharply at his companion. Despite its irony, her speech sounded rather silly; and silliness was not what he expected from this girl, who seemed to have her wits about her. He had a shrewd idea that some definite purpose lay behind this chatter, though what that purpose was, he could not guess. On the face of things, she evidently wanted him to know her exact status at Edgehill; but surely no detailed explanations were needed.

Miss Menteith relaxed her pressure on the accelerator and let the car slow down to a mere twenty-mile-an-hour gait. Evidently she meant to allow herself time for her autobiographical sketch. Her opening was hardly what Jim Brandon had anticipated.

"Suppose for a moment, Mr Brandon, that you were a girl just out of your teens, left stranded in the world with two hundred or two hundred and fifty a year. What could you do with it?"

"Live on it, I suppose. What else?"

Miss Menteith made an attractive grimace.

"Live on it? Yes. But how?"

"Oh, I don't know. Digs, or a boarding-house. Something of that sort, I suppose."

Miss Menteith nodded as though in confirmation.

"Yes, you might live in a women's club or in some boarding-house, of course—very cheap ones. Can you guess what that means? I can remember the animals: the girl who fancies herself at the piano . . . the old lady who always has trouble with her false teeth at meals . . . the woman with a harsh voice that can be heard all over the room . . . the maiden lady who's seen better days when she didn't have to mix with dreadful people like yourself . . . and the rest. Bright companions! No privacy unless you shut yourself up in a cheerless bedroom with a slot radiator and a penny-a-night book from a lending library. And most likely the whole establishment will be bathed in an inescapable smell of boiled cabbage or fried onions."

"It doesn't sound very bright," Jim Brandon admitted cautiously. "But you might take a flat."

"Well, I've tried that too. Half your income goes in rent, and that leaves you so short that you have to cling to every penny of the rest, as if it were a family heirloom. Spend your mornings trailing from one local greengrocer to another, in the hope of getting potatoes a halfpenny a stone cheaper than last time. Shop at Woolworth's, or in the Caledonian Market, or at the street stalls in—where is it?—Farringdon Road, I think, trying to pick up bargains in odd cups or job lots of oilcloth. You can't afford a decent dressmaker. You wear somebody else's cast-offs —'only been worn three times, moddom'—from the second-hand dealers in Bayswater. The theatre, when you can afford a splash, means standing at the pit-door. And when you get home after it, the fire's been smoking before it went out; and you yearn for company—any sort—just someone to talk to, something to take the edge off the loneliness that comes over you when you're all by yourself in the flat before you get to bed. And the people in the other flats may not be as quiet as you'd like, when you want to get to sleep and forget it all. It's not much catch, I assure you. London's the only place worth living in; but it's merely tantalising to live in it when you have to look twice at a bus-fare before you spend it."

"There's something in that," Jim Brandon agreed, thinking of his own experiences. "But what about a provincial town, or the country?"

"Same drawbacks and none of the advantages," Miss Menteith commented.

"And so. . . ?"

"Well, I thought it out; and finally I put an advertisement into *The Times* and *The Morning Post*. Something like this. '*Young Gentlewoman, age 23, capable, musical, child lover, many useful qualities, seeks post: highest references: salary secondary consideration.*' That threw the net wide enough. Some very rum fish came up in it, I can assure you. I wish I'd kept a few of the replies. Elderly gentlemen pining for Bright Young Society and asking for my photograph to see if I'd suit them. Ancient ladies, a bit uncertain in their spelling, who seemed to want either a maid-of-all-work or else someone to amuse their male friends in the evening. And so on. Rather amusing, really. I felt as if I'd paid my fee and was getting a correspondence course on Human Nature."

She paused for a moment as though to give Jim Brandon his

turn in the dialogue; but he merely waited for her to continue.

"The Laxfords saw my advertisement," she went on, with a momentary smile at some covert jest of her own. "They offered me just the sort of thing I wanted. Two children, seven and five, with a nurse to take them off my hands part of the time. They stay with a grandmother for two months in the summer, and I can go abroad or take a cruise then, if I want to. I love these cruises. Such a weird gang one meets on board at times."

Jim Brandon fancied he noticed a faint flush under; the light tan on Miss Menteith's cheek. She ran on with her description of her position.

"Anyhow, that's how it works out. I live rent-free as one of the family in nice big houses. I can dress decently and I can just manage to run a car. Besides, it's the gypsy sort of life I like."

"Gypsy sort of life?" queried Jim Brandon. "I don't see that side of it. Do you go caravanning between whiles?"

"No, I'd loathe caravanning," Miss Menteith retorted. "I don't mean that. But in some ways life with the Laxfords is a hugger-mugger sort of affair," she explained vaguely. "Rather fun, if you have a sense of humour. It might not suit some people, of course."

Jim Brandon picked his words carefully in his next remark.

"It seems a sound proposition, if you like the Laxfords," he said at last. "With your two hundred and fifty a year, plus your salary, you ought to be able to turn round comfortably enough."

"The salary doesn't worry me," answered Miss Menteith in an unusually dry tone.

Jim Brandon had his own ideas about the state of the Laxford finances, and he idly wondered how much Miss Menteith's salary was in arrear at that moment. It might suit her to take a post with the Laxfords, but it would doubtless suit the Laxfords equally well to have a governess to whom salary was "a secondary consideration." He could hardly push this subject further without risk of offence, so he turned the talk into a fresh channel.

"Is Johnnie getting on well with this work of his?"

"As well as can be expected, I think," Miss Menteith answered rather evasively. "He certainly works. Mr Laxford seems well enough pleased with his progress, I gather."

Jim Brandon laughed unkindly.

"Translated into English, that means that he plods away but doesn't make much of it. Johnnie was always a bonehead. A rabbit would be hard put to it to earn a living if it changed brains with my young brother. In some ways, he's exasperating, especially if you have to explain anything to him."

Miss Menteith seemed more than a little annoyed by the gloss put on her description.

"He's very likeable," she declared rather irrelevantly. "I'm rather fond of Johnnie. He's pathetically young in some ways, and frightfully earnest about some silly schemes; but he's not a bit priggish or conceited over them. I'm not sure . . ."

She broke off her sentence abruptly as though her tongue had run away with her. Jim Brandon guessed what she was avoiding. But this was a matter on which he wanted an outsider's view; and he deliberately forced the subject upon her.

"He's very young for his age, as you say," he agreed at once. "A case of arrested development on some sides, perhaps. And that makes him easily influenced by some people. He might pick up ideas from anybody who chose to throw them in his way, especially if he liked the author."

Miss Menteith kept her eyes fixed on the road with unnecessary intentness.

"He's at the hero-worshipping stage, I think," she confirmed.

Something in her tone suggested that this phase in a youth's development might not be an altogether desirable one.

"And there's only one hero on the premises for him to worship just now?" Jim Brandon suggested, with a trace of acidity in his voice.

"Mr Laxford seems to have a lot of influence with him," Miss Menteith admitted with a certain reluctance, as though she felt that she might be going too far.

Jim Brandon detected the faint critical inflexion in her voice, and he wondered if by any chance she felt a touch of jealousy in the matter. She seemed to have a fancy for Johnnie, to judge by the way she had almost fired up when she heard the youngster disparaged. If she were keen on Johnnie, it would be natural enough to find her resenting Laxford's preponderant influence.

"You don't seem to approve, altogether," he suggested by way of probing further.

But evidently Miss Menteith thought she had gone far enough.

"What business is it of mine?" she retorted sharply. "Your family put Johnnie into Mr Laxford's charge, didn't they? Well, it's their affair; and if they're satisfied with the result, there's no more to be said, is there?"

Johnnie must have been talking, Jim Brandon reflected; or else this girl had kept her ears open to some purpose. She seemed to have a pretty good idea of the lie of the land; and her sympathy was not on Laxford's side, to judge by her tone rather than her actual words. She might make a useful ally, if he could enlist her; and even if he stopped short of that, he might be able to utilize her in furthering his plans. In the meanwhile, he decided, he had better drop this rather ticklish subject.

The car rose and dipped as they ran across a culvert, and Jim Brandon caught a glimpse of a swollen little stream swirling brown and foam-flecked as it swept into the archway.

"Lot of rain you must have had lately," he said with a gesture towards the water. "That's fairly high."

Miss Menteith nodded.

"Yes, it's been pretty wet. All the streams are full. There was a lot of rain up in the hills, over yonder, and the water hasn't drained off yet."

"Is Johnnie doing much fishing in his spare time? He used to be rather keen about it."

"He's had to be careful lately, after that sprained ankle he got a month or so ago. Didn't you notice him limping when he was up in town?"

"Up in town, was he?" Jim Brandon had some difficulty in stifling his surprise at this news. "No, I didn't see him. When was he up?"

"Oh, ten days or a fortnight ago," the girl answered. "He and Mr Laxford went up together for the day. I thought Johnnie would be sure to look you up."

Jim Brandon was hard put to it to preserve an air of indifference. Johnnie up in town, along with Laxford? It might mean nothing; perhaps they had merely run up to London on some casual errand which was no concern of his. Still . . . Johnnie hadn't said a word about that excursion in his letters, either beforehand or afterwards; and in that suppression, at least, Laxford's hand was plain. And if Laxford wanted the trip kept dark, there must be something going on behind the scenes. That was one useful bit of news that this girl had given him, though she didn't realise it. Meanwhile, his best policy was to keep his suspicions to himself and not let her guess that she had given anything away.

"Most likely they were very busy," he commented lazily. "There's always so much to do in London when you're only up for the day."

"Well, his ankle's all right again," Miss Menteith volunteered, harking back to the earlier subject. "He had to be careful for a while, you know, and keep off rough ground for fear of giving it a fresh twist. Hard lines on him, being tied by the leg like that. He's quite mad on shooting, just now; and he hated having to hobble about with a stick."

Jim Brandon was glad to get still further away from dangerous ground.

"Not much shooting at this time, surely," he pointed out.

"Not real shooting," the girl agreed. "But Johnnie's quite happy if he has a gun in his hand. He spends most of his time shooting rabbits. In fact, if we lived by his gun, the Edgehill diet would be painfully monotonous. Until the family rebelled, it was a case of the Curate's Grace with us:

Rabbits hot and rabbits cold,
  Rabbits tender and rabbits tough,

Rabbits young and rabbits old:
I thank Thee, Lord, I've had enough.

I don't want to see rabbit pie again in my life—not that I ever doted on it. Australia is the place for me. They don't eat rabbits there, I'm told."

Jim Brandon's mind had gone back to that trip to London. A fresh possibility occurred to him.

"By the way," he asked, "Johnnie didn't go up to town to see a bone-setter, by any chance? About his ankle, I mean?"

Miss Menteith's decided headshake disposed of this comforting hypothesis at once.

"No, I'm pretty sure he didn't do anything of the sort. He's an absurd young Spartan in some ways, you remember. Grin and bear it—all that sort of thing. He wouldn't even let Mr Laxford get a doctor from Talgarth to look at his ankle. There was quite a wrangle over it. I told him he was silly, not having the thing properly looked after. However, he was quite right, as it turned out. The thing got well again of itself, just by taking care."

So that run up to town was still unexplained, Jim Brandon recognised with some uneasiness. London might mean lawyers, when Johnnie was in question; and lawyers might mean the very devil, at this juncture.

"This is Talgarth," his companion explained as they ran into a trim little village. Jim Brandon glanced incuriously at the white thatched cottages, each with its little hedge-enclosed garden, a few larger dwellings, a shop or two, and an old-fashioned half-timbered inn with rambler roses thick on its frontage.

"It seems very neatly kept," he commented.

"Yes, isn't it?" Miss Menteith agreed, with a certain enthusiasm. "It belongs to Mr Wendover—one of the local magnates—and he's a model landlord, they say. He encourages the people to take some pride in the place. It all looks old-fashioned, but everything inside these cottages is modernised. I've been in one or two."

"Must have cost him a pile," Jim Brandon commented, with

something rather grudging in his tone.

"That gate there is the entrance to the Dower House on the Silver Grove estate," Miss Menteith explained as they left the village behind. "It's empty just now. So's the big house itself. There's a very pretty little lake, up yonder behind the trees. If you stay here for a day or two, you ought to go up and have a look at it, it's quite worth seeing. Nobody will mind, so long as you keep to the paths and don't wander at large through the woods."

Jim Brandon had a suspicion that all this local information was not being offered merely for its own; sake. Miss Menteith was using it as a barrier to keep him from putting any more questions about Edgehill affairs. She had given him some information, but it had evidently been carefully selected. Now she was talking to forestall anything savouring of a cross-examination by him.

"That's the entrance to Talgarth Grange," she went on, as they swept past a big ornamental gateway leading into an avenue. "It belongs to that Mr Wendover that I mentioned a minute ago. He's chairman of the County Council, a JP, president of the local Antiquarian Society, something in the Royal Agricultural Society, and all that kind of thing."

"What sort of person is he?" Jim Brandon asked, merely to let her see that he accepted her tacit decision to keep off the Edgehill problem.

"Oh, he's nice. Very nice indeed," Miss Menteith declared with a rather surprising warmth and sincerity. "He's the sort of man one likes at sight. He looks a sort of Ideal Uncle, if you see what I mean. A bit old-fashioned in some ways. Manners dignified, and yet genial, you know, the kind of thing they used to call 'courtly.' He brings it off and makes you feel it's all genuine. He's teaching me golf. He's got a six-hole practice course on his ground up there, and he's been awfully decent in playing with me and giving me a hand. The last man you'd expect to have a taste for crime," she wound up unexpectedly.

"What's that?" queried Jim Brandon. "He isn't a Raffles or what

19

not, is he?"

"No, no. He's a criminologist—dabbles in murder cases, you know. He's a friend of Sir Clinton Driffield, the Chief Constable of the county. I expect that's where he picked it up."

"Rum sort of hobby," Jim Brandon commented with a slight shrug which might have indicated contempt. "Hasn't he grown out of the Sexton Blake stage yet?"

"I can't see the charm in gruesome stuff like that," the girl admitted. "Morbid sort of taste, isn't it? He ought to have got married, and then he'd have had brighter interests."

"A woman-hater, is he?" Jim Brandon hinted, with a side-glance at his companion.

"Not a bit of it," she retorted. "There's nothing of the crusty old bachelor about him. He likes young people. He's been very nice to me."

"What's his friend like? The Chief Constable, I mean."

Miss Menteith reflected for a moment or two before replying. She seemed to have difficulty in recalling salient characteristics which would serve in a description; and when she finally tried to sketch the Chief Constable she produced only a disjointed catalogue of details.

"Oh, well, he's somewhere round about thirty-five, I should think. But it's difficult to guess his age. He's about your height, and he's got a close-clipped moustache and fine teeth. He's got a sort of sardonic way of talking at times. There's a kind of edge on what he says, if you understand what I mean . . . I can't quite describe it. Sometimes it's double-edged. Most of the time he seems politely interested—just on the verge of boredom, but not quite showing it. Then at other times he watches you in a speculative sort of way, not as if he were looking at your nose or your mouth or your eyes, but somehow as if he were seeing you as you really are—your personality, I mean, not your mere outside appearance. But that's only the merest flash. Usually he looks as ordinary as possible,—more ordinary than the man in the street even. He gives you nothing to take hold of, somehow."

"Curious cove, evidently. Doesn't pose as the big official,

then?"

"Not a bit. I only heard what he was by accident. Before that, I hadn't a notion of what his line could be."

"Did you ever meet his wife?"

"He hasn't one," Miss Menteith informed him curtly.

She seemed to have lost interest in Wendover and the Chief Constable. They had served their turn in keeping the conversation off other things. Now her expression betrayed a trace of perplexity, as though she were trying at the last moment to choose between two alternatives which confronted her.

"Here's Edgehill," she explained, turning the car into a lodge-gate which opened on a broad avenue leading upward through a belt of trees.

Then, slowing the car as though to spin out the last few moments, she turned to her passenger.

"You've been trying to size me up, haven't you?" she demanded with a hint of mockery in her tone. "Well, I've been trying an experiment on you. So we're quits, I think."

She pressed the button and sounded a long blast on her horn, apparently to announce her arrival to those in the house, but possibly, Jim Brandon reflected, to prevent him from making any comment on her last speech.

As the car drew up before the house, Johnnie Brandon made his appearance at the front door.

CHAPTER 2 THE BRANDON HERITAGE

Jim Brandon ushered his brother into the Edgehill gun-room; and then, after a cautious glance along the corridor, followed him over the threshold and closed the door.

"Take a pew, Johnnie," he suggested pleasantly, with a nod towards one of the chairs. "I want to have a talk with you. We've not had a minute alone together since I came down."

He propped his gun in a corner. Then, sweeping aside a scratch-brush and some rags, he cleared a space for himself on the table, sat down, and lit a cigarette.

"Have one? No? All right."

For a moment or two Jim smoked in silence, reflecting that he had blundered badly in his opening. 'I want to have a talk with you' had been their father's prelude to the discussion of delinquencies when they were children. That phrase must have struck a wrong note at the very start, as he could see from the expression on Johnnie's face. It suggested that a wigging was coming, and that was the worst kind of beginning for a mission of persuasion. However, it was too late to worry about that.

Johnnie had detached the barrels from the stock of his gun and was preparing to clean them. He took this task seriously, and he went about it with a methodical deliberation which at this moment served to irritate his elder brother, who wanted to secure undivided attention from his junior. One by one, Johnnie collected his requisites with the care of a conjurer running over his properties before a performance. He reached across the table for a cleaning rod and screwed a brass jag to its end with a rather fumbling touch. From a drawer he produced some bristle brushes. He considered the scratch-brush for a moment, hesitating, and then dropped it back into its place. Another drawer was opened to secure clean tow and woollen patches. Then a shelf across the room had to be visited to fetch down bottles of linseed oil and Three-in-One, along with a pot of vaseline. Finally, after a clutch at some of the oily rags across the table, he ranged his collection in neat order before him, looked them over to see that none was missing, and prepared for work.

Jim, fuming internally but outwardly unmoved, watched his brother's awkward movements as he walked to and fro. There had been some excuse for that girl when she miscalculated their ages. For all his twenty-one years, Johnnie had the look of a bulky, overgrown schoolboy; and that frank, freckled, and rather simple face added to the illusion of his immaturity. The blue eyes under the unruly mop of fair hair had still something of child's candour in them. If the mouth showed any firmness at all, it was the firmness of obstinacy rather than of character. Jim reflected sourly on the ill-chance which had made the fortunes of that generation of Brandons dependent on the whim of an inexperienced dullard. Now the danger-period was upon them, and all might turn upon his own diplomacy. He put his cigarette on the table beside him, hitched himself into a more comfortable position, and addressed his brother.

"Why don't you come up to London and see the Governor, Johnnie? He's fond of you, and he feels it more than a bit when you seem to be avoiding him deliberately. He's lonely now, since the Mater died, and it cuts him more than you'd think, your staying away like this. He'd like to see you."

The overgrown schoolboy showed very plainly in Johnnie's attitude in face of this appeal. He looked acutely uncomfortable and tried to conceal it by bending over his task. At last he gave an awkward shrug which revealed his inward discomfort.

"I can't manage it just now, Jim; I can't, really."

Apparently encouraged by the boy's obvious uneasiness, Jim tried a fresh argument.

"There's one thing you might do. You know how much store the Governor sets by anniversaries and all that sort of thing—birthdays, Christmas, and so forth. Rot, I think it, myself. Still, there it is. You know what I mean. For the last month or two he's been brooding over your coming-of-age. He's spoken to me about it more than once. I can see what's worrying him. Of course, in the old days, before he muddled things, it would have been a big spree on the estate. All the tenants to dinner, decorations, flag on the mast, speeches, everybody very mellow and cheery. He'd have spread himself over it and enjoyed every minute. It's the sort of thing where he'd have shone, you know. Bluff old squire, and the young hopeful coming on. Well, that's all dead and done with. . . ."

A slight twitch of his lips betrayed his feelings for a moment. The contrast between the actual state of affairs and the might-have-been was a painful subject. If Johnnie was touched by it, he concealed his feelings by a closer absorption in his cleaning operations and avoided glancing at his brother.

"What he's set his heart on," the elder brother continued, "is just this. He wants you to spend your coming-of-age with him. It means coming up to town tomorrow, first thing. But you'll get back in plenty of time for the partridges."

Johnnie made a sudden gesture of refusal, but Jim continued smoothly as though he had not noticed it.

"'Twon't be exactly a treat, I quite admit, to spend the day with a sick man in frowsy digs. I see that well enough. Still, I thought I'd come down and see if I couldn't persuade you to humour him, Johnnie. 'Tisn't much to ask, is it? The Governor's been an old fool. True enough. Nobody knows it better than I do. Still, he's very keen on you. It would give him no end of pleasure. Just look at it that way, Johnnie. Do the decent thing."

Johnnie's face had grown more and more overcast as the appeal progressed; but the cloud on it was one of worry and perplexity rather than of ill-temper. He appreciated all the points of his brother's argument; but, behind his protective mask of rather surly indifference, a conflict between two loyalties was raging furiously.

Jim felt in his pocket and produced a letter. He held it out towards Johnnie for a moment and then, with an after-thought, drew it back again.

"I'll read it to you. Then you'll hear just how it sounds."

Johnnie had recognised his own scrawling handwriting on the envelope.

"You needn't bother, Jim. It's my last letter to the Governor, isn't it? I know quite well what I said to him."

But Jim Brandon had his own reasons for reading this letter aloud. He knew that he could make it tell more heavily by mere intonations of his voice.

"You know what you said, all right, I expect. But I doubt if you know just how you put it in words. Listen, now."

And with slight touches of emphasis here and there he read out the letter, watching the effect as he accentuated the unintentional cruelty of the wording.

3rd August, 1924.
MY DEAR FATHER,

Thanks for your letter of Tuesday, which I have received. I am indeed very sorry if I have pained you in any way; for of course I had no intention of hurting your feelings in the slightest degree. But I still feel that no useful purpose would be served by my coming to London at the present juncture. It would merely be an extra expense for you, and you say you are short of money. I am afraid we shall all be hard up until I come of age and we can get matters put in better order.

Besides, I am working hard at present with Mr Laxford, and he thinks it would be a grave mistake to interrupt my studies at this particular moment. I must get some real training in book-keeping and estate management generally, as soon as possible.

I think you do Mr Laxford injustice by some of the things you say in your letter. He has, I am quite sure, never misrepresented matters to me, and I am convinced that he has been perfectly straightforward with us all. I see nothing wrong with the negotiations he has been conducting in the matter of the estate; and I think it is very bad policy to pick a quarrel with him, as you seem anxious to do.

I am sorry to disappoint you, and you know I am not finding fault with you; but the plain truth is that you were letting me grow up entirely without any proper education whatsoever; and it is only since Mr Laxford took me in hand that I have learned anything about subjects which I ought to know, in view of my future. I owe him a great deal for that, all the more since he has not received the remuneration agreed upon between you.

You cannot expect me to break into my studies by rushing up to London every now and then. I must have some education. I should feel ashamed to go about, all my life, in utter ignorance of important things.

Your affectionate son,
JOHNNIE.

Jim Brandon folded up the letter deliberately, slipped it into its envelope, and replaced it in his pocket.

"Well, Johnnie? Hear how it reads? A bit sore on the poor old Governor's feelings, eh? That cut about his not having paid Laxford, I think you might have left it out. And you needn't have dragged in that about your education. These things sting, rather. I'm not defending his way of doing things. If a man's left an income of thousands a year and manages to spend half as much again each year, he can't expect much sympathy from his family on that account. Still, you needn't bear a grudge over it, if I don't. You'll come out on velvet at the end of it all."

"I don't bear any grudge at all," Johnnie protested frankly. "I'm downright sorry if I hurt the Governor's feelings, really, Jim. I didn't mean to. Only . . . I don't think any good would come of my going up to town to see him."

"Interrupt your valuable studies too much, eh?"

"Yes."

The rather grudging tone of the reply gave the elder brother an opening.

"Then why," he demanded, "did you go up to town not so long ago?"

Johnnie was plainly confused by this home-thrust. He bit his lip and busied himself with his gun.

"Who told you I was up in town?" he asked rather shame-facedly after a moment or two.

"My detective agency, of course: Messrs. Pry and Trailem . . . No expense spared. . . . As a matter of fact I was told by Laxford's governess—what's her name? Menteith, I think. Nice girl, that. It was she who let out that you'd been up in town with Laxford."

"Oh, Una told you, did she?" said Johnnie rather blankly.

"If that's her name. Well, it seems you spent a whole day in London not so long ago. And never looked near the Governor. How did you fill in your time?"

"We went to a show," Johnnie admitted haltingly.

"Must have given you value for money, there, if you sat in it from ten in the morning until you had to sprint for your last train. What else did you do?"

Johnnie seemed to have some good reason for evading a discussion of his doings in London. Instead of answering the question, he took up fresh ground.

"I'm not your kiddie-brother now, Jim. It's my own affair, how I spend my time."

The unwonted asperity of Johnnie's tone gave warning that his brother had overstepped the bounds of diplomacy. Jim saw that he might lose points by pursuing the subject further. He harked back to the sentimental argument, which put Johnnie morally in the wrong.

"Well, you might have looked the Governor up, Johnnie. Kindness would have cost nothing more than a bus-fare."

Then, without a change in tone, he edged in a fresh subject:

"Besides, you're on the edge of twenty-one now, and we ought all to be putting our heads together to see what can be done about the estate."

This was evidently the last topic that Johnnie wished to discuss. He turned awkwardly in his chair, stared out of the window, and muttered that he understood nothing about financial transactions.

"Then it's time you waked up and took some notice," his brother retorted rather sharply. "Is this just a pose of yours, or do you really not understand?"

"If I can't understand money matters, whose fault is it?" Johnnie countered, without heat. "I'm like the Governor, I've no head for them. The Governor has talked to me often enough about it all; but you know what he's like, Jim. He just burbles along without making it any clearer, and if you ask him to explain anything he just goes back to the beginning and muddles it up worse than ever, until my head begins to go round. It's not my fault if he hasn't made me understand."

"There's something in that," his brother admitted in a less impatient tone. "The Governor's no flyer at making anything clear, least of all finance. Perhaps I can do better. But *listen*, Johnnie, for it's a thing you ought to know the ins and outs of. Something will have to be done about it."

He paused momentarily as though a suspicion had crossed his mind.

"Has Laxford talked to you about it all?"

"He did, once or twice," Johnnie confessed honestly. "But somehow he didn't make it any clearer than the Governor did. Usually he explains things plainly enough, but he seemed to slip a cog in this affair. Or perhaps I was extra dull that day. All I've got out of the two of them is some notion about barring the entail and getting control of the estate again. Is that right?"

Jim Brandon nodded thoughtfully. He was not surprised to learn that Laxford had lost his usual clarity when he came to elucidate the estate question for Johnnie's benefit. It would hardly have suited the Laxford book if Johnnie mastered all the ins and outs of that complex problem. Johnnie was anything but bright; and it must have been easy enough for Laxford to muddle his ideas, already sufficiently confused by doses of his father's explanations which explained nothing.

"That's the main idea: barring the entail and getting control of the estate again. You've picked up the backbone of the thing, anyhow. It's the only way out, so far as I can see. Now just listen carefully, Johnnie. Stop me if you don't grip it. I want you to have the thing clear."

Johnnie apparently resigned himself to the inevitable. He put down his gun-barrels and turned towards his brother with at least an outward semblance of attention.

"Here's the thing in a nutshell," his brother began. "The Governor's life-tenant of Burling Thorn. That means he can't sell the estate, no matter how hard up he is. All he can do is to draw the rents during *his* lifetime. When he passes in his checks, the next heir steps in, draws the rents during his lifetime, and when he goes out, the next heir steps into his shoes. The estate remains in the family, no matter what happens."

"Oh, I knew *that* well enough," Johnnie interjected. "It's the rest of it I can't make head or tail of."

Jim made a gesture as though asking for time.

"We're coming to that. You know what the Governor did. He went the pace, horses and the Stock Exchange, ran up the devil's own debts which he couldn't pay out of income. And then the creditors came down on him. That was before your time, of course. You never lived at Burling Thorn."

Johnnie shook his head regretfully.

"No, I wish I had. It was one London suburb after another, when I was a kid. And we never seemed to stay long enough in one place to get used to it."

"True enough," Jim confirmed with a wry expression. "But let's stick to the point. The creditors came down and demanded their money. The Governor had no cash. You can't collect rents twenty years in advance, and rents were all he had. Somehow or other he had to raise the wind to the tune of thousands and thousands in spot cash. The Osprey Insurance people helped him out of the mess—at a price."

"This is a bit I never really got hold of," Johnnie volunteered. "The Governor always slid over it as if he hardly understood what it was all about himself. He just said the lawyers arranged it, and then he used to damn the lawyers and say it was all their fault, and I never got the thing clear yet."

"Don't you worry. I'll make it clear enough," his brother assured him confidently. "Here's what happened. The Osprey people advanced enough in hard cash to pay off the creditors. I'm not going to muddle you up with figures, Johnnie, but it was a hell of a sum. Now that, of course, didn't really help to better the Governor's position. He was just as much in debt as ever. All it meant was that he owed the cash to the Osprey people instead of to a whole flock of duns."

"I see that, all right," said Johnnie hopefully. "But I don't see what good it did the Governor if he was still up to the ears in debt."

"I'm coming to that. Of course the Osprey people aren't philanthropists, and they wanted two things. They wanted interest on the money they lent the Governor, and they wanted to be sure of seeing their capital back again in the long-run. They'd no claim on the estate itself, you see? All the Governor had was the income from rents. And that only lasted, so far as they were concerned, as long as the Governor lived."

"I think I see that," Johnnie admitted with a certain pride. "Nobody ever put it to me like that before. It isn't so bad as I thought. Go on."

Jim Brandon felt it worth while to throw out a sprat of flattery at this point.

"I knew you'd see it all right if it was put plainly," he said in an encouraging tone. "Now here's what the Osprey crowd did. They made the Governor take out an insurance policy on his life, for a figure that covered the money they'd lent him. That means that when he dies they'll collect the insurance money and get their capital back again, all OK. Of course this means the devil's own insurance premium to pay each year, and the Governor had to find that somehow. Besides that, he had to pay

30

interest to the Osprey people, interest on the capital they'd lent him; and that was no small beer either, though I needn't give you the figures. Of course they had to get some guarantee that these payments would be made. They couldn't take the estate itself as security, because it belongs to the family and not to the Governor personally. So they took a mortgage on his life-interest in the estate."

"Hold on a mo'," Johnnie interrupted. "What d'you mean, exactly? I'm not quite clear about mortgages and such-like."

Jim Brandon reflected sourly that Laxford's tuition had tactfully omitted mortgages from the course of training in estate-management. He could guess the reason for that easily enough, he thought.

"It'll be quite clear in a moment or two," he assured Johnnie. "Just take it as it comes. When the Governor got his rents in he had to pay away ever so much cash to the Osprey people to cover the interest on the loan and the insurance premium on that life policy. That meant, of course, that there wasn't enough left over to keep up Burling Thorn any longer. It had to be leased and all of us had to skip to London. It meant living on a pittance compared with the income the Governor had before he began playing the fool. And, of course, being the Governor, he couldn't realise the position even then, and he made a further muddle of his affairs. That mightn't have been fatal. But unfortunately income tax began to go up and land began to go down, just then. It didn't pay. Tenants cleared out. Rents didn't come in as they used to do. Between that and the Governor's extravagance, things got to a crisis. An instalment wasn't paid when it fell due. The Osprey people got the wind up and they foreclosed immediately."

"I don't see what they got by that," Johnnie interjected with a puzzled air. "They couldn't touch the estate, you said."

"What happened was that they stepped in—legally, of course —and collected the rents themselves from the estate. The Governor lost any claim he had to the rent-moneys. The Osprey people gave him something to live on. You know for yourself what it amounts to, and you know the sort of life the Governor's been leading on it. It killed the Mater. Since then, the Governor's been drifting from one set of shabby digs to another, pursued by clouds of duns after him for five bob or ten bob accounts which he never seems able to square off. And he's a very sick man, Johnnie."

Jim paused, as though hoping that this sentimental touch would produce an effect, but Johnnie had returned to his cleaning and made no remark. The elder brother frowned slightly. He was coming to the really important step in his negotiation, and he had hoped for a more favourable atmosphere. Johnnie had certainly shown some interest, but it was not the kind of interest that Jim wanted. However, he had to go through with the business now.

"Well, that's the mess the Governor got into and stayed in," he continued. "Question is: how can we clean it up? One thing's to the good. You know that disease of his? Well, he's been overhauled by two of the best men in London in that line, and there's no doubt about his being what the lawyers call 'a tenant with possibility of issue extinct,' so far as the future goes."

"I don't understand that," Johnnie interrupted. "What does it mean, exactly?"

Jim's lips curved in a sardonic smile.

"It means you needn't expect any more little brothers or sisters in our family, even if the Governor found anyone who'd marry him after this. That's that."

Johnnie seemed to shy away from this subject.

"Go on," he said rather gruffly. "I've understood all that, so far."

Jim Brandon pitched the end of his cigarette on to the hearth and pulled his case from his pocket. He had reached the crucial stage of this interview. Everything depended on convincing Johnnie now. There might be no other opportunity before it was too late, for on the following day Johnnie was to come of age and anything might happen then. Laxford might move suddenly, and the whole affair might be complicated beyond unravelment. Jim lit his fresh cigarette with unnecessary care, in order to give himself time to think. When he spoke again it was in a more deliberate tone than before, for he wanted every word to sink in.

"This is what we ought to do, Johnnie. You're the youngest, and there aren't going to be any more of us. So when you come of age we can bar the entail by agreement and convert the estate into a fee-simple. That means we can do anything we like with it, sell it if we choose, for all the present restrictions will go by the board if the entail's barred. Suppose it's sold. The cash it fetches will pay off the Osprey people completely and leave us with a big surplus, even at the present value of land. The Osprey people naturally left a wide margin for contingencies when they lent the money. Besides that, we don't need to go on paying the premiums on the Governor's insurance policy. He can take the surrender value of that. Between what he gets for his policy and what surplus is left after the Osprey people are paid off, there'll be a tidy little fortune in hand. Do you follow that?"

Johnnie, too, seemed to recognise that they had reached the crisis in the interview, but his reaction was not encouraging. He shifted awkwardly in his chair, glanced despairingly out of the window, and seemed a prey to minor fidgets which ill suited his bulky figure. At last he screwed himself up to a decision and spoke out.

"Mr Laxford doesn't seem to think that scheme would be fair to me," he declared rather unwillingly, though with a certain obstinacy in his tone.

So Laxford had primed the boy after all, Jim reflected angrily. Damn the fellow! If it hadn't been for him they could have got Johnnie to agree to anything. This initial proposal was an extreme one. If Johnnie had accepted it, well and good. If not, then something more moderate would have to be substituted instead. But Laxford, playing his own game, had been cute enough to foresee their tactics. His objection, voiced by Johnnie, was a sound one, for the scheme certainly involved a certain unfairness to Johnnie.

Jim Brandon thought he had better discover whether his

brother really grasped the arguments against the proposal.

"What's Laxford's objection?" he asked suavely.

Johnnie was obviously a little embarrassed by this demand for details.

"I didn't understand what Mr Laxford said about it, except this: that if we did what you say, the Governor might make hay of any money he got, just as he did before; and his share would be a dead loss."

"There's something in that," Jim conceded in a conciliatory tone. "Well, then, I suppose we could go on paying the premiums on the life insurance policy. Then, when the Governor dies, there'll be just as much cash as there was when he came into the estate at the very first. But it'll mean a good deal less money in the meantime, Johnnie. Still, if you want to have it that way, I don't mind."

But Johnnie was not to be bribed by the concession.

"Mr Laxford doesn't think I ought to come in on that arrangement at all."

Jim Brandon stifled a desire to say what he thought of Laxford's interference in very blunt language. Instead, he tried a fresh line of persuasion.

"I've given you the Governor's side of the thing, Johnnie, first of all; but the fact is, I've got an axe of my own to grind in the matter. It would suit me down to the ground if the affair could be fixed up as I explained to you. I'm rather keen on a girl, as it happens. She's not the sort to marry on the miserable pittance I draw from my office. I haven't asked her. I know she wouldn't look at the prospect. If I had an extra hundred or two on my income it might make all the difference. We've always been good pals, Johnnie. Doesn't that make some difference in your ideas? It means a hell of a lot to me."

He glanced anxiously at his brother, but Johnnie shook his head mulishly. When he answered, it was plain that the second appeal to sentiment had failed completely.

"I'm not going to do it, Jim. Not, at present, anyhow. Mr Laxford advised me not to let myself be rushed into anything. He thinks I ought to have proper legal advice about it all, from someone who's got no axe to grind. Besides, I've got plans of my own, and I don't think your ideas and the Governor's would fit in with them. I'm sorry, you know, but still that's how it is."

Jim Brandon recognised that he had made no impression. There was an obstinate set in Johnnie's mouth which he knew well from childhood onwards. In one of his stubborn moods, Johnnie was unshakable by argument. Further persuasion was useless, and Jim vented his disappointment savagely under his breath:

"Damn this custom of borough English! If it had been the other way round Oswald would have shown more sense."

Oswald was the eldest of the three brothers. As a child he had a craving for the sea, and his ambition had been to enter the Navy. When the financial collapse of his father dashed this hope, he turned to the mercantile marine for the satisfaction of his desire for a sea career. He had started as an apprentice, worked his way up, passed his examinations, and was now third officer on a converted liner which cruised in leisurely fashion down the Mediterranean, carrying tourists to stare at the Sphinx, the minarets of Istanbul, and the pillars of the Erechtheion.

His self-made career had cut him off from the rest of the family. Johnnie got a letter now and again. His father had to be content with what Oswald himself sardonically termed his "Annual Bulletin." Jim hardly ever saw his own name in Oswald's handwriting. Oswald was no letter-writer. And nowadays, even when his ship put into Southampton, he never came to London. He seemed to have other fish to fry. They had seen so little of him that they hardly missed him, now that he had drifted away.

Oswald might have made a better job of this persuasion business, Jim reflected rather bitterly. Johnnie had a certain admiration for his eldest brother, and Oswald had kept in touch with the youngster to some extent through his letters. But where Oswald was at that moment Jim had no idea, since he had long ago ceased to follow the movements of the *Ithaca*. For all he knew, Oswald might be sauntering with some girl under the tree arcades of the Paseo de la Alameda at that moment, or helping her to chaffer for embroideries with the boat pedlars in some port or other. That kind of thing was in Oswald's line, to judge by stray snapshots which he sent home from time to time. They could get no help from him in overcoming Johnnie's pig-headedness.

But if Johnnie was obstinate, Jim Brandon was tenacious; and even at this stage he had not given up hope of achieving something. Persuasion had failed; he might as well try a different line, so in a rather sharper tone than he had used before, he demanded:

"You won't come back to the Governor? Why not? It seems the decent thing to do. He needs someone to keep him company. I can't be with him except in the evenings, and I've got to get fresh air sometimes. I can't spend my whole time between an office and a sick-room. You ought to do your share, if you've any decency."

The prospect seemed to shake Johnnie out of his indifference.

"Me go back to the Governor? I won't do it, Jim, that's flat. I know what it'd be like if I went back. Stuffy digs and rows with frowsy landladies, because the Governor can't pay his way. Getting shoved out into the street when they lose patience, and having to hunt for fresh digs worse than the last ones. And keeping an ear cocked for every ring at the front-door bell because a tradesman may be squalling for his bill of the month before last. No, I'm sorry for the Governor, and all that, Jim, but it's his own muddling that landed him in Queer Street, after all. He never thought of us, or he wouldn't have made such a mess of things."

Jim Brandon's lips curved in a scornful expression.

"Whereas, of course," he suggested acidly, "you can live here with all sorts of luxuries and take no share in family bothers, eh? Who pays for all this?"

"Mr Laxford," Johnnie retorted triumphantly. "Or Mrs Laxford. Anyhow, the Governor doesn't. He hasn't even paid the fees he promised when the arrangement was made."

Jim evaded this issue by a counter-attack which he hoped

might get home on Johnnie's vanity.

"H'm! Laxford seems to bulk very big on your horizon. Shoved the poor old Governor off the stage and got you completely under his thumb, apparently.

"He hasn't," Johnnie denied heatedly.

"Indeed?" The elder brother's tone was contemptuous, now that diplomacy had definitely failed. "What's the use of lying, Johnnie? You remember that letter I read to you? He dictated it to you, didn't he? Of course he did. I know the kind of letter you write off your own bat. *'Dear Father, I am quite well. Are you quite well? I hope you are quite well. . . .'* That's how you write. You couldn't have put that last letter together yourself if you'd tried for a week. It's outside your limits, especially the nasty bits—I'll say that for you. It's plain that Laxford has you under his thumb, even to the extent of dictating your letters to the Governor. Pretty doings! Now, Johnnie, give yourself a fair chance. Get away from that man. Come up to London by yourself and let's all talk things over with no outsiders poking their fingers into our family affairs. You've nothing to lose by agreeing to the entail being barred. Why not come in with us?"

Johnnie evidently felt that he might be worsted if he allowed himself to be entrapped into detailed argument. He contented himself with a clumsy gesture of his hand which abruptly dismissed his brother's proposal. The furrows between Jim's brows deepened, and his lips tightened at this cavalier rejection of his final effort.

"You seem to think that Laxford's a whole-hog idealist, or altruist, or whatever they call it," he said scornfully. 'That he's simply out to do good in this wicked world? You young fool! Shows how much you know about life. He's got his own axe to grind. When all's squared up, you'll have lashings of money. He knows that well enough. And it'll be damned convenient for him, then, to have a rich young mug ready to put his paw in his pocket for his dear old tutor. That's his game, and anyone but you could see it."

The sneers and the charge together stung Johnnie into active protest. He sat up in his chair and faced his brother more boldly than he had done hitherto.

"That just shows you don't understand him in the least," he said, not without dignity. "He isn't that sort at all, and I can prove it, too, Jim."

His brother's brows tilted upward slightly with a hint of weary increduality.

"Really?"

"Yes, really," Johnnie retorted. "Look here, Jim. I've been thinking a lot, lately. I'm not clever, I know that well enough. Still, some things stare one in the face. It's like this . . ."

He paused, trying to find words for his confession of faith, while his brother waited with a certain sardonic politeness.

"It's like this," Johnnie repeated at last. "Things aren't properly distributed. Some of us have far more money than we need. Other people haven't got enough to live decently."

"Like the Governor?" his brother suggested blandly.

"The Governor had far more than enough, at one time," Johnnie rejoined hastily. "He wasted it. That's just my point, Jim. He ought to have thought of all the good he could do with his cash. Instead of that, he just splashed it away on horses, betting, speculating, and all that kind of thing. If he'd any imagination, he'd never have done it. He'd have used his cash to help people worse off than himself. He never thought of them at all. He never even thought of us. But never mind him. Think of the slums, Jim. Think of all those poor devils cooped up in those dens. Some of them never see a green field in their lives. They ought to have a chance. They ought to be taken clean out of these beastly rookeries and planted down in the country with allotments and small holdings. . . ."

As he went on, he warmed to his subject. There was no art or persuasiveness in the curt, jerky sentences, but their very breathlessness betrayed the intensity of the enthusiasm behind them. It was the crude socialism of adolescence, a froth of generous feeling untempered by the slightest experience of the world; and the other descendant of ten generations of squires listened to it with an increasingly evident contempt. At last he broke silence.

"Very pretty, Johnnie. I seem to have heard something like it before, though. And what does it all amount to, when you come down to dots?"

Johnnie was evidently stung by the cool disdain in his brother's tone.

"It comes down to this, Jim. I'm not going to be a second edition of the Governor. Money's a trust. That's what I feel. It's got to be used for the benefit of other people. Land's in the same boat. It ought to be used to help as many people as possible and not just for a landowner or two. Take Burling Thorn. There's land enough to support dozens and dozens of families. You know there is. They could grow potatoes, or keep pigs, and chickens, and sheep, and cattle. A cow, anyway. That's what ought to be done with big estates. They ought to be split up among people who could use the land properly. That's what I'd do, if I had Burling Thorn tomorrow."

Jim glanced rather curiously at his brother, as though speculating on something suggested by Johnnie's outburst. Then, in a single word, he summarised his own opinion of these ideas.

"Rubbish!"

Johnnie was nettled by this blunt verdict.

"Oh, indeed? You think so? Well, some other people think differently. Mr Laxford thinks it's a splendid scheme."

Jim's eyes narrowed as he heard this revelation. It hardly squared with his own opinion of Laxford's character; and for a moment or two he pondered over the point in silence, trying to fathom what lay behind the tutor's approval of such wild-cat schemes.

"Laxford thinks well of these half-baked notions, does he?" he said thoughtfully, and his tone in itself was a comment on the tutor. "Do you know, Johnnie, I hardly think Laxford's just the person for you to associate with. He seems to be a bad influence, and he's getting you right under his thumb, if you ask me. That's no sound position for you, or any of us. You'd be much better away from him and with us, even if it's not the lap of luxury."

The change from irony to thoughtfulness in Jim's tone seemed to impress Johnnie despite himself.

"I can't see why you're so set against Mr Laxford," he protested in a faintly aggrieved voice. "He's been a lot of use to me, Jim. He's broadened my mind. He's educated me. He's taught me to think for myself. . . ."

Jim Brandon ignored the opening offered to him in this last sentence. He shrugged his shoulders almost imperceptibly as though recognising that Johnnie had chosen his own fate and must be allowed to tread the path he had marked out. Getting up from his chair he took his gun from the corner and dismembered it for cleaning. Then, instead of pursuing his arguments, he passed to another subject; and, in doing so, altered his tone to one of friendly interest.

"Well, we needn't discuss these affairs where we don't see eye to eye, Johnnie. No good getting ratty with each other when I'm only here for so short a time. Was it a good show you saw when you were up in town?"

"Top-hole and farther up the strap," Johnnie declared with enthusiasm. "You ought to go and see it, Jim. I haven't laughed so much since the cat died."

He ran on into a long, detailed, and extremely wearisome account of a revue he had seen; but his brother, diligently cleaning his gun, showed no signs of boredom. On the contrary, he listened with well-feigned interest, and even stimulated the narrator with questions when the stream of dull description showed signs of drying up. At last, under this skilful treatment, Johnnie talked himself back into good humour and seemed to have forgotten their earlier disagreement, which was what his brother wanted. Jim had still some information to extract before he could feel satisfied.

"Not a bad scheme, going up to town now and again to see a show," he commented. "Nothing like a little judicious levity, as somebody says. And what else did you do with yourself in town? Lunched somewhere? And you must have had dinner before the show, I suppose. How did you fill in the rest of the time?"

But this innocently worded feeler met with no better fate than earlier probings of the same subject. Johnnie relapsed into his awkward manner, though it was clear that his hostility had died down.

"Oh, we buzzed about a bit. Here and there, you know. I had to buy some things: shirts, collars, and some shoe-laces."

"You weren't seeing a lawyer, were you?" Jim demanded with marked suspicion in his tone.

Curiously enough, Johnnie seemed quite relieved by this question.

"A lawyer? Oh, no, nothing of that sort."

"I thought perhaps you were hunting for advice behind our backs," Jim confessed.

"No, really, Jim, I wasn't."

This denial satisfied Jim as to the lawyer, for lying was unheard-of in Johnnie's code. Still, he had noted that faint uneasiness in his brother's manner, and he guessed that business of some sort—quite apart from the buying of shirts and collars—had been at the back of that trip to London. It puzzled him; but he saw from Johnnie's manner that nothing would be gained by further questions. He rose from his chair and walked over to the window which looked out upon a rather neglected lawn.

"Seems a pretty fair-sized place, this," he commented. "Some partridge-shooting, isn't there? Who's paying for it all? The rent of it, I mean."

"Di's finding the money just now," Johnnie admitted incautiously, and then seemed to wish he had not spoken. "I'm to pay her back, some time," he added.

"Who's Di?" his brother demanded, turning round.

"Mrs Laxford," Johnnie explained with a flush, as though he had been caught in a fault.

Jim Brandon frowned heavily.

"H'm! I knew it could hardly be coming out of Laxford's vast resources. D'you know, Johnnie, if I were you, I shouldn't borrow from a woman. It's done, of course. But not by people of our sort."

"Oh, that's all right, really," Johnnie assured him with a pretence of indifference which was belied by his heightened colour. "Mr Laxford knows all about it, of course. In fact, he suggested it. Besides, Di only signs the cheques; she's got nothing to do with the money, really."

"Indeed? That's a bit rum, isn't it?"

Johnnie disregarded this question and Jim, forbearing to press it, continued:

"And she keeps you in pocket-money too, I suppose. Well, see you make a note of what you get from her—every penny, mind. That sort of transaction ought to be done shipshape fashion, if it's done at all."

Johnnie had his excuse ready.

"Well, I have to have *some* cash to spend, you know, Jim. And the Governor never sends me a stiver. In fact, it's t'other way about, sometimes. Mr Laxford's been giving him a pound or two, now and again. Anyway, he used to."

"Is that so?"

Jim Brandon's tone showed that he disliked this subject, just as Johnnie fought shy of discussing his business in town. It was no pleasure to the elder brother to be reminded that his father had come so low as to sponge on the tutor whom he distrusted. He dropped the matter, came away from the window, and halted before the glass-fronted gun-cabinet in which three shot-guns stood amid a long row of empty places.

"Not an impressive show," Jim commented with a faint sneer. "A bit lonesome, they look, don't they? Who owns this one?"

He opened the cabinet and lifted one of the guns to examine it.

"That's a house-gun," Johnnie explained. "I mean, it was left here when we took over the place. The keeper uses it sometimes."

Jim replaced the gun and took up another.

"Is this another of the same?"

"Yes. The third's Mr Laxford's."

Jim replaced the gun in the cabinet without comment and closed the glass door.

"I see you've got a new 12-bore yourself," he said, turning to his brother. "Found your old 20-bore getting a bit light for you, eh? I wish I could afford a new one, but the old cylinder has to do for all the shooting I ever get, these days."

Johnnie evidently felt the implied comparison between them.

"Oh, mine isn't an eighty-guinea one," he explained with a slight titter. "Mr Laxford picked it up for me second-hand."

Then, apparently feeling that the introduction of Laxford's name was tactless, he hurried on:

"Are you still in your Company Team in the Terriers, Jim?"

His brother nodded.

"That's about all the shooting I've had for ever so long. Still, I think I can still hit a haystack as well as the next man. I'll take you on again, Johnnie, tomorrow morning, if you like."

Johnnie grinned approvingly.

"All right. Only you'll need to get up decently early."

A thought seemed to cross Jim's mind and he paused before replying.

"One thing," he qualified his challenge, "you'll have to be a bit less careless with your gun than you were this afternoon, if you get me to go out with you again. I don't want an ear blown off as an object-lesson to you in gun sense. Why the devil can't you learn to handle guns with proper care?"

"I'm careful enough," Johnnie protested sulkily.

"Meaning that you haven't blown your skull inside out, so far? You're damned easily satisfied. But you'll kindly not shoot to my side, if it's all the same to you. It shakes my nerve."

"Oh, all right. I'll remember," Johnnie assured him.

Jim picked up his own gun, assembled it, and placed it in one of the vacant places in the cabinet.

"It's a pity I've got to get back to town. I'd like to stay for the partridges, but it can't be done. By the way, Johnnie, send the

43

Governor a brace, will you? Or a couple of brace, say. It would please him, you know. He doesn't see game once in a blue moon nowadays. Treat for him to get 'em. He'd appreciate it, poor old boy."

Johnnie nodded his agreement to the suggestion, as he rose to his feet. He put his gun into the cabinet beside his brother's and then moved towards the door.

"Dinner'll be pretty soon," he informed Jim. "I've got something to do before then. You know your way about?"

"Yes. All right, see you later," Jim answered, without showing any desire to follow.

When the door closed behind his brother, Jim Brandon suddenly relaxed from the genial attitude which he had assumed at the end of the interview. His brows knitted angrily and he walked over to the window to watch the sky, which seemed to hint at more rain in the near future.

What was Laxford up to now? He hadn't taken the cub up to town to get his hair cut, that was plain enough. And he'd given Johnnie the straight tip to keep it dark, whatever it was. And the way he was fooling the young pup to the top of his bent over all these cracked notions of his. Good God! Burling Thorn cut up into allotments! What a scheme. And yet, what was Laxford himself going to get out of it? There must be a snag somewhere, if he knew Laxford. Well, Laxford would find that Jim could put a spike through his scheme no matter what it cost to do it. If the family was going to lose Burling Thorn, they'd have to get something more out of it than the pleasure of providing for slum-dwellers.

CHAPTER 3 THE SNARE

As the four men filed into the long drawing-room after dinner, Una Menteith hastily caught Jim Brandon's eye, and then made a slight but urgent gesture inviting him to sit beside her on the chesterfield. He skilfully blocked the passage of his fellow guest, who was making in that direction, and crossed over to join the girl. Hay, finding himself forestalled, gave Jim an ugly look and retired unwillingly to the far end of the room, where Laxford and Johnnie had settled themselves in arm-chairs. Una Menteith's glance followed him for a moment, and a curious expression of mingled relief and distaste flitted across her expressive face. She turned to Jim with a welcoming smile.

"I hope you enjoyed your food as much as Mr Hay did," she said crudely as he took his place beside her.

"Couldn't say more than that, could one?" he retorted.

There was every excuse for the girl's lapse into bad taste, he reflected. He had a mental vision of Hay's close-cropped bullet-head bent low over his plate, the little pale piggish eyes intent on the victuals, the red face congested with the effort of over-swift feeding. A pretty sight. No wonder the girl was disgusted.

But it seemed that there was more behind her dislike for Hay.

"I was afraid he might tack himself on to me after dinner," Una explained coolly. "He's rather ... enterprising."

Jim nodded understandingly. On the way upstairs to dress, he had surprised Hay embracing a reluctant maid, and had earned a sour look for his adventitious interruption. Apparently the fellow had tried the same trick with the governess. She must have choked him off pretty sharply, Jim surmised from what he had seen. But a man of Hay's stamp is not easily discouraged. He had evidently meant to force himself on the girl that evening; and even a room full of people might not have been a complete protection—after dinner. She had been wise to avoid trouble by calling Jim to her aid.

"He doesn't seem to fit in here, somehow," Jim volunteered in an undertone which established a certain intimacy between himself and the girl at his side.

"Of course he doesn't," she agreed contemptuously. "Look at him. His clothes are all right; he goes to a first-class tailor. And yet he manages to look over-dressed even in a short coat and black tie. You'd know there was something wrong, even before he opens his mouth."

Jim glanced across the room and inwardly admitted the shrewdness of that observation. He himself moved now among people to whom dressing for dinner was an event, and he knew the symptoms. They fumbled in the wrong pockets for their cigarettes or their pince-nez, they groped after diaries or papers they had left at home, or in extreme cases they grew embarrassed in the search for pocket-handkerchiefs. In a dozen different little ways they betrayed that they were clothed in unaccustomed garments. But Hay had none of these troubles. His hand went automatically to his cigar-case when he wanted it. He carried his dinner-jacket as though it were part of his habitual wear. And yet in some subtle way the coat and the man inside it failed to harmonise.

"Another thing," Una Menteith pointed out. "His manners are imitative and not natural, if you see what I mean. He knows what to do when he can't help sneezing, for he's seen well-bred people in that fix, and he copies what he saw them do. The same with shaking hands and not shaking hands. He's kept his eyes open, and he knows when to do it and when not to. But he swills his drink like . . . like a cow, because that's natural to him and he probably doesn't notice that he's different from his models in that. Or he may be a bit deaf," she added acidly.

Then, with a gleam of her natural irony, she turned to Jim and put an apparently innocent question:

"Are business men like that?"

"Only some of them," he countered with a smile. "We have better goods at the next counter, madam."

He guessed, easily enough, that her question had a second meaning which he was not meant to discuss just then. Was Hay a 'business man' at all? And if he were not, why had Laxford tried to pass him off as one?

But the problem of Hay was only one facet on the general situation at Edgehill. Jim Brandon was too much of an egoist to possess much of that mysterious sixth sense which detects and measures the unvoiced ebbs and flows of mood and emotion in alien minds. That insensitiveness to the imponderables made him a bad diplomatist. But tonight even his blunted perception had been enough to warn him that he was moving in a strained atmosphere.

And, rather puzzlingly, it was not the sort of tension which he had anticipated when he made up his mind to come as an unwelcome guest to Edgehill. Laxford had behaved perfectly and had not even taken an attitude of armed neutrality. There had been no sign of hostility, even involuntary.

True enough, when Jim tried to get Johnnie to himself by taking a gun into one of the spinneys after rabbits, Mrs Laxford had joined the two of them and prevented any intimate talk. It was only near the house, on their return, that they had shaken her off. Una Menteith had come out to meet them with some message which took Laxford's wife away from them. He had a suspicion that the girl had deliberately contrived that opportunity for him to talk to Johnnie alone; and that was one reason why he had gone to her aid in the drawing-room.

At the dinner-table, Laxford had exerted himself to be pleasant. He had tried to draw Jim out, deferred tactfully to his views, broached subjects which led to easy talk, and avoided any topic on which opinions might differ. His wife had seconded him in his effort to put the intruder at his ease. She was a slim, fair-haired, restless little woman, under thirty, with good looks of a rather hectic type and curiously disturbing hot eyes. She had the gift of an agreeable laugh which she was clever enough to use sparingly.

Johnnie, on her left, was obviously pleased to see his brother and his tutor on apparently amicable terms. From time to time he blundered into that nicely calculated conversation with all the innocent clumsiness of a puppy at play. More than once, in his adolescent earnestness, he began to enlarge on some topic which Laxford wished to dismiss before it grew dangerous. But then, Jim noticed, Johnnie's flow of eloquence suffered an abrupt check for no obvious reason. It needed little intuition to guess that a pressure of Mrs Laxford's tiny Louis-heeled shoe had played its unseen part on these occasions.

Miss Menteith had been a courteous but rather detached spectator. She had refrained from taking any initiative in the talk, contenting herself with answering questions addressed directly to her. Yet there had been nothing of the wet blanket about her. She had the knack of seeming a good listener, always with an alert glance for the speaker of the moment and a smile of appreciation for the point he made.

Throughout the meal, Hay had displayed no conversational talent whatever. He devoted himself wholeheartedly to his dinner, speaking only to comment favourably upon some dish which specially pleased him. Over the wine, when the women had left the room, he had grown more expansive. He seemed to have a vast store of personal anecdotes which, in most cases, depended for their points on a complete disregard for all ordinary decencies, moral or financial. He and Johnnie had finally become hotly involved in an argument about free love, which was apparently being continued in lower tones at the far end of the drawing-room.

No, Jim Brandon reflected, this queer tension in the air had nothing to do with his presence. It was not the strain of a suppressed hostility. It was the tension of expectancy. Each of them, even that gross brute Hay, was on tenterhooks, awaiting —something.

Jim's imperfect comprehension of other people's mental processes had sharpened his study of behaviour. Noumena meant nothing to him; but he could observe phenomena and draw his inferences. So now, as he made idle conversation with Una Menteith, he racked his memory for significant details at the dinner-table.

A series of pictures rose in his mind. Mrs Laxford quickening the service from time to time with a low-voiced order, and crumbling her bread with nervous fingers like a high-strung bride at her first dinner-party. Curious behaviour, that, in an experienced hostess. Johnnie, usually a hearty trencherman, toying hastily with his food and refusing to help himself twice to any dish lest he should thus spin out the meal. Hay, that glutton, furtively consulting his wrist-watch between the courses, as though worried by an approaching appointment. Even Una Menteith had betrayed herself once. She had shown a momentary hesitation in answering a direct question, as though her thoughts had been elsewhere just then. And Laxford? Jim glanced across the room at that heavy mouth, the well-marked nose, the narrow forehead sloping too sharply back to the prematurely-silvered hair. Laxford's face had given nothing away, even when he exchanged glances with his wife. But there had been something arbitrary in the way he had hindered any lingering over the wine. Hay had made a rude protest against being hustled, but Laxford had politely cut him short. And Hay had seemed to understand and had given in, gulping down a last glass as he rose to his feet.

Jim's train of thought was interrupted by Hay raising his voice at the termination of the argument at the far end of the drawing-room.

"Well, there's one thing to be said for this Free Love of yours, Mr Brandon. It 'ud come cheaper, for some of us. I'm all for it, on that side. But human natur's human natur'—you can take my word for that. A man doesn't like another man starin' at his wife's ankles and wonderin' if the rest's up to sample. And he won't stand for his wife goin' off on the sly with a fancy Joseph, neither. By no manner of means, I warn you out of my experience. See?"

Laxford seemed amused by Hay's unexpected vehemence in support of strict matrimony.

"I didn't know you were married, Hay," he interjected with a smile.

"Married? Me? You'll wait a while 'fore you see me enterin' a filly for the Parson's Stakes. It's not personal with me. I'm speakin' thee-eretically. But it's so, Mr Brandon, for all your idees. When a man gets tied up, first thing he does is to hang up a ticket: 'Hands Off! Don't Paw the Goods About!' That's human natur'. And if you don't bother about the ticket, you've got to pay. It costs you umpteen thou' in the Divorce Court, if you live in the West End, or a clip on the jaw and a thick ear if you live in the New Cut. Principle's the same, if the details are different. And quite right too."

Laxford laughed, not unkindly.

"You're prehistoric. Hay. People are more broadminded nowadays. Women aren't private property as they used to be."

"Some of 'em are common property, same as they always was," Hay retorted with a hearty guffaw.

Laxford disregarded this. He leaned forward in his chair and spoke with a certain earnestness.

"Things are changing; one can't stick to the old lines, merely because they *are* the old lines. Women are individuals nowadays, not just bits of property. Galsworthy, Wells, and all the rest of them agree on that. This personal jealousy will have to give way to something more civilised. Treaties only hold so long as both parties profit by them. One has to recognise it."

Hay seemed unimpressed.

"Well, then, there's a good time comin' for some people," he admitted jovially.

Laxford was evidently afraid of Hay going still farther over the score in his reflections, for he hastened to change the subject.

"Talking of poachers on men's preserves," he said, "the keeper here seems to think we may lose some birds if we don't look out. That's a brand of poaching I *do* dislike."

While he seemed to ponder over this, Johnnie struck in, perhaps to show Hay that he bore no malice over the argument.

"Care to have a shot at the rabbits tomorrow morning, Mr Hay? We can't touch the partridges yet."

"I don't mind," was Hay's ungracious form of acceptance.

"You'll need to get up early," Johnnie warned him. "I generally start off before breakfast, while they're at their early-morning feed. Say seven?"

"I don't mind," Hay repeated, though without enthusiasm.

"Seven, then. I'll see you're knocked up in time."

"You're coming, too, Jim?" Johnnie demanded, turning to his brother.

"Very good."

Laxford showed no signs of disturbance, but he included himself in the projected party.

"I'll come along also, Johnnie."

"Right!"

Laxford glanced at his watch and then turned to Hay.

"Care to knock the balls about? Couple of hundred up?"

Hay accepted with alacrity and the two men left the room. Johnnie made no offer to mark for them, but sat down again in his chair.

Jim Brandon had been faintly puzzled by the demeanour of Hay and Laxford during the closing stage of the argument about marriage. There had been occasional hesitations, as though that part of the dialogue had been pre-arranged but not sufficiently rehearsed. Hay, especially, had given the impression of a word-faulty actor who was too slow in picking up his cues. Besides, the idea of that fellow posing as a defender of rigid wedlock! It was laughable. Finally, he and Laxford had made their exit abruptly, like a pair of incompetent minor players huddling themselves off the stage to make way for the principals.

Jim's glance went round to Mrs Laxford, over there beside the french window. She had curled herself up on a couch with the lithe grace of a kitten, and she seemed to be engrossed in a book. When the men came into the drawing-room, she had glanced up, but had gone back to her reading with a pretty little gesture of apology.

Yet Jim easily detected that this interest in her novel was the merest pretence. She lifted her eyes from the page too frequently for an attentive reader. The mental tension he had noted at dinner still persisted, and its tell-tale physical reactions were even intensified. From time to time she shifted her attitude, as though on pins and needles, crossed and uncrossed her ankles, smoothed down her skirt mechanically, or toyed restlessly with the string of beads she was wearing. Each of her cigarettes lasted but a few minutes; one followed another in swift succession, as though she had made a bet to smoke them against time; and there was a nervous twitch in her gesture as she flicked the ash into the tray beside her on the arm of the couch. Behind the fence of her book, she seemed feverishly alert, as though chafing in expectation of some imminent and decisive call.

She looked up for a moment as the two men left the room, but it was towards Johnnie that she glanced. She bent her eyes to her book again, turned a page, and then, with what might have been an involuntary movement, upset her ashtray on to the carpet. Johnnie was on his feet in an instant, as though he had been watching for a signal. Before Jim could intervene, he had crossed the whole length of the room, retrieved the ashtray, and replaced it. Mrs Laxford gave Jim a smile of thanks for his unavailing attempt and then, with a natural movement, made a place for Johnnie on the couch beside her, putting her book down as though she were glad to be done with it.

"What sort of a night is it?" she asked. "There seems to be a thundery feeling in the air."

Jim stepped over to the french window, threw it open, and

looked at the sky.

"Cloudy, but quite dry," he reported. "It does feel a bit close."

Mrs Laxford bent over and switched off the reading lamp she had been using.

"Thunder in the air always affects me," she explained. "I must be extra sensitive. It seems to sharpen my nerves and make me ready to do the maddest things. Please leave the window open, Mr Brandon."

Then, as Jim turned back to Una Menteith, Mrs Laxford tactfully left him to his own devices and began a low-voiced conversation with Johnnie.

"It's a *new* moon just now, isn't it?" Una inquired carelessly as Jim came back and took his seat beside her on the chesterfield.

"I suppose it is. It's dark enough, outside."

He wondered if Una's remark was another specimen of her irony, a sly dig at Mrs Laxford for saying she felt off her balance that evening. Was the girl hinting that a full moon would have fitted the case better? It was under the full moon, of course, that lunatics were supposed to work up to a crisis.

It crossed Jim's mind that there might be something in Mrs Laxford's admission. Certain people were undoubtedly sensitive to a supercharge of electricity in the air; and for a moment he was inclined to accept that as a possible explanation of her restlessness; but he dismissed the idea almost as soon as it presented itself. To make it fit the facts, one would have to assume that all of them—except himself—were electrically sensitive and over-stimulated. That was nonsense. Besides, it was not such a thundery evening as all that.

"A nice night for poachers, I suppose," Una suggested, dropping into an intimate undertone so as not to disturb the conversation across the room. "Or is it 'a shiny night' they prefer? I never can remember. I expect a dark night's best if you're setting snares for rabbits."

"I suppose so," Jim agreed, not seeing much point in her remark.

Una glanced sidelong at him, with a faint trace of mockery at the corners of her lips.

"You're a very literal-minded person, aren't you, Mr Brandon?" she queried, rather irrelevantly as it seemed to him.

"I suppose I am," he admitted indifferently.

Una Menteith made the faintest gesture of vexation, as though giving him up as hopeless. She leaned back in the chesterfield with her arms behind her head and for some moments she seemed engrossed in studying the lines of her evening shoes. Apparently they suggested a fresh topic.

"I take four and a half in shoes," she said, glancing down at her neatly-shod feet with a serio-comic disapproval. "That's one of the things I envy in Mrs Laxford. She can wear threes. And, naturally, she always chooses extra smart ones. Did you notice the shoes she's wearing tonight?"

Jim Brandon had seen them, but they had not struck him as anything out of the common—smart, undoubtedly, and small, of course, but 'nothing special,' he reflected. But Una's remark stimulated a natural curiosity to examine them more carefully, and on looking across to the couch he found it easy to verify his original impression. In one of her restless movements Mrs Laxford had crossed her knees, rucking up her skirt; and, apparently unconsciously, she was stroking her ankle with a nervous action. Johnnie, as though fascinated, was intent on the little hand as it moved, slowly and caressingly, to and fro over the gossamer silk only a few inches from his knee. Suddenly Mrs Laxford became aware that Jim was watching her. She took her hand away to smooth down her skirt.

"Caught me at one of my bad habits, I'm afraid," she admitted with a smile. "I like to have my ankle stroked. There's something . . . what's the word? . . . titillating about it, with a silk stocking. It gives me a funny feeling all over, like . . ."

"Like a kitten having its fur stroked?" Una suggested, filling the gap.

"Thanks for 'kitten,'" Mrs Laxford retorted with her attractive laugh. "You always manage to avoid the worst by a hair's breadth, Una. Some people would have said 'cat' outright."

Una Menteith, with a gesture, disclaimed any wounding intention.

"I was just praising your shoes to Mr Brandon," she explained.

Mrs Laxford seemed not unwilling that they should be fully admired.

"They're rather pretty, aren't they?" she said, pulling up her skirt and moving her feet gracefully to show off the special beauties of the shoes. "You like them, Johnnie?"

She shook down her skirt with a lithe movement and threw away the end of her cigarette. It failed to go through the french window and Johnnie's dash to remove it from the carpet effectually broke up the conversation into its original pairs.

At this stage, Una Menteith seemed to exert herself more than before. Her talk lost its earlier inconsecutiveness and she drew Jim into a discussion of plays then running at the theatres in town. Here he was able to keep pace with her, though he did not think it necessary to mention that he himself had seen them from the gods and not from the stalls. There was just enough difference in their tastes to make the talk enlivening, and Jim soon forgot the rate at which time was passing. He was surprised when Mrs Laxford suddenly rose to her feet.

"I must say good night," she explained as she passed towards the door. "I've got a dreadful headache. There's nothing for it but aspirin and a soft pillow."

When she had gone, Johnnie showed no inclination to join the other two. He glanced at his wrist-watch as he sat down on the couch again. Then, switching on the reading-lamp beside him, he picked up the novel Mrs Laxford had left behind and began to read it in the middle, without paying any attention to Una and his brother. Knowing Johnnie to be a non-reader, Jim was not surprised to see him grow fidgety. He turned over three or four pages *en bloc*, skipped another page, and finally switched off the lamp again. Almost at once he got up from his seat, wandered over to the french window, and stood on the threshold, gazing up at the darkened sky. When Jim looked again, he had vanished into the garden.

Jim caught Una consulting her watch with a furtive glance, and it struck him that everyone seemed very anxious about the time that evening. Hay had been busy with his watch at dinnertime. Mrs Laxford had glanced at hers just as she said good night. Johnnie had twitched up his sleeve and looked at his watch twice, once when Mrs Laxford went away and again, within five minutes, when he rose to go to the french window. And now Una Menteith had looked at hers. One would think all these people had trains to catch, he reflected rather crossly. Or else that there was to be a murder on the premises that night, and that they were all taking precautions about alibis. And then, moved by a common human peculiarity, he glanced at his own watch and found that it was half-past ten o'clock.

As he did so, the drawing-room door opened, and a visitor was ushered in. Jim Brandon's first impression was of a man about middle height with a genial manner, kindly blue eyes, a sensitive humorous mouth under a grey moustache, and with something in his bearing which spoke plainly of unemphasised authority.

Una Menteith rose to her feet with a smile which proved that she was genuinely pleased to see the new-comer.

"It's very nice of you to come across, Mr Wendover," she greeted him. Then, introducing Jim, she added, "This is Mr Brandon—Johnnie's brother."

As Wendover acknowledged the introduction, Jim Brandon looked at him in some surprise. So this was the local criminologist that Una Menteith had mentioned when she drove him from the station. Somehow, he had pictured him differently: a trifle pompous as became a local magnate, and perhaps rather sillily interested in crimes which he read about in the newspapers. Wendover's shrewd, cataloguing glance dispelled several illusions.

"I've only dropped in for a minute or two," Wendover explained to Una. "I tried to ring you up, but my line's out of order, it seems. So I came across instead."

"Mrs Laxford's gone to bed, with a headache," Una explained. "Mr Laxford's playing billiards, I think. Shall I get him?"

Wendover brushed the suggestion aside.

"I'm sorry to hear Mrs Laxford's out of sorts. No, don't bother about Mr Laxford, please. I merely came over to ask if you'd care to play a hole or two tomorrow morning over at my place. All you need now is plenty of practice—and more follow-through," he added honestly.

Rather to Jim's surprise, Una hesitated before replying and finally declined.

"I'm afraid I can't manage it tomorrow morning," she said with obvious regret. "Nor any time during the week-end. And, of course, after that you'll be busy with the partridges. Like David—slaying your tens of thousands."

"We shan't reach even Saul's modest total, I'm afraid," Wendover retorted with a smile. "Our birds aren't quite so thick on the ground as the Philistines seem to have been at Ephes Dammin."

"Is Sir Clinton coming for the First?"

"No. I asked him, of course, but he's up to the eyes in work just now, it seems, and he can't possibly get away. He may come for a day or two, later on; but the shooting will be over long before that, I'm afraid."

"I'd like to see him again," Una said, though without any special eagerness in her tone.

Wendover had a weakness for a pretty girl, and Una Menteith's personality amused him; but he had no middle-aged illusions about his capacity to compete with younger men. Still less did he imagine that Una would find a threesome as interesting as the tête-à-tête which his arrival had interrupted. These two young people had been getting on very well together when he came in, he judged, and he had no wish to play the elderly spoil-sport.

"Well, I must be getting back to the Grange," he said. "I only came across because I couldn't telephone; and, if you'll excuse me, I've a lot of things to clear up tonight."

"Thanks for asking me to play," Una answered. "I'm very sorry I can't manage it."

She glanced at her watch, seemed to make a mental calculation, and then continued:

"It's rather stuffy, tonight, isn't it? I'd like a breath of fresh air. You've got your car, Mr Wendover? Would you mind taking me as far as the lodge-gate and dropping me there? The walk back would freshen me up a bit. You'll come too, won't you?" she asked, turning to Jim.

"I'd like to," he responded.

"That's settled then. Come along."

"But aren't you going to put on something stouter than these things?" Wendover asked with a downward glance at the delicate high-heeled slippers Una was wearing.

She hesitated for a moment over this obviously sensible suggestion, then refused as though she were anxious to get away at once.

"Oh, they'll do well enough," she said with a touch of impatience. "I don't think it's going to rain, just yet."

In the car, Wendover spoke over his shoulder to Jim, who had taken the back seat.

"I've got some young people coming at the weekend. They'll be having a dance of sorts on Monday night. Miss Menteith and your brother are coming. Would you care to join them?"

"Thanks, but I'm afraid I can't," Jim declined. "I'd like to, but I shall be leaving before then."

"I'm sorry."

Wendover seemed genuinely disappointed. After a moment or two he added inconsequently:

"I like that young brother of yours, Mr Brandon. Some of his ideas are a bit too advanced for a prehistoric survival like myself, I must admit; but I expect he'll grow out of them, just as most of us have done in our day."

"It's to be hoped so," Jim growled.

So that young fool had been jabbering his nonsense to Wendover. Nice notions to thrust on a man who owned a good estate and was obviously proud of it. Johnnie was evidently quite hopeless.

Wendover drew up the car just inside the lodge-gates.

"Well, Miss Menteith, we must try to fix up some other time for your practice. If you'll ring me up later on, when we've got our visitors off our hands . . .? Good, then that's settled. And now I must be getting along. Good night!"

"Good night!" Una called after him as the car passed on through the gates and swung into the high road with all its lights aglare.

CHAPTER 4 THE RABBIT

As the lights of the car vanished down the road, Una turned away from the lodge-gates and, with Jim at her side, paced up the avenue towards the house. When she spoke again, it was merely to break the awkwardness of a silence.

"Over yonder, on the left—you can't see it in the dark, of course—is what they call the Cottage. It's really quite a decent-sized two-storey affair. I expect it was built as a sort of dower-house for Edgehill, somewhere to stow a dowager in, if they had one on hand."

"Empty at present, then?" Jim asked indifferently.

"Yes. I believe they sometimes let it in the summer, to bring in a few pounds. It's fully furnished, I know. But no one lives there at present."

Jim made no comment, and they walked on again in silence. But it seemed that Una had not exhausted her talent for apparently inconsecutive conversation. When she spoke again, it was on an entirely fresh topic.

"Suppose you went to the telephone, Mr Brandon, and found the wires crossed, so that you overheard a conversation you weren't meant to hear. Say you heard a man give a friend some inside information that might be worth something on the Stock Exchange. What would you do about it?"

"Ring up a broker at once and put a deal through," Jim answered with a hard laugh. "That is, if I was sure the information was OK. But tips of that sort don't come my way, unfortunately."

"You'd have no scruples in the matter, then? Your finer feelings wouldn't revolt, or anything of that sort?"

If there was irony here, Jim ignored it.

"No. Why should I have scruples? If they wanted the thing kept quiet, they should not let themselves be overheard. I'm entitled to profit by anything I hear. I wouldn't be breaking any confidence."

Una neither approved nor disapproved, so far as words went.

"I'm in a curious position," she went on. "I happen to have extra-sharp ears, though I don't brag about them. And sometimes I catch things I'm not meant to hear. Tonight I heard something that might be profitable—like the Stock Exchange tip on the telephone. Or again, there may be nothing in it. It's really your affair more than mine. Should one use information got in that way?"

"Why not?" Jim demanded, in a tone that showed he himself would have no hesitation in the matter.

"All's fair in love and war, you think? Especially if the other side begins it. Very well."

She seemed to consider carefully for a moment or two, while Jim waited on tenterhooks.

"I'll do it," she said at length, "but only on one condition. You'll leave yourself entirely in my hands in the matter. I've got my own interests to look after," she added drily.

Jim's shrug was apparent, even in the dark.

"As you like," he agreed.

"Then, unless it goes too much against the grain with you"—her sneer was obvious even to Jim—"you'd better do a bit of deliberate eavesdropping. I shan't join you in it. I'm losing enough self-respect for my taste in going this length to help you. Now listen carefully."

She gave him some brief directions in a low voice, winding up with a final caution.

"I'll wait for you here. Go as quietly as you can. And remember, no matter what you hear, you're not to say a word or interfere in any way."

"Very well," Jim agreed, not too cordially.

This girl seemed to think she could order him about as she chose, he reflected crossly as he left her. However, he was in her hands to some extent and must perforce agree to her conditions. He left the path, crossed a dew-laden lawn, reached the barrier of a hedge and turned along it, according to her directions, moving with the utmost caution to avoid a noise. At length, glancing upward, he saw beyond the hedge the roof of an arbour dimly outlined against the gloomy sky; and as he came to a halt, he heard the sound of people talking in subdued tones. Jim strained his ears to catch the words.

"Don't let's stay here, Di. Let's go to the Cottage. It's a better place than this."

It was Johnnie's voice, low and urgent.

"No." Jim knew it was Mrs Laxford speaking. "I'm not going there. We can talk quite well here, Johnnie."

"I can get the key in half a jiffy," Johnnie persisted. "It's in the drawer of the hall table. No one would see me take it. Come on, Di. We'll be all alone there, with no one to disturb us."

"Nobody ever comes here at night, you silly boy."

"Please do come," Johnnie urged. "Please, Di."

"No. Don't worry me so," Mrs Laxford said pettishly. "You're as bad as a husband."

The words and tone together seemed to suggest something to Johnnie. It was a moment or two before he spoke again.

"What d'you mean?" he asked hesitatingly, as though the words went against the grain even as he said them. "He isn't beastly to you, Di?"

Mrs Laxford gave a faint laugh which seemed to have a touch of bitterness in it.

"No, he isn't. He doesn't beat me, ii that's what you mean. But we've nothing in common now, he and I—not even a bedroom. We never quarrel. He's easy-tempered and all that, but . . ."

She paused, evidently to let Johnnie fill in the gap for himself.

When she spoke again, the words came faster and a more emotional tone crept into her voice.

"Oh, I suppose it's partly my fault, Johnnie; but marriage isn't what I expected, somehow. He's got used to me, I suppose. He's long past the stage where there's any attraction in my looks or anything else about me. He takes it all for granted. He never looks at what I put on, now. These shoes and stockings I have on tonight, I saw you admiring them. It's the first time I've had them on. But he never even noticed, he didn't give them a glance. I'm nothing to him nowadays, except that I run the house and play hostess for him. That's all my marriage has come to, Johnnie."

She paused again with a little catch in her breath. Then, without giving Johnnie a chance to break in, she continued haltingly.

"I looked for something quite different when I married him. You know what I mean . . . passion . . . desire . . . a thrill every time we kissed . . . something that would make the world into a sort of dream. And I've missed it all. So far as I'm concerned, he's like ice. I don't stir him now. I can't stir him. I've tried . . . It's no good . . . And yet, if he knew I was letting you kiss me, he might . . . I don't know what he might do."

"If he's like that, he wouldn't mind, no matter what you did," said Johnnie with blundering reassurance, failing to see the double-edge in his remark. "He's broad-minded. He looks at things from a different angle from the ordinary hide-bound lot. He's often told me that."

"Yes," said Mrs Laxford scornfully, "because he feels sure of me. I'm not so sure of myself, when I think what I'm missing. I want to live differently. I'd like to feel that someone really wants me, longs for me, can't do without me. If I had that . . . Oh, I do wish I could start afresh, all over again with someone who wasn't all ice. I want something . . . Oh, I don't know what I want, but I feel so lonely and so wretched. I want someone to be kind to me, to pet me—yes, I mean it, to pet me physically just as if I were an animal that he was soothing. That's what I'm missing so much. It makes me miserable. . . ."

Her voice broke as though her emotion overpowered her, and a burst of low weeping followed. Jim heard a movement in the arbour and some stumbling words of comfort from his brother. After awhile, the sobbing died away and there was silence, broken occasionally by murmurs of inarticulate tenderness. Then at last, very clearly, Mrs Laxford's voice was raised in a half-hearted protest:

"No, Johnnie.... No, you mustn't, dear.... No, *please!*"

Instantly, as though at a signal, an electric pocket lamp flashed in the darkness beyond the arbour. Then Hay's voice, jeering and triumphant, broke in:

"Caught you, have I? I knew there was some funny business goin' on tonight. Wish I'd a flashlight camera with me. 'Twould have made a pretty picture, wouldn't it?"

Then, as he switched off his lamp, he added:

"So that was why you signed that thing, eh? For value received? That's a good joke on my pal Laxford, isn't it?"

Jim, separated from the others by the hedge, could not have intervened effectively even had he given no promise to Una. He heard a sudden movement in the arbour as though Johnnie had sprung to his feet and then a vehement whisper from Mrs Laxford:

"No, Johnnie. We can't risk a row. We must talk to him. Sit down. Sit down, do you hear?"

Evidently Johnnie reluctantly obeyed, for when she spoke again it was to Hay:

"Well, what are you going to do?"

Her voice was quite firm and showed no trace of the recent emotion. She did not even seem shaken by the rudeness of the surprise which Hay had given them. Jim began to think that he had under-estimated her character.

"What am I going to do?" Hay repeated out of the darkness. "There's one question comes before that. What is there in it for me? That'll take a bit of thinkin' over, that will."

"Be quiet, Johnnie!" Mrs Laxford exclaimed with almost savage emphasis. "Leave me to manage this." Then she continued in a more even tone. "You mean, Mr Hay, that you'll tell my husband about this if it pays you, and that you'll refrain from telling him if that pays you better?"

"You've hit it at once," Hay concurred.

Mrs Laxford seemed to ponder for a moment or two.

"Very well," she said at last, "we'll have to think this out. Suppose you go away now and leave us to talk it over. In the meantime, you'll say nothing to my husband, of course?"

"Not likely," Hay assured her. "But just you remember this, young Mr Brandon. You may swallow all that talk about free love that Laxford's been givin' you. But Laxford'll look at it a bit harder if he finds it on his own doorstep, I can tell you. He won't be so airy-fairy about it when he finds you've been cuddlin' his wife. I know him. Just you make a note of that, for the good of your health."

And with this parting shot he moved off in the darkness.

"Let's get out of this," Jim heard Johnnie suggest in the tone of a nervous schoolboy. "We can walk about, Di. I don't want to stay here any longer."

"Very well," Mrs Laxford agreed without protest.

Jim heard them rise and move out of the arbour. He paused for a moment or two, in order to let them get out of earshot, and then he made his way back to where he had left Una. When he rejoined her, she asked only one question:

"Well, are you satisfied?"

"I heard my young brother making love to Mrs Laxford, if that's what you mean, and then Hay came and caught them at it."

"I don't want to hear anything about it," Una interrupted angrily. "The only interest I have in it is on Johnnie's account. . . . Oh, I'm not jealous of Mrs Laxford. You needn't imagine that. I'm interested in Johnnie, but not in that way at all. Get that quite clear in your mind."

Then, after a momentary pause, she added:

"You didn't give yourself away, I hope."

"No, they didn't guess I was there."

Una seemed to ponder for a while before she spoke again.

"If you take my advice, Mr Brandon, you'll make no move until tomorrow."

"Why?" Jim demanded bluntly.

This girl seemed to imagine that she could dictate to him as she pleased. She had been helpful, of course; but that didn't entitle her to carry on like a commander-in-chief.

"Haven't I given you sound advice, so far?" she queried in her turn, with a tinge of disdain in her tone. "Would you have got wind of this affair if you'd taken your own course and stayed at the Talgarth Arms? Not a bit of it! You'd have been stumbling about, playing your game in the dark, if I hadn't helped to open your eyes."

"I'll admit that," said Jim curtly. "But why shouldn't I speak to Johnnie about it tonight?"

"For three reasons," the girl replied coolly. "First, because you're a bad diplomatist and you'd probably make a bungle of the business. It needs very careful handling. Second, because you've no plan ready. That's true, isn't it? You'll need a night to think the thing out in all its bearings and make up your mind on the best line to follow. And, third, because I've called up reinforcements that may be useful."

Jim felt the contempt in her first two statements, and he winced the more since he recognised that there was some basis for it. To rush in tonight, with no settled plan, would be the worst kind of diplomacy. He let this go by default and fastened on her third reason.

"Reinforcements? What sort of reinforcements?"

"Something that may help to turn the scale." Una seemed nettled by his attitude. "And as you aren't calling them up it'll be time enough to discuss them when they appear. You're not a very grateful person, Mr Brandon, it seems to me."

She had a remarkable knack of putting one in the wrong, Jim reflected ruefully. It was true enough that he had forgotten to thank her for the help she had already given him. He had been so intent on the main problem that he had spared no thought for graces or even for simple courtesy to her. And now she was paying him back by this bit of petty mystery-mongering. He shrugged his shoulders angrily in the dark. Let her keep her two-penny little secret if she wanted to! He didn't intend to crawl to her, merely to learn it.

Una had paused, evidently to allow him a chance of putting himself right. As he did not seize it, she went on smoothly, but with that assumption of command which irritated him:

"I'm going to leave you here. It won't do for us to go back together to the house. Someone might see us and put two and two together, though it's not likely. I'll go first and get in by the side door, through the conservatory. You'll wait here for five minutes and then follow up, but you'd better go in by the front door. I'd go straight to my room, if I were you. You'd better not meet any of these people tonight."

She bade him no formal good night but slipped away abruptly into the darkness. Jim gave her the five minutes' grace and then made his way back to the house in leisurely fashion. As he passed the french window of the drawing-room he noticed that it was now closed, and through the uncurtained panes he caught a glimpse of Hay and Laxford sitting there, deep in consultation, with glasses of whisky and soda beside them. Hay seemed to be doing most of the talking, whilst Laxford listened, cheek on hand and elbow on the arm of his chair, his face betraying nothing of his thoughts.

Jim found the front door ajar and entered with caution. No sound of conversation reached him through the closed drawing-room door as he passed it on his way to the stairs. He had an impulse to listen for a moment or two; but eavesdropping there was too risky. There was always the chance that a servant might come into the hall and catch him at it. He climbed the stair and went along a corridor towards his own room. As he passed John-nie's bedroom, he noticed that the door was wide open. Evidently Johnnie was still in the gardens, settling his account with Mrs Laxford.

Once in his own room, Jim Brandon switched on the light,

closed the door, and flung himself angrily into an arm-chair. He had no intention of going to bed just then. He had too much to think about. He lit a cigarette and for a while he smoked, turning over in his mind the events of the last two or three hours.

Of course, he reflected, this affair hadn't been planned on the spur of the moment; they must have been leading up to it for days—or weeks, most likely. No doubt Mrs Laxford had put Johnnie through a progressive course in philandering: holding hands, toying with shoes under the table, minor caresses in odd corners, hurried embraces with a watchful eye for intruders, kissing on the sly, and all with the extra spice of something forbidden. That preparation had been carried out before he himself appeared at Edgehill; but anyone could see that it was an essential preliminary before they risked their final stroke in the arbour.

Jim's habitual dependence upon superficial symptoms drove him to recall what he had observed, consciously or subconsciously, since the gong sounded for dinner. Bit by bit, each detail fell into place, until in the new context even Una Menteith's disjointed remarks became infused with fresh meanings. That night, everything had been directed towards a single end.

This accounted for the curious tension at dinner, the air of expectancy which had puzzled him at the time. They'd been following a pre-arranged time-table. So long for dinner, with Mrs Laxford's shoe at work under the table. She had made it serve two purposes, only one of which Jim had understood at the time. Besides acting as a check on Johnnie's blundering conversation, that tiny shoe had given his senses a preliminary canter, in preparation for the second stage.

Next Hay had been utilised, with his after-dinner stories, to attack Johnnie's equilibrium from a new angle. And then, having set his imagination grossly afire, they had turned to the task of weakening his inhibitions. That was what lay behind that grotesque discussion on free love, Jim could now see clearly. Laxford had let Johnnie infer that so far as Mrs Laxford was concerned, Johnnie had a free hand. Hay's part in the argument was evidently contrived to make his coming intervention more plausible. A very ingenious bit of work, Jim admitted to himself. No wonder they had talked like inferior actors. The whole thing must have been memorised beforehand.

And, meanwhile, a fresh attack had begun in the drawing-room. That hot-eyed little jade on the couch had played her part better than the two men, Jim judged. Each of these restless movements was meant to catch Johnnie's eye and make him restless too. And when Johnnie joined her on the couch there was that hint about the thunder: 'It seems to sharpen my nerves and make me ready to do the maddest things.' And then all that 'show-a-leg business,' as he brutally described it to himself, that stroking of her ankle: 'There's something . . . titillating about it with a silk stocking. It gives me a funny feeling all over.' No doubt Johnnie was expected to make a note of that idiosyncrasy, although the words had actually been addressed to himself. And when she saw she had the game in her hands, she must have made an appointment at the arbour.

Even there, she had managed to kill two birds with one stone. To avoid Jim's suspicions, she had made that excuse about a headache and had gone out of the drawing-room, leaving Johnnie to wander out through the french window, apparently alone. But before she slipped out of the front door to rejoin him, Jim guessed, she had passed the word to the couple in the billiard-room, so that Hay might know that he must go to the rendezvous.

As to the business in the arbour, he had missed a lot of it, no doubt. From his own point of view, her pose as a misunderstood wife was a poor affair; but it had worked well enough with Johnnie who had no experience of the world and who, by that time, had probably no wits left in control. And, obviously, that cry of semi-surrender had been the prearranged signal for Hay to come out of the darkness and play his part.

And then, with a final stroke of cleverness, she had taken control of the situation, pushed Johnnie aside, and negotiated with Hay herself.

"Damnably smart bit of business, the whole thing," Jim confessed to himself with a scowl. "Laxford's cuter than I took him for."

He had no doubt that Laxford had planned the whole affair. The other two were mere subordinates coached for their parts by the leading spirit.

Then his thoughts turned to Una Menteith and he paid a grudging tribute to her astuteness. These apparently aimless remarks of hers had their hidden meaning, if he had only been sharp enough to catch it at the time. That one about the new moon had been double-edged. It was meant to draw his attention specially to Mrs Laxford's talk about 'being ready to do the maddest things,' and it was also to remind him that the night was dark. 'A nice night for poachers,' she had called it, just after Laxford had spoken of people 'poaching on men's preserves' in the matrimonial sense. And she had underscored that by talking about setting snares for rabbits on a dark night. Of course Johnnie was the rabbit she meant. And when she saw that Jim was too dull to notice her hints, she had given him a straight tip: 'You're a very literal-minded person, aren't you?' Jim winced as he thought of the mocking expression which had gone with the words. After that she had resorted to more direct methods. That apparently pointless talk about shoes had been meant to draw his attention to Mrs Laxford's manoeuvres on the couch across the room—the ankle-stroking and all that sort of thing. Una Menteith had succeeded there, without committing herself in the slightest.

His mind passed to Wendover's visit. Why had she refused that invitation so definitely? Of course! Because she had 'called up reinforcements,' as she put it; and she had to keep herself free on that account. That meant the reinforcements might turn up tomorrow. What did she mean by 'reinforcements'? Jim wondered.

But Una Menteith was only a minor character in the Edgehill drama. His mind went back to Laxford and his scheme. Hitherto Laxford had only his moral influence with Johnnie to throw into the scale against the Brandon interests; but that coup in the arbour had given him a double hold on the youngster. By remaining in pretended ignorance, Laxford could retain his old mastery while using his wife and Hay to play on Johnnie's fears of discovery and make him amenable. Johnnie had enough decency in him to feel ashamed of what he had done, Jim suspected; and a boy in that state would be mere clay in the hands of a clever scoundrel like Laxford, aided by his confederates. Jim bit his lip as he explored one possible course after another which Laxford might choose.

Then a fresh idea crossed his mind. Why had Laxford chosen to execute his plan at the very moment when Jim was on the premises? That seemed like taking unnecessary risks. Why hadn't they waited over the week-end and sprung their mine after he had cleared out? Then he remembered the people who were coming for the shooting next week; the house would be crowded; and the chance of carrying out a carefully timed scheme would be gone. The coup had been planned for that night, and when he made his unexpected incursion they had to take the risks, whether they liked it or not. It was a case of now or never. Besides, if they had waited, Johnnie in his excited state might have forced the pace with Mrs Laxford and taken the bit in his teeth at a moment when Hay was not available. That would have complicated matters, for Jim had a shrewd suspicion that Laxford didn't mean his wife to go to extremes. Obviously their best policy had been to go through with their original plans even under Jim's very nose. As he admitted to himself, resentfully, he'd never have seen through their game without Una Menteith's help.

He glanced at his watch and found that it was later than he thought. He switched off the light, opened his door, and glanced out. The house was dark and silent; everyone must have gone to bed.

Cautiously he made his way down the corridor and tried the door of his brother's room. He wanted to see how Johnnie was taking it; and it would be easy enough to fake up some excuse for disturbing him, even at that hour. But the door was locked; and when Jim knocked gently there was no response. His ear caught a faint sound of movement in the room. Evidently Johnnie was awake. It was hardly likely that he'd be asleep after his evening's experiences. Jim tapped again on the door.

"Johnnie!" he called softly, to let his brother know who was there.

But Johnnie evidently had no wish for visitors. Jim heard him move again, but he made no answer. Jim turned away and went back to his own room, fretting with rage. A pretty business! The whole Brandon position shaken because a damned young cub couldn't keep control of himself for an evening! This was the end of all his own hopes for a diplomatic settlement. And then, into his mind flashed Hay's words at the arbour:

"So that's why you signed that thing, eh? For value received?"

What had Johnnie signed? Jim pondered over that problem with growing perturbation. It must have been a business paper; the phrase 'for value received' made that clear enough. So Laxford had already attained to the stage of documents and signatures. Johnnie had promised something—'for value received'— and that something could only concern the Brandon inheritance. And then, with a kindred menace, the recollection of that unexplained trip to London edged itself up in Jim's thoughts.

He was so engrossed in his reflections that the bursting of the long-heralded storm failed to rouse him. Roll after roll of thunder shook the windows, followed by the heavy beat of straight-falling rain upon the ground outside. At last Jim woke from his introspection with a muttered comment:

"That'll bring the streams down, bank-full, if it goes on."

Suddenly a flood of relief swept over his mind as he realised that no real damage could have been done yet. Johnnie was a minor. In legal transactions, his signature was not worth the paper it was written upon. He breathed more freely as he remembered this. Curious that it should have slipped his mind! Then came a fresh doubt. Laxford must be quite well aware that Johnnie's signature had no binding power; and still he had persuaded the cub to put his name to some paper. It must be yet another move in that twister's crooked game, Jim reflected, if only one could spot the meaning of it.

It was invalid now. But tomorrow Johnnie came of age and his signature would be effective. And after this night's work, Laxford had in his hands a weapon of coercion which might make it easy to extort a second signature, an effective one, from a cowed and repentant youngster.

CHAPTER 5 THE HA-HA OF DEATH

Jim Brandon always began the day badly if he had less than eight hours of undisturbed sleep. His prolonged and anxious cogitation overnight had sent him to bed far in the small hours; time and again in the night he had wakened to a fresh consideration of his problem, and when a gentle knock on his door aroused him at an unaccustomed hour, he was in anything but good fettle for another day of strain and diplomacy. He got out of bed reluctantly at the summons, drew aside the window-curtains, and looked out disgustedly at a rainy, squally morning with heavy clouds racing over a leaden sky. A nice day for Johnnie's coming-of-age, he reflected grimly.

Once fully aroused, he wasted no time but dressed quickly. The danger-period had begun. Johnnie's signature to a document would now be valid; and it was essential, if possible, to prevent Hay or Laxford from contriving a private interview with the boy and inveigling him into signing anything.

When he was ready he made his way quietly along the corridor to his brother's room, hoping to catch him before he went downstairs to join the others. When Jim passed it on the way to his bath, Johnnie's door had been closed; but it was now half-open, and a glance inside showed that the room was empty. The untidiness of the place jarred on Jim's orderly mind. On the previous night Johnnie seemed to have walked about as he undressed, flinging each discarded article of clothing on the chair which happened to be nearest when he stripped it off. The confusion was symptomatic of his mental perturbation when he returned after his interview with Mrs Laxford. And the tumbled bedclothes, witnesses of long-continued turning and tossing, were proof enough that sleep had forsaken him even when he got between the sheets. Jim, from his own experience, could make a guess at how Johnnie must have felt as he lay there, confronting the first grave problem that he had ever had to face in his twenty years of life. Well, if cubs made damned fools of themselves, they had to pay for it; that was the way of the world.

Jim descended the staircase, and at the foot he encountered the butler.

"The other gentlemen are in the dining-room, sir," the man informed him. "I brought them some sandwiches. If there's anything you would like...?"

"No, nothing, thanks," Jim answered. "Is Mrs Laxford there?"

As he uttered the words he felt that his tongue had run away with him. No one would expect her to be downstairs at this time in the morning. He had merely blurted out his question because his thoughts had been running on her so much. Fortunately the butler's answer relieved his mind.

"No, sir. Mrs Laxford is breakfasting in her room. She is catching the early train, with the children, to do some shopping in Town; but she will not be down for some time yet."

Jim nodded, and the butler threw open the dining-room door for him. His first glance showed him Hay recharging his glass of whisky and soda at the sideboard. Johnnie was sitting at the table, with a glass of milk and a plate of sandwiches beside him; but it was clear that he had made no headway with either of them. He did not look up as his brother entered the room, but kept his eyes on his plate with a hang-dog air. Jim could not see his face. Laxford, leaning against the mantelpiece, seemed to be fidgeting slightly as though anxious to get started. There was no sign of any document; but Jim felt no reassurance at that. A fountain-pen makes no show, and a paper can be pocketed in a moment.

Laxford looked up as Jim came into the room.

"A miserable sort of morning, I'm afraid," he greeted Jim with the same polite cordiality which he had shown overnight. "Edgehill's hardly showing you its best side, Mr Brandon. Would you care to have a sandwich . . . or biscuits, perhaps? This is a rather early start, and it'll be a while before you get breakfast, you know."

Jim shook his head.

"I'm not hungry, thanks," he said curtly.

He watched with mild surprise the generous dose of liquor which Hay was pouring out for himself. It was beyond his experience to see a man beginning the day with whisky and soda on an empty stomach, and the sandwiches had been left untouched, apart from the one which Johnnie was making a pretence of nibbling. Hay caught Jim's eye, grinned broadly, and lifted his glass as if giving a toast.

"Well, here's to a good shoot up West, the night I get back to Town!" he said with a coarse guffaw. "This country air of yours is a fair corpse-reviver, Laxford, I'll say that for it. Makes me feel like twenty-one again," he added, with a sidelong leer in Johnnie's direction.

At this thrust Johnnie lifted his head involuntarily, as if stung by some noxious insect; and in that instant Jim caught a glimpse of his brother's face. It was hardly recognisable. Only a few hours ago it had been the face of a rather simple, trusting, and care-free youngster, ignorant of the seamy side of life. Now bitter experience had re-drawn its lines, transforming it into something with a different meaning. Shame, remorse, misery, fear, and despair: all seemed to have left their marks on those tragic lineaments. The whole agony of Johnnie's sleepless night was written in his reddened eyes. He looked like some dumb creature, caught and tortured in a trap from which there was no escape. Even the faculty of resistance seemed to have faded out in him. "I'm at the end of my tether!" was the abject confession in his pose as he sat hunched in his chair. Without looking towards any of the other three he bent his head again and made a futile pretence of finishing his sandwich.

Hay gulped down his whisky, emitted a loud gasp of satisfaction, and replaced his empty tumbler on the sideboard.

"About time we were moving, eh?"

Laxford nodded and turned towards the door. Johnnie heaved himself clumsily to his feet. His whole bearing reminded his brother of a dog which has just been soundly thrashed for some fault. Jim bit his lip at the sight.

"Takes his medicine badly," he reflected pitilessly. "If he'd any spunk in him, he'd keep a stiffer upper lip for the credit of the rest of us. Oswald wouldn't have lost his grit like this."

It never occurred to him that Oswald was a man of the world with hard experiences behind him, whereas Johnnie was suffering from an initial contact with a world of which he had never dreamed.

In the gun-room only one of the house-guns stood on the rack; the other one had disappeared. Jim picked up his own gun; Johnnie secured his private 12-bore.

"The keeper must have taken our other gun," Laxford explained to Hay. "He sometimes uses it. This one I'm accustomed to myself, but you can have it if you like. It's all the same to me."

Hay grunted something in response, took down the spare gun, gave it a trial, and seemed satisfied.

"It'll do me," he said. "Keep your pet one if you want to."

"Very well," Laxford agreed.

Johnnie had gone to a drawer and was putting some cartridges in his pockets. Jim crossed to his side.

"What are you using?"

"Number Fives," Johnnie mumbled.

"Number Sevens give you fifty per cent more chance of a hit," Jim commented rather absently. "Still, it's a gusty morning and Number Seven might be on the light side. Give me the same as you're using."

Johnnie obediently handed out a supply to him, and then served Hay and Laxford before he closed the drawer. With an unobtrusive movement Jim blocked his brother's way until the other two had left the room.

"These fellows haven't been getting you to sign anything this morning before I turned up?" he demanded roughly.

"No," Johnnie answered dully.

He seemed as though he meant to add something to the monosyllable, but apparently changed his mind.

"H'm! Well, you're of age now, Johnnie. Congratulations."

Despite his relief at Johnnie's admission, Jim betrayed no warmth in his felicitation. Johnnie evidently felt his brother's coldness, for he acknowledged the cavalier good wishes only with a gloomy nod, and, evidently glad to escape, followed the others out of the room. Hay and Laxford were at the front door, staring at the windy sky and apparently not too pleased with the weather.

"Are you taking the keeper with you?" Jim inquired as he joined them.

Johnnie shook his head without speaking. Laxford evidently agreed with him.

"Hardly worth while," he explained. "Johnnie's been shooting so much that it isn't possible to drag a keeper about every time he goes out, and we've fallen out of the way of bringing him along. We'll do without him this morning."

Jim made a gesture of agreement.

"I was only thinking of someone to carry any rabbits we shoot," he said indifferently. "By the way, Johnnie, if it's all the same to the others, I'd rather go over the ground we covered yesterday afternoon. I know it, more or less, and it's easier shooting when you know where you are."

"Where was that, Johnnie?" Laxford demanded.

Johnnie muttered a word or two.

"Oh, you mean the Long Plantation?" Laxford continued. "I don't mind, Mr Brandon. Certainly, if you like it. We can walk down the road to the far end and do our shooting as we come up again through the wood. That suits you? Devilish rainy morning," he added with a glance at the sky. "We can always shelter under a tree if it gets much worse."

They moved off through the gardens and struck a rough wood road which ran more or less parallel to the edge of the Long Plantation. The track was narrow for four abreast, and Johnnie dropped behind the others. An awkward silence fell upon the group; even Hay's coarse humour failed. This squally morning, with its heavy sky and burst of rain promised nothing to the shooting-party but a dreary fiasco.

After a time Jim glanced over his shoulder at the dejected figure lagging in the rear. Johnnie's eyes were bent on the ground. Rapt in his miserable thoughts, he seemed heedless of the outer world and trudged listlessly along the track with his gun held so carelessly that it pointed straight towards the group in front of him.

"Damn you, Johnnie!" Jim protested sharply. "Don't carry your gun at the trail like that. You'll be holding it in your mouth, next. Have some pity on our feelings."

At the fretful rebuke, Johnnie lifted his sombre eyes for a moment. Mechanically he shifted his gun to the 'secure' and then seemed to lapse again into his thoughts. Laxford and Hay had looked behind them as Jim remonstrated with his brother, but when they saw the gun in a safer position they turned again without comment and plodded on along the track.

As they came to the lower end of the plantation, where a little house abutted on the wood road, the rain suddenly broke on them in a heavy downpour.

"Better shelter in the porch of the gardener's cottage," Laxford suggested. "This won't last long, and there's no use standing out in it."

They broke into a run and crowded under the cover of the little penthouse roof which screened the cottage door. Johnnie, coming last, had to stand partly in the lashing rain.

"I'd've had another go of whisky, if I'd guessed it'd be like this," Hay declared regretfully. "I take back what I said about your air, Laxford. It's mostly water. Fair drowns the miller, it does. Good for frogs and nothing else."

The cottage door opened and a roughly-clad man appeared.

"Oh, it's you, sir?" he said, as his eye fell on the group. "Won't you step inside, out of the wet? The worst of it'll soon be over," he added, after casting a weather-wise glance skyward.

"It's all right, thanks." Laxford declined the invitation. "We'd make a mess of your floor, Stoke, with boots like these. Besides, as you say, it won't be more than a short burst."

They waited on the threshold, chatting aimlessly with the gardener, until a faint blink of whiter light heralded the end of the downpour.

"About time we moved on," Laxford suggested, setting the example with a nod of farewell to the gardener.

The others followed him, Johnnie still lagging in the rear. The gardener watched them as they turned past his garden and made for the square end of the Long Plantation.

"We'll need to spread out, here," Laxford pointed out as they neared the edge of the wood. "The undergrowth's fairly thick in parts, and we might be shooting into each other if we don't keep well apart."

Jim made a gesture of agreement.

"If it's all the same to you," he said, "I'll take the east side, beyond that stream. I was over that ground yesterday afternoon and I'd rather have that beat."

Laxford seemed to hesitate over this proposal.

"The Carron's pretty full, with all this rain," he pointed out. "It's on the cards that the stepping-stones may be under water over there, and there's no other way of getting across until you come to the foot-bridge just above the house."

"I'll manage it all right," Jim assured him with a certain stiffness. "I'm not afraid of getting my feet wet."

Laxford at once gave in.

"Very well, just as you please. Johnnie, you'd better walk up the line of the ha-ha. I'll take the middle line up the wood. You can take the west side, Hay. If we stick to that, we shan't poach on each other's preserves."

No one objected to this arrangement, and the party split up.

Hay moved towards the western fringe of the plantation, Laxford went straight forward, whilst Jim, with Johnnie lagging at his heels, took an eastward direction. He had no need to appeal to his brother for guidance. The previous day's excursion had taken him over this ground, and he had the gift of memorising unconsciously not only the general lie of a country-side but even individual landmarks.

From its crest near Edgehill the Long Plantation sloped down obliquely towards the south-east; but the incline terminated on the edge of an almost level tract bordering the little Carron, whilst the wood itself extended beyond the stream. The junction of high and low ground was demarcated by a ha-ha: a four-foot stone wall forming a tiny cliff, its top flush with the slope and its base resting on the horizontal stretch below.

The plantation was a mixed one, with patches of heavy undergrowth which impeded direct progress; but Jim had no difficulty in striking a path which led, he remembered, to the stepping-stones over the Carron. The track was narrow, winding in and out among the trees, and the brothers had to go in Indian file. When they came to the ha-ha Jim halted and turned to his brother.

"You're going to walk along the top of the sunk fence, aren't you? I go farther on, across the stream."

Johnnie nodded rather absent-mindedly.

"Bet you five bob my bag's bigger than yours," Jim continued. "Take it?"

For the first time that morning Johnnie seemed to rouse himself. Apparently the inveterate sporting instinct momentarily conquered. Shooting was his favourite pastime, and even in his troubles it held its place in his mind.

"Done!" he agreed briefly.

Jim stepped to the edge of the miniature cliff and glanced down into the ditch running along the foot of the wall.

"Not much of a jump," he commented. "But the landing-place looks pretty muddy. I can't afford to sprain my ankle."

He laid his gun down on the grass on the top of the sunk fence, chose his ground carefully, and made his leap, landing with a stagger on the far side of the ditch. Johnnie handed him his gun.

"See you later."

Johnnie, standing on the higher ground at the crest of the sunk fence, watched his brother's figure receding among the trees until it vanished behind one of the clumps of undergrowth. Then he turned northward and began to walk up the line of the ha-ha, keeping close to the edge so that he could overlook the lower ground on his right as well as the upward slope on his left. He did his best to concentrate his mind on the wager with Jim and to forget, even for a few minutes, the troubles which beset him.

A white scut caught his eye, and he fired at the little scurrying brown thing just as it dodged behind the roots of a fallen tree. It reappeared momentarily and then vanished among some tall grass. Almost at the same instant two shots in rapid succession sounded from the left, where Laxford's beat lay. Johnnie reloaded his empty barrel and continued his way along the top of the ha-ha.

Jim heard these three shots as he reached the stepping-stones. The little stream was in spate, bank full, and the stones were covered by a swirl of foam-flecked brown water. Jim stepped cautiously out on to the first stone, and a wave swept over his ankles, almost dislodging him from his foothold. He picked his way judiciously from stone to stone till he came to mid-stream, where he paused for a moment to gauge his next stride. As he stood poised he heard behind him the sound of people shouting —a brief dialogue. He guessed that the voices were Johnnie's and Laxford's, but the gusts which swept the plantation made clear hearing difficult.

He got across the stream without mishap. With the Carron in high flood like this there would be no chance of crossing it again until he came to the foot-bridge above Edgehill. He listened for a moment or two, but the voices had ceased; and without paying more attention he climbed the little bank before him and turned up-stream.

Within fifty yards he flushed a rabbit and brought it down with a clean shot. Then he was faced by a difficulty. To carry it was to hamper himself so much that he might give up any further shooting, whilst if he left it lying where it was, he might have to come back later to retrieve it, or else direct the keeper to pick it up. Without hesitation he decided to leave it behind.

He continued on his way, keeping a sharp look-out for the chance of a shot. Owing to a curve in the Carron's course, he was drawing in towards the line of the ha-ha as he walked upstream; and when two reports reached his ears almost simultaneously, they were much louder than the earlier ones. From the relative intensities he guessed that Hay and Johnnie had fired. Then came another shot from the nearer gun. Johnnie seemed to have aroused himself, put aside his troubles for the time being, and bent his energies to winning his bet.

"Nothing like a little shooting to blow away the cobwebs," Jim reflected rather grimly.

His eye caught a rabbit as it took fright and fled up the slope, and he sent it rolling head over heels with a snap shot. Then, leaving it lying, he continued his way. By this time he had climbed well above the stream, for at this stage in its course the Carron ran through a tiny steep-sided glen hardly fifty feet in breadth, with patches of heavy undergrowth growing on the edges of the chasm. It was only here and there that Jim could catch a glimpse of the ha-ha on the farther side. Once he saw Johnnie's figure moving cautiously on the slope at the top of the sunk fence, and he regulated his own pace to keep level with him. It struck him as curious that with three of them on the far side of the stream, there should be so little shooting. He heard one report in the farther part of the plantation after a time, but that was all.

*

But Tragedy was afoot in the Long Plantation that morning.

A gunshot. The noise of the wind tearing at the tree-tops. In the lull between two gusts a voice called:

"Did you hit…?"

No answer. After a minute or more a second gunshot, followed by a fresh call from the same voice:

"Did you get anything, Johnnie?"

A longer pause. Sounds of movements in the wood, drowned almost completely by the intermittent blasts. Then, suddenly, there came a shout:

"Brandon! Brandon!! There's been an accident. Your brother's shot himself."

A startled ejaculation from Jim came down the wind from fifty yards up-stream on the farther bank.

"Come here, quick, Brandon," Laxford's voice ordered. "Go round by the foot-bridge; it's the nearest way. He's shot in the head. Must have fallen over the edge of the ha-ha, and his gun's gone off."

Owing to a bend in the Carron's course and an intervening belt of undergrowth, the actual site of the tragedy was hidden from Jim. He set off, hot-foot, for the bridge, crossed it, and followed the line of the ha-ha down-stream. He had not far to go before catching sight of Hay and Laxford, on the top of the sunk fence, bending over something which lay between them. In a moment or two he came close enough to see Johnnie's body, face downward, with a pool of blood on the grass where the head lay.

The tragedy had been enacted in a tiny glade, surrounded on one side by a rough semicircle of thick bushes of which the line of the ha-ha formed the chord. Below the sunk fence the ground fell away down a short and steep grass slope towards the chasm through which roared the swollen waters of the stream; and on the far side of the Carron was a thick belt of shrubs and undergrowth.

Jim knelt down when he reached the body. That gaping wound behind the right ear told its own story plainly enough, even to his inexperienced eyes.

"Bad job, this," said Hay dully.

Jim glanced up at the words. And as he did so, from behind the screen of undergrowth appeared the figure of a total stranger with a gun in his hand.

CHAPTER 6 MAN IN
THE BIG HOUSE

Mr Kenneth Dunne of Fairlawns was in many ways a fortunate man. He lived in a roomy mansion surrounded by spacious grounds; and in the well-tended flower-gardens he whiled away his time pleasantly enough, when weather permitted, for he was interested in horticulture. A large and expensive staff ministered to his needs and saw to it that the comfortable routine of his existence ran, week in and week out, with the smoothness of a dynamo. His private fortune was more than sufficient for all his needs, and he was never heard to grumble about the size of his income tax, large though it was.

Although he paid no visits to his neighbours in the country-side there was nothing of the misanthropist about him; and he never lacked congenial company when he desired it, for he was both likeable and accomplished. He was a fine billiard-player; he could do more than hold his own at the bridge-table; though he never went up to Lord's now, he was a reliable stone-wall batsman in village matches; and, despite the fact that he had become a strict teetotaller, he could discuss wines and vintages with an authority based upon the long and varied experience of a trained and sensitive palate. Having literary tastes, he edited a magazine which had some merit, though its circulation was small; and he had won a reputation as a producer of amateur dramatic performances which his friends gave, from time to time, on a stage specially erected in one of the long high-ceilinged rooms of his residence.

With all these advantages, it might be supposed that Mr Dunne was an enviable man, and that many, less fortunately situated, would gladly have exchanged places with him. Actually, however, no one envied him and few indeed would have agreed to fill his shoes.

On most subjects he was a pleasant talker, interested in what others had to say; but his hobby was Celtic second sight, and once launched upon that his politeness failed him, and he was merciless to his unfortunate hearers. He knew every detail of the prophecies made by Thomas of Erceldoun, the Lady of Lawers, and Coinneach Odhar Fiosaiche; and he would reel them off on the slightest provocation, paralleling each with the historical incident which fulfilled the prediction. If he were allowed to run on, his enthusiasm lent to his discourse a convincingness which left some of his hearers uneasily wondering 'if there wasn't perhaps *something* behind all that damned rubbish, after all.'

This was the stranger who had blundered upon the scene as the three men were grouped about Johnnie Brandon's body.

At the first glance Jim Brandon got the impression that Mr Dunne was drunk. He stood, gun in hand, staring at them in a dazed fashion, as though he were not quite in possession of all his faculties. Then, as a cloud drifts off the sun, the bewildered look passed from his face, and the light of intelligence came back to his eyes. He glanced at the gun in his hand as though it were some unfamiliar object; then, after a moment, he raised his head and faced the onlookers.

"I don't quite know how I came to get here," he said hesitatingly, as though he were merely thinking aloud.

Then his eye wandered to Johnnie's body, prone on the grass, and he seemed to recover himself completely.

"What's this?" he demanded in a firm tone.

"A damned bad job, cully," said Hay, before either of the others could reply. "That's just what it is: a damned bad job. This young fellow's shot himself. Stumbled on the rough ground, dropped his gun—and there you are!"

"Dreadful!" said Mr Dunne, with a sympathetic shudder.

A thought seemed to strike him, and he gave a furtive glance at the weapon in his hand. There was a moment of very apparent hesitation; then he opened the gun. It was fitted only with an extractor, and he pulled out the cartridges in turn and examined them with the air of a man who fears what he may find.

"Both barrels have been fired," he reported in a peculiar tone as he pushed the empty cases back into place.

He closed the breech and leaned the gun against a tree, still with a half-puzzled expression on his face.

Jim Brandon was in the act of rising to his feet when his eye caught a small detached piece of bone which lay in the pool of blood by Johnnie's head. Very gingerly he picked it up, wrapped his handkerchief round it, and laid the little parcel down beside the body. When he straightened himself again it was clear that he was making a tremendous effort to hold his emotions in check.

"We'll have to get him up to the house," he said to Laxford in a deliberately matter-of-fact tone. "And then we'll need a doctor, though I don't suppose he'll be able to do anything. And the police . . . what about them? I suppose they ought to be informed. And the coroner, too. There'll have to be an inquest, won't there?"

"I'll see to all that," Laxford assured him, with a certain nervous readiness. "We'd better get one of the farm-carts and some men to help. I'll go and see about it now, if you'll wait here."

Jim nodded assent, but Laxford lingered for a moment before going.

"I'm sorrier than I can tell you, over this affair," he said awkwardly. "Poor Johnnie! I wish to Heaven we'd never thought of shooting this morning. It's left me stunned—so absolutely unexpected."

His face spoke plainer than his words. No one, looking at it, could have failed to see that he was suffering under some very strong emotion. He hesitated for a moment; then, with an almost meaningless gesture, he turned and walked up the sunk fence towards the house.

Hay gulped convulsively once or twice. His face was several shades paler than its normal.

"Sight of blood always makes me sick," he explained abruptly. "Better get it over."

He turned and walked stumblingly into the shelter of the plantation. When he returned, Jim Brandon was still standing beside the body, but Mr Dunne had climbed down the face of the ha-ha and was aimlessly examining the grass at the foot of the wall. He extended his vague investigation towards the lip of the little chasm only a few yards away; and for some moments he stood listening to the torment of the swollen stream below. He took a step or two back towards the sunk fence, then suddenly stooped to pick some object from the grass. When he rose again he seemed almost to have forgotten the tragedy in some fresh excitement.

"Look!" he said, with a touch of triumph in his tone. "I knew I'd find it sometime. I've been hunting for it long enough, but something told me I'd find it. It's just what I want to fit the hole in my white stone."

He held up between his fingers a little hollow cylinder of green pasteboard, about two inches long and three-quarters of an inch in diameter. It looked rather like the body of an elongated pill-box minus top and bottom.

There was something inhuman in Mr Dunne's complete disregard of the tragic surroundings. Jim Brandon shrugged his shoulders with an undisguisedly hostile gesture and knelt down once more beside his brother's body; but Hay seemed rather glad of the diversion. He held out his hand for the tiny object, as though he wished to examine it. Mr Dunne, however, seemed loath to trust him, and stowed the little cylinder in his pocket with the air of a man making sure of a treasure.

"I've got Coinneach Odhar Fiosaiche's white stone at home," he explained. "The one with a hole in it, you know. But the hole's very rough at the edges, and one can't see through it properly. This thing that I've found will make a clear field of vision. I knew I'd come across it sooner or later. Bound to, on the face of things. You see, my name's Kenneth Dunne."

"Oh, it is, is it?" said Hay rather blankly. "Pleased to meet you, Mr Dunne."

He turned aside and began to pace restlessly up and down the little glade, his hands in his pockets and his head bent in obviously uncomfortable thought. Mr Dunne also seemed sunk in reflections, but they were seemingly of a pleasanter sort than Hay's. Jim Brandon rose to his feet and stood with a frown on his face, as though the unsympathetic presence of the other two men irked him.

At last a clank of cart-wheels announced the arrival of the assistance Laxford had gone to summon; and a few minutes later he and three estate hands appeared among the trees, two of the men carrying a hurdle. Johnnie's body was covered with a rug and lifted on to the improvised stretcher. Two of the men carried it off towards the cart, which had been brought up as near as possible on a wood-track through the plantation.

Mr Dunne, tired of wandering about, swung himself up to a seat on the turf at the top of the ha-ha wall. Laxford fidgeted for a moment or two, then his eye caught the gun which Mr Dunne had propped against a tree, and he went forward to examine it. As he picked it up he gave a start of surprise.

"This is my gun," he ejaculated as he recognised it. Then, with a change in tone, he demanded: "Where did you get it?"

Mr Dunne passed his hand across his brow with a mechanical movement, and a curiously puzzled expression overspread his face.

"I can't remember," he asserted. "I must have picked it up somewhere; but my memory's treacherous at times and I can't really recall finding that gun. I had it in my hand when I came upon you here; but beyond that I really haven't any recollection of it."

The perplexed expression on his features changed gradually to one of deepening dismay; but he evidently meant to keep his own counsel, for he offered no further information.

"To hell with that!" Hay broke in brutally. "Nobody picks up a gun without remembering it."

Mr Dunne was not provoked by this bluntness. He passed his hand again over his forehead, apparently striving fruitlessly to jog his memory.

"I don't remember," he repeated, after a prolonged interval.

Jim threw an inquiring glance at Laxford.

"I left my gun back yonder in the plantation, propped up against a tree," Laxford explained hurriedly. "I was carrying these rabbits, you see, and couldn't shoot."

He pointed to five dead rabbits lying half-hidden among some tall grass. Jim seemed to accept the explanation as sufficient for the moment. He bent down, lifted Johnnie's gun which was lying near the pool of blood, and ran his eye over it.

"The safety catch isn't on, of course," he commented, tucking the gun under his arm mechanically as he spoke. "He never took the most ordinary precautions, poor chap, no matter what one said to him. And of course, sooner or later, something happens."

He paused irresolutely for a moment or two before continuing:

"Better be getting along to the house, I suppose? There's nothing we can do here. You'll come along with us, Mr Dunne? The police will want to know about this accident, and you may as well see them now and get it over."

Mr Dunne rose without demur from his seat on the edge of the ha-ha. He said nothing, but his face showed plainly enough that he was still deeply perturbed by his undisclosed problem. Jim turned to the third man whom Laxford had summoned: the gardener at whose cottage they had taken shelter earlier in the morning.

"You might bring that up to the house, please," he said, pointing to his own gun which lay where he had dropped it when he came upon the scene. "I'll carry this of my brother's."

"Very good, sir. And the rabbits?"

"Oh, damn the rabbits," said Jim irascibly. "Who cares about them? Keep them for yourself, if you want to."

Laxford and Hay set off side by side along the line of the sunk fence in the direction of Edgehill. After a few moments Mr Dunne followed them hesitatingly, like a man whose wits have gone wool-gathering. Jim looked after him.

"You'd better show him the way," he suggested to the gardener.

He himself did not linger on the scene of the tragedy, but followed in the wake of the others.

The cart carrying Johnnie's body had been forced to take a more circuitous route than the line of the ha-ha; and when Jim Brandon reached the front door of Edgehill he saw no sign of its arrival. He entered the house and went straight to the gun-room where he found the remainder of the party. Hay and Laxford were just replacing their guns on the rack; and Jim followed their example, putting Johnnie's 12-bore in a place slightly isolated from the others. When he had done so he found the gardener beside him with Jim's own gun in his hands and evidently awaiting instructions.

"Put it over yonder, in the corner," Jim directed, with a gesture towards the spot where his leather gun-case stood. "I'll clean it and put it away later on."

Stoke obeyed him promptly; but then he showed signs of lingering, as though anxious to hear anything that might be said. Laxford dashed any such hopes by ordering him to go and bring word as soon as the cart appeared. The gardener retired with obvious reluctance; but in less than a minute he was back again with the news that the cart had already reached the house and had been taken round to the back. Cranley, the butler, was awaiting instructions.

"We'd better have him taken up to his own room," Jim decided.

Laxford made no objection.

"We'd better be there," he suggested, leading the way out of the room.

Jim and Hay followed him. Mr Dunne, after a momentary hesitation, fell in behind them, leaving Stoke alone in the gun-room.

This was the opportunity for which the gardener had been waiting. Two strides took him to the gun-rack, and his hand went out to the fatal 12-bore. With a glance to see that no one was observing him, he pressed the lever and extracted the cartridges. One of them was undischarged, and he replaced it in the barrel. The empty case he transferred stealthily to his pocket.

Then he seemed to reflect, and stood for a moment on the *qui vive* seeking a solution of his problem. He put down Johnnie's gun and lifted Hay's weapon from the rack. Opening the breech he picked the two empty cartridge cases out of the extractor, slipped one of them into the vacant place in Johnnie's gun, replaced both guns on the rack, and threw Hay's second empty case out of the window into a clump of bushes. Then, still with a certain furtiveness, he stole out of the gun-room and made his way to the back premises. In these two minutes alone Stoke had 'done a good stroke o' business,' as he himself would have phrased it.

When Johnnie's body had been carried upstairs and placed upon his own bed Jim and the others came downstairs again. Now that the first shock of the tragedy was over their emotions seemed to relax, and a faint air of constraint crept over the group.

"I've a word to say to you, Laxford," Hay announced as he reached the hall. "We'll go into the smoking-room, eh?"

His tone made it plain enough that he wanted to have his host to himself. Laxford obediently followed him, and Jim was left confronting Mr Dunne, whom he plainly wished at the other end of the world. His politeness came to the rescue, however.

"Shall we go into the drawing-room? I expect the police will be here, any minute now; and then you'll be free of this business."

Mr Dunne made a gesture of consent; but when they reached the drawing-room he seemed to have nothing to say. Without being asked, he dropped into an easy-chair, rested his head on his hand, and with down-bent face plunged again into that latent problem which so perplexed him. Jim had no inclination for talk; but the mere presence of this stranger irritated him, and he began to pace up and down the room with nervous strides like an imprisoned animal.

His ordeal ended much sooner than he expected. The drawing-room door opened and a scared-looking maid announced:

"Two gentlemen wish to see Mr Dunne, sir."

At her heels there entered two fresh visitors: big broad-shouldered men whose general appearance suggested a queer similarity in type. Each wore a blue double-breasted overcoat and carried a bowler hat in his hand. Each had the same air of watchful and confident authority. Close-cropped hair, cheeks showing blue under the razor, square uncompromising jaws, and hard, steady eyes, completed the resemblance. They looked efficient machines endowed with intelligence.

As they came into the room Mr Dunne glanced up with obvious recognition but without any show of surprise. His face, in fact, betrayed something almost like relief.

"Oh, it's you, Connel?" he greeted the first-comer, rather in the tone of one addressing an inferior with whom he is on good terms.

"Yes. You've led us a bit of a dance, Mr Dunne; but we got news of you, you see. The car's waiting for you, outside."

Mr Dunne rose to his feet without ado.

"That was very clever of you, Connel," he said. "We must have a little chat about it, later on, perhaps. Shall we go, now? I'm afraid I must leave you," he added, turning to Jim.

The second burly man stood aside to let Mr Dunne pass out of the room. Jim made a movement of protest, but before he could open his mouth the man Connel gave him a quick significant look which arrested the verbal expostulation on his lips. Mr Dunne, closely followed by the big man in the blue overcoat, went out into the hall.

"Look here," Jim broke out as the door closed behind the pair, "are you the police?"

Connel seemed surprised by the question.

"No," he replied tersely, without volunteering any further information.

"Then you can't take this Mr Dunne—whoever he is—away from here until the police turn up. There's been a shooting accident—my brother's killed—and we need Mr Dunne as a witness. He was near the place at the time, and the police will perhaps want his evidence."

"They won't," Connel said confidently. "I'm sorry about your brother, sir. Very sad affair indeed, that is. I sympathise, sir. But as to Mr Dunne, if the police want to ask him questions they'll have to come to Fairlawns. We're going there now."

He seemed to think that this made the matter clear beyond any argument.

"Fairlawns?" Jim demanded. "Where's that?"

Connel seemed a trifle surprised.

"It's the big house with large grounds, up Stanningleigh way."

He paused for a moment, scrutinising Jim's face as though perplexed by his dullness of apprehension. Then his own face cleared and he went on:

"You're a stranger here, perhaps, sir? Ah, of course, or you'd have tumbled to it as soon as I mentioned the name."

"Tumbled to what?" Jim asked, irritably.

"Well, sir, Fairlawns is Dr Barreman's place. It's a private institution where rich people can go to get over a nervous breakdown, or what not."

A light broke on Jim's mind as he translated this delicate euphemism.

"A private lunatic asylum, you mean?"

"You might call it that, if you like," Connel admitted, as though personally disclaiming responsibility for the definition.

Now Jim understood whom he was dealing with: one of the asylum attendants.

"And this man Dunne?" he demanded. "He's one of the patients? Escaped from your charge, evidently."

"He got away early in the morning, before sunrise," the warder admitted.

"What's his trouble?" Jim asked with some interest. "He seemed sane enough to me, barring that he looked a bit dazed when he came up to us in the plantation."

"We're not allowed to discuss the residents, sir," Connel declared with a bluntness so uncompromising that it sounded like a snub to Jim. "If Mr Dunne's needed by the police, they'll have to apply to Dr Barreman about it."

There was a downrightness in Connel's manner which, quite involuntarily, roused a suspicion that professional secrecy alone was not at the back of his abruptness. He gave the impression, quite against his intentions, that he felt himself on slippery ice and that he wanted to get off it before he came a cropper. Mr Dunne suffered from bats in the belfry; that was undeniable. But at least Connel could keep his own counsel as to the nature of these bats. Discussion on that subject might lead him farther than he thought desirable. It was Dr Barreman's affair, not his; and he had no wish to burn his fingers by blabbing to a stranger.

"That's all I can say, sir," he concluded after a pause. "I'll wish you good morning. We must get back to Fairlawns. Dr Barreman's a bit anxious, naturally."

"But . . ." Jim began.

"Can't stay, sir. Good morning."

With his air of cool authority he bowed himself out; and a moment or two later Jim heard the purring of a car as it receded into the distance.

CHAPTER 7 OSWALD BRANDON

Once rid of Mr Dunne and his keepers, Jim Brandon might well have hoped to be left undisturbed after his tragic experiences. But his respite was of the briefest. To him it seemed only a moment or two after Connel's departure when the drawing-room door reopened and Una Menteith appeared on the threshold. One glance told Jim that she had heard the news of Johnnie's disaster; and that it had hit her harder than he expected. Outwardly she was calm, but her eyes showed traces of recent tears. When she caught sight of Jim she turned to address someone behind her.

"He's here, Oswald. Come in."

Over her shoulder, Jim caught a glimpse of his elder brother's face, serious and tight-lipped. Una came forward, and Oswald followed her into the room.

"Hullo, Jim," was his curt greeting. "Didn't look for me, did you?"

In appearance, Oswald Brandon faintly recalled both his brothers. He had Johnnie's ready smile without Johnnie's boyishness; and he had Jim's aquiline features, unspoiled by the shade of discontent which marred Jim's expression. The steady grey eyes and firm lips had served him well in many a game of poker, for they betrayed nothing which it did not suit him to reveal. His vocabulary was mainly monosyllabic, so that even in his less laconic sentences his speech had a trenchant note. Altogether, he looked a more formidable character than Jim, and in his presence the younger man seemed slightly over-shadowed.

"I suppose you've heard about it?" Jim asked, without showing surprise at his brother's advent.

His tone was almost perfunctory, for Una's face had already given the answer to his question.

"Yes," Oswald replied. "A man told us, on the road up here. It's true, is it? He's dead, I mean, not just badly hurt?"

"He's quite dead," Jim explained soberly. "He shot himself in the head, you know, behind the ear. A doctor'll be here any minute now; but he won't be able to do anything. Poor Johnnie's gone."

Oswald accepted the main fact without futile questions.

"How did it happen?"

Jim's involuntary gesture expressed total ignorance.

"I don't know; I wasn't in sight of him at the time. He was walking along the top of a sunk fence, perhaps he tripped and his gun went off. I don't know. The other two got there long before I did."

Oswald seemed to ponder over this for a moment or two, but his face gave no clue to his thoughts.

"H'm!" he said. "What did he look like this morning? White about the gills? Una's told me some queer yarns."

"He looked damnably worried," Jim admitted, with a certain reluctance.

"Why did you let him go out shooting at all when he was in that state?" Una demanded, with a note of accusation in her tone. "You knew quite well..."

She broke off as though she could not trust herself to keep her voice under control.

For a moment or two Jim seemed puzzled by her vehemence. Then, apparently, an underlying meaning in her words suggested itself to his mind, and he stared at her with an air of incredulity which slowly changed to one of doubt.

"What d'you mean, exactly?" he demanded.

Oswald exchanged a quick glance with Una, and then intervened to save the girl from having to put her idea into words.

"No use codding ourselves, Jim. It stares you in the face. Last night—so Una tells me—Johnnie got into a fix with Laxford's wife. I knew poor Johnnie better than you did, for he liked me; and I can guess how he took it. Went to bed, scared stiff by the mess he'd got into. Got no sleep for thinking about it. Cubs are like that—always thinking the hole they're in is the worst that ever was. After a night like that Johnnie's nerves would be just fiddle-strings. Send him out in that state with a gun in his hand . . . it's as good as giving him the key to a short road out of his fix."

He paused for a moment and then added:

"Una blames herself for not letting you butt in last night. She did it for the best. She knew I was due here today, and she thought the pair of us could deal with Laxford better than you alone."

Jim seemed to pay no attention to the last three sentences. He fastened on the main implication of Oswald's speech, which had evidently thrown a fresh light on the situation for him.

"Good Lord!" he ejaculated in obvious surprise. "You think he shot himself on purpose? I don't believe it. He was badly under the weather this morning; I could see that well enough. But from that to suicide's too big a jump."

Oswald looked at him keenly.

"Think so? All the better, then, especially for Una's feelings. Now here's the point. We want no talk about this thing. Poor Johnnie's gone. We don't want this affair with Laxford's wife raked up for gossip. You're with me there? Right. Say 'Suicide,' and every old wife in the place will be nosing in, trying to guess what was at the back of it. Let's keep Johnnie's name clear of all that sort of stuff."

"Of course," Jim agreed instantly.

"Then mind what you say," Oswald warned him. "Keep your thumb on anything that might give a hint. There'll be an inquest. You'll need to be careful at it. He had no worries of any sort. That's our line."

"I'll take care of that," Jim agreed. "It'll be easy enough. The only other people who could let it out are the Laxfords and Hay; and I don't suppose they'll want to brag much about their share in the business."

"Nor do I, from what Una's told me," Oswald concurred grimly.

He had no chance to say more, for at that moment the door opened and the maid announced:

"Dr Brinkworth, sir."

Dr Aloysius X. Brinkworth exemplified one of the minor tragedies of the medical profession: a competent doctor handicapped by a bad bedside manner. He cured his patients; but he never inspired them with that confidence which often wins half the battle. The continual struggle against a marked inferiority complex gave him an air of nervousness and indecision, even when he had settled in his mind the best course of treatment. He brought with him into the sick-room a faint suggestion of flurry, as though he had fallen behind his time-table and was on pins and needles to get away again to visit the next case on his list. He was a little bald man, with large round glasses and a pair of flat feet of which he was acutely conscious.

"Er . . . Mr Brandon?" he inquired vaguely, being evidently taken aback at finding more than one person in the room.

"My name's Brandon," Oswald explained. "This is my brother. He can give you the facts you need. I know nothing at first hand."

Dr Brinkworth looked rather flustered at this, but he turned to Jim.

"Er . . . Yes, I see . . . A very distressing affair, Mr Brandon. I knew your brother by sight, poor young man. Er . . . can you throw any light on this accident? I'd like to have some details, if possible, before I make an examination of . . ."

His voice tailed off as he realised that the completion of the sentence might be untactful.

"I'm afraid I can throw no light on the accident," Jim answered readily. "Mr Laxford or Mr Hay might know more about it. They were on the spot long before I got there. But I'll tell you what I saw myself, if it's of any service to you."

Oswald and Una listened with strained attention while he gave a concise account of his discovery of Johnnie's body, with Hay and Laxford beside it; then he described how Mr Dunne had supervened. At Dunne's name Jim saw Dr Brinkworth's eyebrows lift momentarily in what might have been an expression of surprise; but almost immediately the physician regained control of his features.

"Mr Dunne?" he echoed. "From Fairlawns, you say? Ah! I know him . . . er . . . at least I've played cricket with him, once or twice. I doubt if it's worth troubling him for his account of the affair, Mr Brandon. He suffers from . . . er . . . slight lapses of memory, at times. His recollections might not be altogether reliable. Or so I've found them, once or twice. I think Mr Laxford and . . . er . . . Mr Hay, most likely will be able to give me all the details I need."

He glanced furtively at his wrist-watch and seemed perturbed to find how time was passing.

"Perhaps I might see them now?" he suggested in a faintly fussy tone, "and then go . . . er . . . upstairs. I've a case waiting for me . . . giving me some anxiety, you understand? Urgent, in fact. So I oughtn't to delay too long."

At the door he turned back.

"Er . . . Your brother, Mr Brandon, was he careful in handling his gun? I mean, was he likely to have handled it so as to make this accident more likely in his case than it would have been with yourself, for instance, if you had tripped in walking along the sunk fence?"

"He was very careless," Jim answered unhesitatingly. "I had to check him for it this morning, before the accident happened."

Una forced herself to offer her testimony also.

"Everybody complained of poor Johnnie's light-hearted way of treating a gun, Dr Brinkworth. I always felt a little anxious myself if I was out with him when he was shooting."

"So if he tripped . . . ?" Dr Brinkworth began.

"The safety slide must have been out of action if the gun went off," Oswald pointed out.

"Er . . . Yes, of course," Dr Brinkworth agreed at once. "And so, if his gun slipped from his hold and fell the whole height of the ha-ha, there would be nothing to prevent it exploding with a jar like that. Er . . . When he was walking up the sunk fence, Mr Brandon, had he the ha-ha on his right or his left hand?"

"On his right," Jim explained.

"So the wound is on the right side? Of course. Thanks for making it clear. And now . . . er . . ."

An inarticulate murmur represented the tail-end of the sentence, and with a hurried bow in Una's direction, Dr Brinkworth passed out of the room. For a few seconds after he had gone the three stood silent, listening to his footfalls on the parquet of the hall.

"Think that's nailed it down?" Oswald queried at last when it was evident that Dr Brinkworth was not going to return again. "We overdid it a bit—all shouting at once about poor Johnnie's carelessness. Still, no harm in zeal. He seemed to gulp it down. And that's the main thing."

"Suicide isn't likely to cross his mind," Jim said, without noticing Una's shudder at the word. "Why should it?"

Oswald nodded thoughtfully, as though not altogether sure.

"Well, one hopes so. Come to think of it, we don't know ourselves which it was. But," he added with an ugly scowl, "if he did himself in, I'd like to get my knife in Laxford, just to put things square. We've a score to pay there, Jim, if the chance comes our way. That's a hound's trick he played on poor Johnnie."

Una took his arm as though to coax him out of his black mood; and at her touch he made an effort to curb his vindictiveness. He threw a quizzical glance at his brother.

"You didn't guess Una knew me, Jim?"

"She said nothing to me about you, if that's what you mean," Jim admitted. "I suppose . . ."

"Yes, we fixed it up this morning. I've only been waiting till the Company gave me a shore job, and I've got that now. Heard the news yesterday when we got in. So I sent Una a wire and came on here at once."

Jim's manner, as he offered his congratulations, was perhaps a trifle absent-minded. Something had stirred in his memory, and the effort to bring it into clear focus occupied part of his attention. Then, a few seconds later, his face cleared and he turned to Una.

"Of course, that's it! You talked about going on some of these summer cruises. I suppose you met Oswald on the *Ithaca*. But why didn't you say you knew him, when you met me at the station yesterday?"

Una seemed a shade disconcerted by the question.

"Well, you see . . . I suppose I call you Jim, now? . . . I could hardly say: 'I'm Una Menteith, the girl your brother's going to get engaged to, sometime.' And besides, nobody's ever natural when they're introduced to a total stranger as a prospective relation-in-law. It's a strained business, with both on their best behaviour and both feeling critical and being afraid to show it. So I thought, since I had the chance, I'd say nothing about Oswald and just get to know you as an ordinary human being. Fairer to both parties. Partly for the fun of the thing, I kept it up and swore Johnnie to secrecy; and I couldn't help playing the mystery-monger a little, just to make you inquisitive about me. Any kind of interest's better than none, you know. And you didn't seem particularly interested in me at the start."

"Oh, that was it, was it?" said Jim, without much cordiality in his tone.

Oswald intervened swiftly and changed the subject.

"Una's told me a few things, Jim. We'll need to get our bearings in this affair. Una can't stay on with the Laxfords after this."

"No, of course not," Jim agreed, but he contributed no suggestion.

Oswald took a pace or two, as though movement helped his thought.

"Do you know who pays the rent of this place?" he demanded, coming to a halt before his brother.

"Johnnie told me that Mrs Laxford was finding the money, but that he was to pay her back later on."

Oswald exchanged a glance with Una which showed that this was no news to either of them. Oswald swung round again to face his brother.

"Yes. Laxford's an undischarged bankrupt. You know that? And his wife hasn't a stiver of her own, so Una tells me. Where did the cash come from to rent a place like this?"

"That's queer," Jim commented, with awakened interest. "I hadn't thought about that side of it. Where *did* they raise it, d'you know?"

"Search me! They must have raised it from somebody. But that's not the point just now. Point is, Johnnie was supposed to be the lessee; the lease is in his name. That's so, Una?"

"But Johnnie was a minor," Jim objected. "He couldn't make a valid contract."

"Oh, there was some flim-flam bringing in a bogus trustee. Una knows about it. She and Johnnie were good pals. He let out a lot to her without knowing it. Point is, Johnnie was technically the man who leased Edgehill. Laxford's name didn't come in at all. Now Johnnie's dead, poor kid, we've got to make the best of it. He died without making a will, didn't he?"

"He couldn't make a legal will till this morning when he came of age," Jim pointed out, "and I don't expect he made one before we went out shooting."

"Then this lease of Edgehill's part of his estate. It goes to the family—the Governor, I suppose. That's what I'm after, Jim. I don't see much of the Governor. Still, I hate his living in foul digs the way he has to do. Let's bring him here to live for the rest of the year that the lease runs. A blink of sunshine before he goes out, what? And Una can stay on and look after him. Kills two birds with one stone. It's no catch for her, but she says she'll do it. Cheer him up, make him happy while it lasts. What do you say?"

Jim considered for a moment before replying.

"It sounds all right," he agreed. "That is, if you care to take it on," he added turning to Una.

"Of course," the girl replied at once.

"We'll need to cut expenses to the bone," was Jim's comment. Then a thought seemed to strike him, and he asked: "What about the Laxfords?"

"The Laxfords?" Oswald's gesture emphasised his words. "Out they go, neck and crop, today."

Jim gave a curt nod of agreement, but Una showed her discomfort at this proposal of abrupt expulsion. She had been fond of her young charges, and she intervened on their behalf.

"I don't like the idea of turning out those two kiddies, Oswald, without knowing they've some place to go to."

"There's an inn, isn't there? They can go there, can't they?"

Una smiled rather wryly.

"You don't understand, Oswald. One has to pay one's bill at an inn. The Laxfords are broke—really broke, I mean. Why, they had to pawn Di's jewellery to pay their fares up here, when we shifted to Edgehill. You can't turn two children out into the street like that, when their father can't scrape up enough to get a roof over their heads for the night. You mustn't do it."

Oswald's reply showed no yielding on the main point.

"Well, they can't stay here, Una. That's flat."

Una considered for a moment and then hit upon an alternative proposal.

"Why not let them shift into the Cottage? It's empty and ready for occupation. That would give them time to turn round."

"I'd rather be shot of them for good. However . . ."

He consulted Jim with a glance; but Jim was thinking about Una's revelation of the state of Laxford's finances, and his nod of acquiescence was purely perfunctory.

"All right, then," the elder brother conceded. "Have it your way, Una. So long as they get out of here straight off, I don't mind where they go."

Jim was evidently still pondering over Una's disclosure.

"If they're as broke as all that," he said thoughtfully, "I'd like to know where they got the cash to lease this place. The agents would want references or else cash down, you know, and . . ."

"It doesn't matter a damn," Oswald retorted impatiently. "Now look here, Jim. You and I must see Laxford and tell him to clear out. It won't be a cosy chat. I shan't spread butter on it. But we've got to keep our thumbs on one thing. Keep Johnnie's name clean out of it. No talk about blackmail or suicide. We owe that to Johnnie."

"Oh, that's all right," Jim replied rather testily. "I'm not so likely as you are to go off the handle, if you ask me. It was just an accident, of course. The sort of thing that might happen to any-one. We all understand that quite clearly."

Oswald took no notice of his brother's irony.

"Quite so," he said. "And now the next thing. How are we going to break this business to the Governor, Jim? That's going to be a nasty job for somebody."

"Send him a wire," Jim suggested.

Una was revolted by this callous proposal.

"You can't do that," she declared indignantly. "One of you must go up to town and do it as gently as you can. It'll be a fear-ful shock to him. Oswald, you'd better do it."

Jim seemed not to see the implication of her choice.

"Yes, you'd better take on that job, Oswald," he concurred. "After he's got over the worst of it, we can find plenty to divert his attention with. The whole business of Burling Thorn's on our hands now and it'll be enough to keep the Governor busy, once it starts. It'll be good for him."

"All right. I'll go, then. Una can come up with me. You've never met him, Una."

"I don't think he'll want a stranger at a time like that," Una pointed out.

"Something in that. We'll settle it by and by, before train time. And now, Jim, let's get Laxford off our hands."

Jim followed him from the room; and as they emerged into the hall, Dr Brinkworth came downstairs followed by a tall raw-boned man with a solemn face.

"Er . . . Mr Brandon, this is Inspector Hinton of the local constabulary. He came up . . . er . . . a pure matter of form, you understand. And there will have to be an inquest, of course. The Inspector will be able to give you the . . . er . . . necessary particulars."

CHAPTER 8 NON-EXISTENT BLOOD-STAIN

Inspector Hinton's parents had thought fit to have him christened Rufus, and in some ways their choice had been justified. He was red-haired and red-faced. Much to his disgust, his big-boned capable hands were also red. Even his eyes harmonised with the rest of the monochrome, for they had a russet tint like the irises of certain animals. And yet, for all this display of colour, no one would have described him as rubicund. His complexion had a weather-beaten look which matched his tall gaunt figure and his morose mannerisms.

The inspector was just a shade cleverer than the average of humanity. He was not unaware of this. In fact, nobody recognised more clearly than he did himself that he was, as he put it, 'a bit sharper than most.' Unfortunately, he lacked the sense of perspective which might have shown him that he was not so very clever, after all. Secure in his possession of a superior intellect, he was apt to look down on the common run of people with a faintly tolerant contempt. Like Carlyle, he regarded them as 'mostly fools.' He had never read Carlyle. If anyone had shown him the passage in *Latter-day Pamphlets*, he would probably have growled out the tag about "great minds thinking alike," with the kindly intention of paying Carlyle a compliment.

As an offset to his physical uncouthness, Nature had given him a pleasant and sympathetic voice. It was one of the best weapons in his professional armoury, and the use to which he put it was characteristic. Contempt for ordinary humanity had made him an assiduous collector of conversational small change: "Just so," "Now, then," "Of course," "I see," and the like. Continual practice had given him such skill in the use of these depreciated tools that, time and again, they served to loosen the tongues of halting or stubborn witnesses. By his subtle modulations of a mere "Well, well!", Inspector Hinton could feign any emotion from cynical indifference to breathless astonishment. His time-battered interjections became the vocal equivalents of understanding nods or interrogative glances. And, like a nod or a wink, they committed him to nothing. A prisoner, lured into amplifying a voluntary statement by the inspector's interested "H'm?" or "Ah?", could never assert that he had been subjected to illegal questioning; and yet Hinton generally secured the extra information which he wanted.

This mastery of vocal inflection was the inspector's solitary artistic accomplishment. Its exercise gave him more than a little sardonic amusement. He made a hobby of it, elaborated his effects, and furbished up his verbal trivialities with all the care that a master lapidary brings to the polishing of some rare and beautiful gem.

His official superiors were not favoured by displays of his peculiar talent. "Never get funny with the men higher up," was one of the first tenets in his unwritten code. Efficiency was the card he played in their case. He took special pains with his reports, whether oral or written. Invariably they were divided, like ancient Gaul, into three parts: Evidence, Inferences, and General Conclusions. No facts were ever suppressed, even when they happened to tell against his own theories. No inference ever got mixed up with his summary of the actual evidence in a case. "No hugger-mugger methods for me," he would say, with conscious superiority.

In his rare moments of expansion, Inspector Hinton would impress upon his subordinates that a member of the police force should function like a perfect machine, smoothly, efficiently, and without emotion of any sort. "Like me, you understand?" he would add modestly, to make the matter perfectly clear.

Curiously enough, he ignored something which completely invalidated his simile. No machine works in the hope of changing its name; but at the root of his own efficiency lay a burning desire that Inspector Hinton should become Superintendent Hinton at the earliest possible moment. He kept that ambition to himself, naturally; but it flamed all the more fiercely behind the screen. "If one big case comes my way," he told himself confidently, "then I'm sure of my step." It never crossed his mind that he might not be equal to the emergency when it came.

When the news of the disaster in the Long Plantation reached him, his obvious course was to send a sergeant up to Edgehill to take the necessary particulars. From the constabulary point of view, the affair was purely formal: a gun-accident, a coroner's inquest, a verdict of "Death by misadventure." A mere matter of routine.

As it chanced, however, the only sergeant available at the moment was one of the inspector's *bêtes noires*, a man whose reports never satisfied Hinton's refined demands. The fellow had been on the carpet only the day before. He'd bungle the business, somehow, the inspector reflected in wrathful contempt. And then Inspector Hinton would eventually be put to more trouble than it would cost him to go to Edgehill himself in the first place.

Behind all this fuming and fretting, a psycho-analyst would have suspected that Inspector Hinton was rationalising something. As a matter of fact, he hated to delegate responsibility. It was his notorious failing as a superior officer and it had earned him the nickname of "The Grabber." His subordinates disliked him because he was so loath to give them opportunities.

He reached Edgehill in advance of Brinkworth, and, while waiting for the doctor, he filled in time by making some inquiries from the servants. When the physician came on the scene,

Hinton accompanied him upstairs and watched him examine Johnnie's body, jotting down notes from time to time as the doctor described the results of his observations.

"I'll read what I've put down, doctor," he said, when the examination was over. "Just check it, will you? He's quite dead. He may have died a couple of hours ago. The wound's on the right side of the head. It involves the scalp and the bone. It's smooth at the back and rather irregular at the front. The external ear's damaged. There's a hole in the skull, and a bit of bone's detached. There's no apparent singeing or blackening round the wound. There's some blood—not much—on the collar of his jacket which has been removed from the body. There's been a certain amount of blood exuded since he was brought up here, staining the pillow. You conclude he died from a gunshot wound. That's right?"

"Er . . . yes, that's quite right," Dr Brinkworth confirmed. He glanced round the room as though searching for something. "I . . . er . . . suppose we can wash our hands, Inspector. In case we happen to meet anyone. . . ." A gesture completed his meaning.

"I saw a lavatory as we came along the corridor," explained Inspector Hinton, who missed little. "We'd better go there before we go downstairs."

At the foot of the staircase, a minute or two later, they encountered the Brandon brothers. Hinton waited for the doctor's introduction and then, ignoring Oswald, he turned to Jim.

"Sorry to intrude on you with these formalities, sir," he began in his most sympathetic tone. "Nasty shock, it must have been. I knew young Mr Brandon slightly—and liked him, if I may say so."

Jim made an inarticulate acknowledgment.

"We have to make inquiries," the inspector explained, with a semi-apologetic note in his voice, "even in the case of a pure accident like this."

"I'll answer any questions you like," Jim assured him. "I quite understand. But I saw nothing of the accident myself. I was on the other side of the stream when it happened and I didn't get to the spot till some minutes after."

Inspector Hinton might feign sympathy when it suited, but his mind was fixed on one thing only, at the moment: the production of a perfect report. He made a soothing gesture with his hand.

"Let's begin at the beginning," he suggested suavely. "I understand you were out shooting, early this morning, along with Mr John Brandon, Mr Hay, and Mr Laxford. You carried your own gun. Your brother also had his own gun. Mr Laxford and Mr Hay were using guns belonging to the house, I'm told. You all walked in company down the road to the cottage of the gardener, Stoke, where you sheltered for awhile. Then the party split up."

His calculated pause had the effect of a question.

"That's so," Jim agreed. "We were going to shoot in the Long Plantation. Mr Laxford suggested we should spread out well, so as to run no risk of firing into each other. I think perhaps he was afraid of . . ."

He broke off suddenly as if he had said something which he regretted.

"Yes?" said Hinton encouragingly.

Jim apparently fell into the trap baited with the monosyllable.

"Well, perhaps I shouldn't have said that," he explained in a reluctant tone. "It's only a guess. I got the notion that Mr Laxford was a bit nervous. You see," he went on in a burst of apparent frankness, "I'm afraid my brother was careless with his gun. Some people didn't like to shoot with him, just because of that. I spoke to him myself once or twice about it. In fact, I checked him as we were walking down to the gardener's."

Oswald's trained features showed nothing; but he gave Jim high marks for the skilful way he had handled this point. That awkward little pause at the start had riveted the inspector's attention in a way that nothing else would have done, and had made him take special notice of the evidence, apparently so reluctantly given, about Johnnie's careless management of firearms.

"I see," said Hinton concisely.

As though eager to leave the subject, Jim continued his main narrative without further prompting.

"Mr Hay went off towards the west side of the Plantation. Mr Laxford kept straight on till he got to the trees. That was the last I saw of them till after the accident. My brother and I turned to the right—eastward, I think it is—once we got into the Plantation. There's a narrow footpath running that way. We took it and went on till we got to the ha-ha, the sunk fence, you know."

"I know," said the inspector, slightly nettled to find doubt thrown on the extent of his vocabulary.

"We stopped there for a moment or two," Jim continued. "My brother was going to walk up the line of the ha-ha, on top of the sunk fence. I was going on a bit farther, across the Carron, before turning north. When we were all in position, you see, there would be four of us in line: Mr Hay on the far left, then Mr Laxford, then my brother walking along the top of the sunk fence, and I myself on the extreme right, across the stream. That was the last I saw of my brother before the accident."

"Just so," Inspector Hinton murmured. "And then?"

Jim seemed to recollect something.

"Oh, just one other point. It's not important, except that it made me keep my ears open. My brother made a bet with me that he'd get a bigger bag than I could, before we got to the top of the Plantation. I just mention that to let you see why I had my ears cocked to hear his shots—to know how he was getting on, you know."

"Yes, yes," said Hinton encouragingly.

This fellow Brandon, he reflected, seemed to have his wits about him. He told a plain tale, when the ordinary witness would have rambled all over the shop. Young Brandon could write a good report, if he tried his hand at it. Not like that damned sergeant.

"When I got to the stepping-stones," Jim continued, "I heard three shots: two together and then a third, much nearer. Then, up among the trees I heard some shouting. I couldn't hear what

113

they were saying; the wind was gusty and made a lot of noise in the trees round me. Then I shot a rabbit myself and left it. After that I heard two more shots, and then a third. The first one sounded far off, but the other two were quite loud, so I took it they were fired by my brother. Just after that, I think, I shot another rabbit and left it lying to be picked up later on. It must be there still, and that gives you my position at that moment, roughly. And after that I heard another shot, pretty far off."

He broke off here for a moment, fumbled in his pocket for some papers, and then rejected them as unsuitable.

"Can you give me a page from your note-book?" he asked. "I think I can make things clearer with a sketch."

Hinton was using a loose-leaf book, but instead of taking out a sheet he opened the book at a fresh place and handed it across.

"Just use the book. Here's a pencil."

He watched Jim sketch roughly the outline of the Long Plantation, the course of the Carron, and the lie of the ha-ha.

"This is about where I was when I heard another shot," Jim explained. "It was quite near at hand—you see how the stream curves in towards the line of the ha-ha about this point. I was there"—pointing with his pencil—"alongside the top end of that long strip of bushy stuff that lines the Carron bank thereabouts. The bushes grow pretty thick, and I could see nothing of the banks. And of course the ha-ha across the stream was hidden completely from me. A rabbit got up, and I pulled trigger just as it got behind a tree-stump. Then I heard shouting across the stream, but the wind was too gusty to hear words. It was blowing from me towards the Carron, besides. The rabbit bolted from cover and I shot at it. Missed it, though. Then there was more shouting. And, finally, I made out something about an accident. I went down to the bank and when I looked downstream, I saw Mr Laxford with his hands to his mouth, shouting for all he was worth, directing me to go round by the bridge—here—as quick as I could. He said my brother had slipped off the ha-ha and his gun had gone off and shot him. I couldn't get across anywhere nearer than the bridge. It's a sort of chasm there, and the Carron was swirling down almost bank-full. No one could have got over, short of the bridge. So I ran for all I was worth. When I got to where my brother was, I found the other two standing beside him. He was on the top of the bank. . . ."

Hinton made an arresting gesture.

"I thought he'd fallen off the sunk fence."

"I expect they lifted him up, then. He was on the ground at the top of the ha-ha when I saw him first. You'd better ask them about it. I've no first-hand knowledge."

"And then?"

"I examined him. He was quite dead, of course. There was a pool of blood on the grass. Mr Hay, I remember, said something about it being a bad job. Mr Laxford didn't say anything that I can remember. Then a stranger came out from behind some bushes. Thought he looked a bit queer when I saw him, dazed or something, as if he'd had a shock. Rather like a sleepwalker who's been waked up suddenly. It seemed funny at the time, but by and by his keepers came and took him away. One of them told me he was a patient at some place called Fairlawns, a mental case, apparently. That explains things, I suppose."

"Of course!" Hinton interjected, but it was impossible to guess from his tone what he thought of Mr Dunne's incursion.

"After that," Jim went on, "Mr Laxford started off for help. Mr Hay stayed with us. He seemed very upset; pretty sick, I should say. Worse than I was, and I felt sick enough," he confessed, touching for the first time on his emotions of the morning.

"What about your brother's gun?" Hinton inquired.

"His gun? Oh, yes, it was lying beside him."

"On the top of the sunk fence?"

"Yes, close beside him."

Jim looked puzzled for a moment by the expression on Hinton's face, then he seemed to see the point.

"Oh, you mean it ought to have been in the ditch? I suppose they must have lifted it up on to the top when they lifted him."

"I'd better see it, just for form's sake," Hinton suggested.

"Of course. It's in the gun-room. I brought it up myself. One barrel had been fired. There was a live round in the other. And the safety-catch was off, I noticed. Of course it must have been, or the gun couldn't have gone off."

"Naturally," Hinton agreed.

Jim seemed to find nothing further to add to his narrative.

"I think that's all," he said, after a moment or two of thought.

Hinton added a jotting to his notes, and then passed the book to Jim.

"Mind initialling this, sir, after you've read it over? I like to have things in order. By the way, there'll be an inquest, of course, and the coroner will want your evidence. You'll get a subpoena later on. An official notice, I mean."

As Jim was scribbling his signature at the foot of the inspector's notes, Hinton made a further request.

"I'd like to see Mr Brandon's gun, sir, merely as a matter of form."

Jim led him to the gun-room and handed him Johnnie's gun from the rack. The inspector examined it for a moment or two, but his mere handling of it betrayed that he was no expert.

"What sort of gun is it?" he inquired doubtfully.

"A 12-bore, half-choke. I don't know the maker's name."

"Is this the safety-catch?" Hinton demanded, fiddling with the little lever. "It's off now, I think you said?"

"No, it's on at present. It was off when I picked up the gun from the grass," Jim explained, "but when I handle a gun I always push the slide over to 'safety,' and I expect I did it almost without thinking what I was doing. It's one of these movements one makes automatically. It gets to be second nature and one doesn't notice one's doing it."

"I see," Hinton assured him with an understanding air. "Pity everybody isn't as careful."

He fumbled for a moment over opening the breech, extracted the cartridges, and examined them.

"One unused cartridge and one spent one, just as you said. We have to see things with our own eyes," he added, half-apologetically. "'Eley-Kynoch 12.' That 12 is for 12-bore, I suppose. What does this big '5' mean on the cardboard at the other end?"

"Loaded with Number Five shot," Jim explained patiently.

"H'm! The card's been blown away from the other one when it was fired. What had it in it, do you know?"

"It had Number Five in it, too," Jim assured him. "We were all using Number Five this morning. I remember that perfectly well, because we had a little argument about it at the time. Just to be sure ..."

He fished a number of cartridges from his jacket pocket and showed the inspector that each of them had the figure 5 on the wad.

"Quite so," said Hinton. "Now I see three other guns here. These are the ones the rest of the party were carrying?"

Jim confirmed this with a nod.

"This is my own gun," he said, indicating it. "This other one, with the score along the wood of the stock, is the one Mr Laxford was using. The third was in Mr Hay's hands. These two belong to the house, I believe."

"I see, I see," Hinton assured him in a tone which showed no interest in the matter. "And now I think that's all I want with you, Mr Brandon. I've Mr Laxford and Mr Hay to see now."

"They're in the smoking-room, I believe," Jim volunteered. "I'll show you the way, if you'll come with me."

Jim left him at the door, going off to rejoin Oswald. The inspector entered the smoking-room and introduced himself When he went in, Hay was hunched forward in a big saddle-bag chair, a glass of neat whisky in his hand, and a forgotten cigar sending up a spiral of blue smoke from the ashtray at his side. His red face wore an angry and perplexed expression, and there was something like uneasiness in his little pig-like eyes as they swung round to the new-comer. Laxford was standing beside the mantelpiece, aimlessly fidgeting with one of the ornaments. His face was turned away from Hinton, but his whole attitude suggested disquietude of an extreme type. When they saw the inspector, they both did their best to appear at ease; but to Hinton their bearing was eloquent of their having been interrupted in the midst of some uncomfortable discussion.

"Bit of a knock for them, this affair," Hinton reflected, as he remembered the appearance of the body upstairs.

"You've come to make some inquiries, of course," Laxford said, when the inspector had given his name. "Have you seen Mr Brandon? Oh, you have? And Mr Dunne?"

"I've seen Mr Brandon. Mr Dunne's gone away, but I have his address," Hinton explained.

Laxford seemed to hesitate for a moment before speaking again.

"I wonder would it make matters clearer if we went over the ground?" he said tentatively. "I think I could explain better if you saw the actual ground. What do you say, Hay?"

"Suits me. It'll give us a mouthful of fresh air, anyhow," Hay declared ungraciously as he hoisted himself out of his chair. He gulped the rest of his whisky and set down his glass. "Go now, eh?"

As they trudged along the road to the gardener's cottage, Hay left all explanation to Laxford. He volunteered no information, and maintained an attitude of morose aloofness, as though occupied with his own reflections. Laxford gave the inspector the impression of a man who forces himself to talk in order to avoid awkward silences. He, like Hay, seemed to be engrossed by some problem which never came to the surface, but he was evidently trying to conceal his absorption by a flow of trivialities.

"This is where we stood, taking shelter from the rain," he explained, when they reached the cottage. "Stoke came out and invited us into the cottage. It wasn't worth while. We stood in the porch till the shower passed. Ah! There's Stoke. He can tell you what he saw."

The gardener had evidently seen them from the window, for he came out and joined the party.

"One thing at a time, if you please, sir," Hinton suggested. "I'll have your story first. It keeps things ship-shape in my notes," he explained, to avoid giving offence.

"I hadn't thought of that. Of course you're right," Laxford

agreed with a certain eagerness. "Well, after the rain stopped, we went on. We were going to shoot in the Plantation, there, on the way back to the house. We split up, of course, to avoid shooting into one another by accident. Young Brandon, poor chap, was always careless with a gun; and, frankly, I didn't want to be too close to him."

He gave a rather nervous laugh and made a gesture to amplify his meaning.

"I see," the inspector said. "And then?"

"Mr Hay went into the wood on the left," Laxford continued. "Just about that fallen tree, wasn't it, Hay?"

"About there," Hay grunted in confirmation.

"I was next in the line," Laxford went on. "I got into the wood just about where you see that withered branch. That's right, isn't it, Stoke?"

The gardener gave a confirmatory nod and would evidently have spoken if the inspector had not checked him with a frown.

"The two Brandons turned off towards the right. I didn't see them enter the wood, but I believe they went in together. You saw them, Stoke?"

"I did, sir. They went in about fifty yards to the right of you. Then I lost sight of 'em among the trees."

The inspector ran his eye over the end of the plantation, gauging the distances of the landmarks.

"So they went in about a hundred yards west of the line of the ha-ha; you got in about fifty yards to the west of them; and Mr Hay was another fifty yards from you, on the far left? I see."

"When I got into the Plantation," Laxford went on, "I waited for some minutes, to give the Brandons time to get into position. Then I heard a shot, on my right. I guessed, from the sound, that young Mr Brandon had fired. I took it that he must have begun to walk up the line of the ha-ha; so I moved forward myself. If you come with me, I think I can show you where I went."

He led them into the Plantation.

"Here's where I waited. Then I heard the shot and I began to walk forward, this way. Almost at the start, I flushed two rabbits and managed to bring them both down. That was just here, beside this little pool."

He pointed out the spot.

"Then it struck me that we ought to have brought the keeper with us. To carry the dead rabbits, you see. One can't carry a couple of rabbits and use a gun. It was a question of either leaving the rabbits and going on shooting, or else picking them up and not shooting any more. You see the position?"

"I see," the inspector assured him.

"I'm not very keen on shooting," Laxford conferred. "So it occurred to me that the best thing to do would be to carry the rabbits. Then it struck me that, since I wasn't going to shoot any more, I might as well carry for the rest of the party. I shouted to young Mr Brandon and told him I'd carry anything he and his brother got. He called back that his brother had gone across the Carron, so it was no use bothering about him. You can't cross the stream anywhere between the stepping-stones and the footbridge up near the house. Then I called to Mr Hay, on my left, that I'd pick up anything he shot. That's correct, isn't it. Hay?"

"Right," said Hay laconically.

"Then it struck me," Laxford continued, "that if I was going to carry all they got, I might have my hands full. I'd no further use for my gun, so there was no point in hampering myself with it. I leaned it up against that big tree over yonder at the side of the pool in as conspicuous a place as I could find. I meant to tell Stoke to pick up the gun on his way back to his cottage, later on.

"Did you reload, after your two shots?" the inspector inquired casually.

Laxford seemed confused by the unexpected question.

"Did I? I can't quite remember doing it, but I suppose I did. One does these things mechanically, you see. It's hard to recall whether one did or not. I suppose I must have slipped in fresh cartridges. Now I think of it . . ."

He seemed to make an effort to jog his memory, but with no apparent success.

"No, I can't say, really," he concluded, looking rather flustered.

The inspector seemed to attach no great importance to the detail.

"And then?" he queried.

"Then I heard a couple of shots from the ha-ha side. Young Mr Brandon had missed his first shot, I forgot to tell you. When I heard these two shots, I walked over to the ha-ha. If you'll come with me, I'll show you where I went."

He led them through the wood till they reached the line of the sunk fence.

"When I got here," he continued, "young Mr Brandon had gone on farther. He pointed to where the two dead rabbits were, and I picked them up. That was the last I saw of him alive."

The inspector examined the ground at the top of the sunk fence, where the stones cropped up here and there through the turf.

"Not easy walking," he commented. "When you saw him, was he going carefully?"

"No," Laxton said. "He was just taking it at his normal pace without any particular caution. Like this."

He illustrated by walking along the top of the ha-ha; but before he made a dozen steps his foot slipped on a projecting stone and he had a narrow escape of losing his balance. Hay guffawed at the mishap.

"Easy to come a cropper there, Laxford," he commented.

The inspector seemed impressed by the accident.

"Narrow shave of a nasty fall, sir. One can see how the accident could happen. By the way, how was he carrying his gun?"

Laxford thought for a moment.

"I expect he usually carried it at the 'ready'; but when I saw him last he had it at the trail in his right hand and he was fending off a branch—there—with his left hand. You see the branch grows over the line of the ha-ha. He had to push it aside to get past."

The inspector seemed satisfied.

"And after that?"

"I walked back—follow me, please—towards the middle of

the plantation. As I was going, I think I heard a shot from over the stream; but I wasn't paying much attention to shots from that quarter."

After a few moments, Laxford halted again.

"Just about here, I heard Mr Hay's gun. He'd hit a rabbit, so I crossed over—along here—to pick it up for him. . . . This is the place, I think, Hay?"

"Hereabouts," Hay confirmed. "Not that it matters a damn."

"Mr Hay and I walked on together—along this line—till we came to a fallen tree. . . . Here it is. Then we heard a shot to the east; so I left him and hurried off to pick up the game. I took this direction. The undergrowth is pretty thick here and I had to go roundabout at times. . . . I'm not quite sure of my exact route, but it was roughly on the line we're taking. . . . When I got to somewhere about here," he paused at the spot, "I called out to young Mr Brandon to know if he'd hit anything. I got no answer; and I took it that my voice hadn't reached him. He was up-wind and it was very gusty. I went on—this way, please—and as I was going I heard another shot. I called again and got no reply. That surprised me. We're quite near the line of the ha-ha, as you can see, though it's quite out of sight behind all that undergrowth. I went forward, along here, and came out on the edge of a little clearing. Here it is. There was no sign of young Mr Brandon. I went forward to the edge of the ha-ha, to look along it; and then, here, just below me, I saw him lying at the foot of the wall."

The inspector joined him at the top of the dike.

"Just there?" he asked.

"Just there," Laxford confirmed, pointing to the exact spot.

The inspector examined the place for a moment or two, but did not seem to think it worth his while to jump down to the lower ground.

"And then?" he prompted.

"I jumped down and found he was quite dead, so far as I could see. His gun was beside him. I climbed up again and went back into the wood, calling to Mr Hay, who hurried across to join me. I told him what had happened, and we both came back here. I had no notion where Mr James Brandon might be. That screen of bushes across the stream hides everything from here. Then I called, on the off-chance that he was within hearing. He was farther up the stream; but I managed to make him hear; and when he came out on the bank beyond the bushes I directed him to go round by the bridge, up above. Meanwhile Mr Hay and I lifted Mr Brandon's body on to the grass at the top of the ha-ha. Did you lift his gun, Hay?"

"Don't remember doing it," Hay answered. "One of us must've picked it up."

"Which way was he lying down there?" the inspector demanded.

"His head was to the north, up-stream," Laxford replied at once. "We didn't turn him, in lifting him; and his head was to the north when we laid him down—here—on the grass. You can see the blood where it oozed from the wound, if you look."

The inspector apparently took no interest in the matter. He merely emitted one of his battered conversational counters: "Quite so," and waited for further information.

"Mr James Brandon arrived here almost immediately after that," Laxford went on. "Then, while he was examining the body, somebody stepped out from behind the bushes—here—with my gun in his hand. I understand his name was Dunne. He seemed taken aback, which wasn't surprising. In fact, he seemed to me to behave rather strangely altogether. He said he didn't know how he got there."

"I know about Mr Dunne," the inspector admitted, with a touch of impatience in his tone.

"That's really all I can tell you about the affair," Laxford concluded. "I went off to get assistance, and we took the body to the house."

The inspector nodded as though satisfied, but turned to Hay.

"You were here while Mr Laxford was away?"

Hay seemed to have the strongest disinclination to telling anything.

"Right," he agreed, and stopped short at the monosyllable.

"Did you notice anything that seems important?" Hinton demanded bluntly.

"Me? Nothing much. I saw a bit of the bone of his head lying on the grass there. Made me feel sickish, somehow. I catted over yonder among the trees, if you want to know. Blood takes me like that, somehow. This Dunne person didn't seem to mind. He was prowling all over the place, down the slope, there. I don't think that cove's quite right in the head, if you ask me. He talked a lot of stuff about somebody or something he called Cunning Oar Physic or some such stuff—rot! And he picked up a bit of a pill-box and made enough fuss over it for it to have been the Cullinan Diamond complete. Bats in the belfry's his trouble, you take my word."

Inspector Hinton nodded rather absent-mindedly in acknowledgment.

"The coroner will want the evidence of you gentlemen at the inquest," he explained. "You'll get a subpoena later on. And that reminds me to ask your full names."

He produced his note-book ostentatiously and stood with pencil in readiness.

"Thomas Laxford . . . L-A-X-F-O-R-D," Laxford volunteered. "Some people are apt to spell it L-A-C-K-S," he added in explanation.

The inspector turned to Hay.

"Joseph's the first one; and you spell the other one the same way as you spell a donkey's breakfast, so you can't go wrong there," Hay sneered.

"And the address?" demanded Hinton, taking no notice of the rudeness.

Hay seemed confused by this question. He glanced at Laxford before answering.

"I'll be here for a day or two."

"Edgehill," the inspector noted. Then, turning to Laxford, he asked casually, "By the way, sir, you've no doubts about how this happened, I suppose?"

"None whatever," Laxford declared immediately. "He was

coming along the top of the sunk fence, because it makes easier walking than the up-slope, most of the way. He must have tripped or stumbled over something and dropped his gun out of his right hand, so that it fell down the ha-ha. It went off with the jar it got when it hit the ground, with the safety-catch at danger; and his head happened to be in the way of the discharge. That fits everything, doesn't it?"

"It was the first idea that crossed my mind," Hinton said in a faintly superior tone. "I just wondered if you knew anything that didn't fit in with it."

"No, nothing I can think of," Laxford assured him immediately.

"Ah, well, in that case I needn't trouble you gentlemen any further," the inspector concluded with a certain finality in his tone. "The coroner likes to have a little plan made, so I've got to take one or two measurements here. You'd only be in my way, so I'll say good morning, gentlemen."

His air of dismissal, though polite, was too plain to ignore. Laxford wished him good morning. Hay contented himself with a surly nod.

"You wait here and give me a hand, Stoke," Hinton ordered as the other two moved off towards the house.

When they were out of sight among the trees, he produced a surveyor's tape from his pocket and, with Stoke's assistance, proceeded to make a rough sketch-plan of the environment of the tragedy. The farther bank of the stream gave him a little trouble; but he resorted to some rough triangulation with a prismatic compass, a procedure which evidently impressed Stoke considerably. The plotting took Hinton rather longer than he had anticipated; but at last he completed his work and had the sardonic satisfaction of witnessing Stoke's admiration of the result.

"And that's a ship-shape job!" he commented aloud as he filled in the last details; for Inspector Hinton was never slow in drawing attention to his own talents. "Now I'll have a look round."

He went to the edge of the ha-ha at the point indicated by Laxford and climbed gingerly down to the lower level, where he fell to examining the grass. Apparently the thing he was looking for eluded him, and he went over the ground several times with increasing care, but still with obvious ill-success.

"That was just where he must have fell," Stoke declared, seeing the inspector so evidently at fault in some way.

"I can see the grass trampled down," Hinton retorted scornfully.

"Some o' the trampin' was done by that loony Dunne," Stoke pointed out. "I seen him at it. Trampin' all over the place, he was. Lookin' for somethin' or other he'd lost, so he said, an' he fair furraged round till he got it, he did. Then he came and scrambled up here on the dike and sat swingin' his heels, as pleased as Punch, with young Mr Brandon's corpse just behind him. Them loonies is queer, I tell you. And him playin' cricket like he was a sane man. Rum, to think o' that. Wrong in the head, an' holds a bat as straight as I do myself!"

The inspector's only response was a grunt. Not one of those encouraging, interrogative noises which he had practised so often, but a plain grunt which was intentionally meaningless. Hinton had come upon something which puzzled him; and he had no desire to let Stoke guess that he was perplexed. "Never give yourself away," was another tenet in his unwritten code.

He had climbed down the ha-ha merely to verify, for form's sake, Laxford's statement that the body had been found lying at the foot of the wall. If that were true, then there should be some blood on the grass, the inspector argued quite reasonably. But his examination, casual at first and then more and more searching, had failed to reveal any bloodstain whatsoever. He admitted to himself that the grass was wet. Still, considering the size of the pool of blood on the upper level, some trace ought to be detectable on what was supposed to be the place where young Brandon had fallen. And there was none to be found.

As to the grass at this point, nothing could be inferred from it. Mr Dunne had evidently trampled it in the course of his search, and it retained no trace of a heavy body having fallen upon it.

Hinton made a jotting in his note-book: "Found no trace of blood on grass at foot of ha-ha." That was the fact. On the opposite page, which he kept for his inferences, he scribbled; "May have been washed away or . . ." And here he paused.

"Or . . .?"

Or else the body never was at the foot of the ha-ha at all. That was the only alternative, so far as the inspector could see. And in that case, Hay and Laxford had deliberately lied when they said they found young Brandon at the bottom of the wall and lifted him up on to the higher level.

Suppose they had faked their evidence, the inspector reflected, why had they done so? Because the truth didn't suit 'em, obviously. That was the only reason why anybody was tempted to tell a lie. And if the body hadn't been at the foot of the dike, then it must have been somewhere else. Where else? the inspector asked himself; and the only answer he could find was: "On the slope above the ha-ha where the pool of blood was lying." But in that case, the gun hadn't fallen down the ha-ha at all; and the hypothesis based on its exploding with the shock was all nonsense. The youngster must have been shot at the only place where there was blood visible: on the spot where Jim Brandon had found him lying. And Laxford's evidence must be a pack of lies, the inspector concluded, neatly rounding off his argument in a circle.

Viewed in this new light, Laxford's behaviour struck Hinton as suspicious. A bit too ready with needless details: 'I was just here, at that time; and then I went over there; and after that I . . .' and so forth. Too much anxiety to get his evidence 'just right.' These glib witnesses weren't much to Hinton's taste. And suddenly it struck him that Hay had contributed practically nothing to the story, beyond one or two curt corroborations of Laxford's statements.

The inspector realised that his silence might make Stoke inquisitive, so he hastily put aside his preoccupations and turned to the gardener.

"How's the museum getting on, eh?" he inquired, as if he had dismissed the accident from his mind.

Stoke rose at once to the bait. His museum was the thing of which he was proudest.

"Oh, so-so," he admitted with modest satisfaction. "I've got a fresh thing in hand for it, just now, not finished yet. It's a whaler in the ice. I made the boat myself and copied the rigging off an old picture, so it would be right. It's in a tub of brine at present, to get it all coated with salt-crystals—for the snow and ice, you see—and it's coming along fine, I can tell you. After that, I'm going to bed it in some clay and sprinkle salt all over it for the ice-floe. You won't be able to tell it from the real thing, barring the size, I'll guarantee, when it's all fixed up."

"I wonder how you can think of things like that," the inspector mused, in well-feigned admiration.

Stoke failed to see the double edge on the compliment.

"It's just a sort of gift, I suppose," he confessed bashfully. "I keep my eyes open for anything rum that comes my way, of course, and it's queer how many o' them kind o' things you meet with if you keep your eyes open for 'em. And I like makin' curiosities, too. Gives me somethin' to fill in my time with, in the winter evenin's."

"Better get a wife," the inspector suggested genially.

"No, no!" Stoke protested coyly. "You and me's of the same opinion there, Mr Hinton, I think. No use keepin' a cow when you can buy milk, is there? I can hire a woman for to do springcleanin' or anything else I want, and a sight cheaper nor keepin' a wife."

Then, rather timidly, he made a suggestion.

"You've never seen my museum, have you? I'd be glad for to show it to you any time you like, Mr Hinton, if you'd care for to look in and give it a look over. Mr Wendover, he's promised me to come and see it, sometime. Very interested, he was, he told me. He liked to see people with a hobby that made them keep their eyes open. That's what he said. So perhaps you'd care to give me a look up? Night's the best time. There's some o' the things looks best lit up with little candles."

"Yes, yes," Hinton answered, in a non-committal tone.

He felt a good-humoured contempt for Stoke's hobby. Fancy a full-grown man wasting his time with peep-shows and rubbish like that! It strengthened the inspector's feeling of personal superiority to humanity in general.

Now that he had misled Stoke as to the trend of his thoughts, he went back to his own problems. Inspector Hinton had a suspicious mind; but he was too level-headed to ignore the plain proposition that one fact and one inference did not suffice to make a case. The fact was that he had found no blood at the foot of the ha-ha. The inference was that Laxford had told an elaborate series of lies. Suggestive, perhaps, but nothing more, Hinton decided.

And with that, his mind switched over to the coming inquest. What line should he take? He would not be called as a witness: Hay, Laxford, Jim Brandon, and the doctor were the only people who could give first-hand evidence. That left him free to tell the coroner about the ha-ha or to keep his own counsel if he chose to do so.

Should he give the coroner the benefit of his discovery or not? He had a prejudice against the whole business of inquests and coroner's juries, especially when the coroner thought himself clever enough to play Sherlock Holmes and trench on detective work. They ought to leave that to experts like himself. And in this particular case he had nothing to gain by being fussy, whilst it was quite on the cards that he might make a fool of himself if he went too far. He decided to sit tight and say nothing. That left him free to keep his eyes open, in case anything fresh turned up.

CHAPTER 9
COINNEACH ODHAR FIOSAICHE

"You can't call him as a witness, you understand?" Dr Barreman pointed out in a slightly irritated tone. "No Court would take his evidence."

The inspector glanced out of the window at the broad stretches of velvety turf from which Fairlawns took its name.

"Not if he gave this address," he admitted without ado. "No, doctor, that idea never entered my head. It's just a matter of form. Nobody was there, when this young fellow Brandon met his death. We have to get at how it happened, if we can; and all we've got to go on is what people saw when they came up and found him dead. Mr Dunne was on the spot. He's no use to us as a witness; but still he might remember something that would give us the key to the business. Some trifling detail, maybe, that would throw some light on the affair."

Dr Barreman shook his head sceptically.

"He remembers nothing about it. The first thing he can recollect is coming upon a group of three people with young Brandon dead in the middle of them. You must have heard that already," he added, with a sharp look at the inspector.

"So I gathered," Hinton admitted. "But what I'm concerned with is what he saw after he woke up. By the way, how did he come to be on the loose at all?"

Here, intentionally, he put his finger on a sore spot. Dr Barreman was proud of his organisation in Fairlawns, where everything ran like clockwork. But even clockwork may slip a cog. The most trusted keeper may fall into a doze. A wandering fit may come over a patient. The chance that the two things will synchronise is millions to one; but if it falls out so, then the cog slips, and the pride of the head organiser suffers a severe shock. And, by a still more unfortunate coincidence, Mr Dunne had got himself mixed up in this notorious affair in the Long Plantation.

"It won't happen again," Dr Barreman said curtly, with a tightening of his lips.

The inspector had achieved his object. Rather than discuss the escape, Dr Barreman would discourse freely on any other subject which was presented to him.

"What's wrong with Mr Dunne?" Hinton asked in a casual tone. "He's . . . abnormal, of course; but just how?"

A gleam of something in the doctor's eye arrested his attention momentarily, but he refrained from showing that he had seen it.

"I can't discuss a patient's troubles with you, of course," Dr Barreman pointed out stiffly.

Then he seemed to reconsider his position, for he went on in a less reserved tone:

"So far as professional secrecy goes, my hands are tied. But I don't mind telling you what you could ferret out for yourself, since it's public property. A few years ago Mr Dunne was just the same as you or myself. He's a bachelor, with big private means. He was a good all-round sportsman. I don't mean he was first-class, or anywhere near it, of course; but he could sit on a horse, handle a yacht or a gun, play cricket without making a fool of himself—you've seen that for yourself, I expect—and his golf handicap was four, I believe, in those days. He has a literary turn; you know he edits our magazine. Altogether, as you see, he was rather exceptionally gifted. Unfortunately, as it turned out, he was a keen motorist; and one day, through no fault of his own I gather, he got into a bad smash. His car was wrecked, and he got very bad concussion of the brain. There was a law case over it, and the other man was proved to be quite in the wrong. I'm telling you nothing confidential; you can read the case for yourself in the newspaper files. After that," and here the inspector noted that Dr Barreman picked his words carefully, "he began to have lapses of memory. That, you know already, Inspector."

Hinton nodded understanding.

"I see," he said. "You mean he does things, and then forgets he's done 'em?"

Somewhat to his surprise he saw the doctor's lips tighten again as though something had involuntarily escaped him. Then Dr Barreman suddenly became communicative.

"Let's take an ordinary phenomenon," he suggested. "Now most of us fall into a brown study at times. You do yourself, Inspector, I expect. You may be puzzling over something or other while you walk along the street, and all your attention's concentrated on what you're thinking about. And yet you can cross the road and take the right turnings, dodge the traffic, and so forth, can't you? You don't notice where you're going; you just walk along automatically, taking no notice of anything; and if you were asked to describe a man who passed you halfway you wouldn't remember anything about him, most likely. Your mind's working on something else all the time, and your body works on like an automatic machine without you having to exercise a conscious control."

"I see," the inspector declared, but he chose a tone which suggested that the doctor was talking much above his head. "But all I want from Mr Dunne is what he saw when he came out of this 'brown study' of his. He'll remember *that*, all right."

Dr Barreman evidently paused to consider something.

"Very well," he said at length. "If you insist, you may go up and see him. But you mustn't worry him, you understand? He's had a nasty jar, perhaps; and I can't have him heckled and flustered. I'm responsible for his health, and my first duty's towards him. If you excite him, you'll have to come away. That's clear? And if he begins to talk about Dun Kenneth, just let him run on. Don't contradict him, since it's a pet subject of his. I'm stretching a point in letting you see him, and you'll have to play the game, you know."

The inspector made one of those affirmative noises which committed him to nothing definite. It seemed to satisfy Dr Barreman, for he led the way to Mr Dunne's sitting-room. As they entered Mr Dunne was standing at the window with his back to them, apparently gazing up at the sky; but at the sound of their steps he swung round, and the inspector saw that he held in his hand a large white stone. He laid it down on a table as he advanced to meet his visitors.

"This is Inspector Hinton," the doctor explained. "He would like to hear anything you can tell him about the accident this morning, Mr Dunne."

Mr Dunne acknowledged the inspector's greeting politely. He seemed in no way perturbed by this unexpected intrusion.

"I shall be delighted to help you if I can," he said frankly. "Only, I'm afraid I can't tell you much that will be of service. The fact is..." His eye wandered to the doctor for a moment. "The fact is, my memory is rather treacherous at times."

"Quite so," the inspector said sympathetically.

"I really remember nothing between the time I went to bed last night and the moment when I came upon some gentlemen in a little glade in a wood, this morning," Mr Dunne pursued, as if such a phenomenon was one of the commonest. "From that moment onwards, I think I can tell you what happened, clearly enough."

"If you'd be so good," Hinton said, filling in the pause.

"I remember stepping out from behind some bushes," Mr Dunne pursued, knitting his brows slightly as though in an effort to forget nothing. "In front of me two gentlemen were standing. A third was kneeling on the ground. And in the centre of the group was the body of a young man, face downward, with his feet towards me. One of the men standing up had a gun under his arm; the other was empty-handed. I recognised none of them, I may say. They were total strangers to me. The empty-handed man was grey-haired; the one standing near him, with a gun under his arm, was a big red-faced fellow; the third, the kneeling one, was a good deal younger than the other two. He had a gun beside him, as if he'd laid it down when he knelt. There was another gun on the grass . . . let me see . . ." He passed his hand over his brow as if to concentrate his thoughts. "Yes . . . I think I can recall it. It was a little farther away from me than the young man's body."

The inspector suddenly pricked up his ears.

"Can you remember it distinctly?" he asked in. a carefully neutral tone. "I mean, which way the muzzle pointed, and so forth."

Mr Dunne reflected for some moments as though striving to clarify his mental picture.

"My impression is that it lay rather beyond the body, from my own position I mean, past the head. And I think . . . I can't be absolutely sure . . . but I think the muzzle pointed away from me. Yes, I think so."

"And then?" prompted Hinton.

"I think I stepped forward and asked what it all meant. The red-faced man—a rather vulgar fellow, he appeared to me—explained that there had been a shooting accident. Then I suddenly realised that I was carrying a gun myself, though how I came by it I can't imagine. Quite mechanically, without thinking what I was doing, I opened the breech and found two spent cartridges in the barrels. Just then the young man who was kneeling beside the body seemed to find something which he wrapped in his handkerchief and laid back again on the grass. I have no idea what it was. Then they all began talking about the accident and about removing the body. The grey-haired man finally went off for assistance. The red-faced man went off into the wood, saying he was sick. There was nothing I could do, and to fill in the time I began to search about on the grass. I suppose it was seeing the young man find something that suggested that to me. I got down the ha-ha on to the patch of grass between it and the river. And . . ." Mr Dunne's voice changed its note. "I suddenly discovered something I've been hunting for, the very thing I needed. Wonderful piece of luck, wasn't it?"

"Wonderful!" echoes Hinton. "What was it, sir?"

Mr Dunne turned to the table and lifted from it the white stone which had been in his hand when the inspector came in.

"This is the White Stone of Coinneach Odhar Fiosaiche," he said solemnly.

"Oh, it is, is it?" said the inspector blankly, for the words conveyed nothing to him.

Inwardly he was cursing bitterly. Obviously this subject was the 'hobby' about which the doctor had warned him. He had let himself in for it now, he reflected ruefully. It might be risky to try to switch Mr Dunne back to the main question until he chose to return to it voluntarily. Better let him get his wind out on his 'hobby,' and then bring him round to business tactfully.

"Yes," continued Mr Dunne, handling the treasure reverently. "This is, I am convinced, the actual stone which belonged to Coinneach Odhar Fiosaiche—Dun Kenneth the Seer of Brahan. When he was put to death, after prophesying the Doom of the Seaforths, he threw his white stone into Loch Ussie and predicted that whoever found it would inherit his gift of foretelling the future. One day it happened that I was walking on the shore of the lake, when this white stone caught my eye. The curious hole through it attracted my attention. And then it flashed on me that this was Coinneach Odhar's talisman. Besides, the name made it almost certain. His name was Coinneach Odhar—Dun Kenneth is the English of it. And my own name is Kenneth Dunne. That would be a very strange coincidence if it were mere chance."

The inspector's gift of counterfeiting emotions served him well at this stage.

"And you can see the future when you look through it?" he asked in a respectful tone.

Mr Dunne's eyes clouded slightly at the question.

"No," he admitted grudgingly. "I haven't developed the gift —as yet. I get glimpses, sometimes, but they're nothing more.

There's something missing, evidently, something to clarify the vision. Lying in that lake so long, the hole in the stone got bigger, most likely. If I could bring it back to the proper size, I might see the picture sharper."

"Yes, yes," agreed Hinton, who was on pins and needles to get back to the main question.

"You think so?" Mr Dunne was evidently pleased to hear this endorsement of his scheme. "I think there's certainly something in the idea. That's why I've been on the hunt for something to fit the hole and narrow it down a trifle. I picked up this bit of pasteboard in the wood this morning. You see it fits neatly in. It seems to me to make some improvement, though the pictures are still very vague, too vague to show anything definite, so far."

He held the white stone out for inspection so that Hinton could see how he had fitted the little pasteboard ring to form a lining to the central aperture.

"That's very interesting, sir," said the inspector cautiously.

He refrained from taking the stone into his own hand, lest that should prolong this, to him, worthless discourse. But Mr Dunne was by no means discouraged. While the inspector writhed at the waste of time Mr Dunne delivered a short lecture on the chief prophecies of the Brahan Seer, carefully distinguishing between those which might be attributed to natural shrewdness and those which demanded something less normal in the maker of them.

"Wonderful!" Hinton declared at last, as though he could stand no more marvels that day.

Mr Dunne, having ridden a long course on his hobby, seemed to recover his natural good manners.

"I'm afraid I have taken up your time unduly," he said in an apologetic tone. "Is there anything further you'd like to know?"

It was evident that he meant to clear up any doubts in Hinton's mind about the Seer of Brahan, but the inspector chose to interpret the question otherwise.

"Just one or two points I'd like cleared up," he said gratefully. "You'd got to where one of the party went off for assistance.

What happened after that?"

Mr Dunne had the air of a man interrupted in affairs of importance by the intrusion of a child; but his courtesy stood the strain.

"Oh, after that?" he answered. "I remember. The grey-haired man came back with a cart and some men; and the young man's body was taken away to the house. Then the grey-haired man came up to me and claimed the gun I was carrying. It was his, apparently, so I handed it over to him. The red-faced fellow was rather offensive because I couldn't recall how I came to have it in my hand. I gave it up to the grey-haired man."

"And then?" Hinton prompted.

"Let me think," Mr Dunne replied, with a gesture which begged for time to assemble his recollections. "Oh, yes. The youngest of the three handed his own gun to a labourer who had come on the scene, and picked up the dead man's gun himself. I remember that quite well because he spoke of it as his brother's gun, and that was how I learned the relationship between them. The two older fellows set off towards the house, and I followed them at a little distance. The young man came behind. The labouring man joined me after a moment or two, to act as guide, apparently. And shortly after we reached the house two attendants appeared and I accompanied them back here," Mr Dunn concluded, as though it were the most natural thing in the world.

"I see," said the inspector with a note of finality in his tone, for he was afraid that Coinneach Odhar Fiosaiche might crop up again if he remained there for a moment more. "And now, Mr Dunne, I must thank you for your patience. Most interesting," he added, as a dishonest tribute to the lecture on the Brahan Seer.

As he walked down the Fairlawns avenue he thought over the strange phenomenon presented by Mr Dunne's behaviour. Here was a man whose memory had been blotted out completely over a fairly extended period; and yet, when he regained his normal faculties again he had shown a power of exact recollection rather better than that possessed by the average person.

"If this business were a case for us," Hinton refleeted, "that loony would make a better witness than a good many—and yet we couldn't put him into the box, no matter how much we needed him."

From that his mind turned to other peculiarities of Mr Dunne's mental make-up. The evident reluctance of Dr Barreman to discuss his patient came back to him. And suddenly the inspector pulled up short, arrested by a thought which flashed into his mind. When he moved on again, it was to take the road to Dr Brinkworth's house. He was fortunate enough to find the doctor at home and disengaged at the moment.

"There's a thing I ought to have asked you about when I saw you this morning," he said disingenuously, after apologising for his intrusion. "It's come up in connection with a case, and I'd like an expert opinion. This is it. Suppose there was a theft in a house one night. All the doors and windows found secure in the morning. An inside job, on the face of it. And suppose one of the family is a sleep-walker. Would you say it was possible that that sleep-walker had got up—asleep—in the middle of the night and stolen the article, concealed it, and then gone back to bed without the faintest recollection of the whole affair?"

Dr Brinkworth reflected for some moments before replying.

"Er . . . it's possible, I suppose," he admitted grudgingly, "but I never came across any case like it."

"It's a puzzling case," the inspector went on with a well-feigned semblance of perplexity. "I hardly know what to make of it. Somebody in the house must have done it, and yet . . . well, none of 'em shows the slightest symptom of knowing anything about it. I was just wondering. These loss-of-memory cases one hears about in the newspapers might give one a hint, I thought, even if it wasn't sleep-walking. Is there any other trouble that would fit? I'm putting it to you as a mere John Doe and Richard Roe case, you understand? I'm not fishing for information about any somnambulist you may have among your patients. I hope that's quite clear?"

"As a matter of fact, I haven't anything of the sort," the doctor answered, "so . . . er . . . you're quite free to ask whatever you choose."

"Well, then, isn't there some disease or other that works like sleep-walking—where a man does things and remembers nothing about them afterwards? Automatic something-or-other, isn't it?"

Dr Brinkworth rose to the bait.

"Er . . . perhaps you're thinking of post-epileptic automatism," he suggested. "That might fit your case."

The inspector shook his head doubtfully.

"Don't epileptics fall down in fits, froth at the mouth, bite their tongues, and so forth?" he demanded. "None of the people I'm dealing with do that."

"Not necessarily," Dr Brinkworth asserted, and as he came to definite technicalities his usual nervous manner faded out. "These fits you speak of are a symptom of one variety of epilepsy, a type that's called *le grand mal*. But there's another type, *le petit mal*, where all the visible symptoms may be pallor, a slight twitching of the muscles, a movement of the eyes. The whole thing's hardly noticeable in some cases. In both the *grand mal* and the *petit mal* there's a lapse of consciousness. During that lapse of consciousness, the patient may do things and have no recollection whatever of having done them, once he wakes up again. That's the sort of thing you're looking for, isn't it? That's what they call post-epileptic automatism."

The door-bell rang at this moment, and Dr Brinkworth fell back into his usual semi-flurried condition.

"I'm sorry," he apologised. "That's a patient come by appointment. I'm afraid I'll have to go. But see, here's a book that will give you something more about the thing."

He turned to his shelves and took down a volume on forensic medicine.

"You'll get what you want here," he said, fluttering the pages until he found the passage he wanted.

"Just sit down and read it for yourself. You'll be able to find your way out when you've finished, won't you? Er . . . I'm sorry ... but ..."

And with that Dr Brinkworth left the inspector to his own devices.

Hinton opened the book at the place indicated and read over the paragraph, muttering the crucial passages aloud to reinforce his memory.

"... 'Automatism is, as a rule, more pronounced after an attack of *petit mal* than after a typical fit' ... Ah! ... 'but this is not always so.' ... Mmm! ... 'The automatic action is either a habitual action of the patient in his normal life, or a caricature of that action.' ... This looks like something! ... 'In illustration, take the case of a man who walks into a shop, picks up something, and walks out again, and is then arrested for thieving' ... Well, well! ... *'or a person accustomed to firearms may shoot somebody'* ... The devil he may! ..."

The inspector paused for a moment as this last ejaculation was drawn from him by the textbook's meaning. Then he went on eagerly.

"... 'Epileptic equivalents (sometimes termed masked epilepsy) are mental disorders which exist in some epileptics without the occurrence of fits.' ... Oh, indeed! ... 'For instance, instead of falling into a fit, the patient may do some act such as a brutal murder' ... Whew! ... 'without motive and without the slightest recollection of having committed the act! ..."

"This looks like getting warm!" Hinton muttered to himself.

He hurried on to the final phrases of the section.

"... 'These cases are characterised by the fact that the victim is usually unknown to the assailant, by a total absence of motive, and from the fact that no attempt is made to escape or to conceal the crime.' ... Well! That's torn it!" exclaimed the inspector, who was at times apt to recur to old-fashioned slang.

He copied out the relevant sentences in his notebook, took a note of the book's title and author and then, more thoughtful than usual in his demeanour, he let himself out of the house.

Now he thought he understood Dr Barreman's behaviour not so long ago. 'Lapses of memory?' Oh, yes. We admit them because we can't deny 'em, after Dunne had given himself away in the Plantation. But post-epileptic automatism? Oh, no. We never mention it. And why? 'Cause it might be awkward for us if an epileptic got loose from our establishment and shot a man. Damned awkward, in fact. So we keep our thumb on Mr Dunne's particular trouble, and very firmly too. Professional secrecy, of course. Quite all right. And so much for Dr Barreman. No use expecting any further help from that quarter.

Viewed in the light of the textbook of forensic medicine, the affair in the Plantation seemed plain enough now. A fit of post-epileptic automatism on Dunne's part; his discovery of Laxford's gun beside the pool; the sportsman's habituation to the use of firearms; the tendency to repeat some normal action in distorted form; a motiveless attack on young Brandon from behind the screen of the bushes: the whole thing fitted together like a jig-saw puzzle. In the first flush of his discovery, Inspector Hinton believed that he had stumbled upon the truth of the business.

Then came calmer reflection, with less satisfactory results. That case depended on Laxford having reloaded his gun before he left it beside the pool; and Laxford had been unable to say 'yes' or 'no' when Hinton had quizzed him on the point. If Laxford had not reloaded, then Dunne could not have fired a shot, since he had no cartridges of his own. And, as the inspector realised, the act of reloading is so automatic that a man might well be doubtful whether he had slipped fresh cartridges into his gun or not.

Further, and still more awkward to Hinton's logical mind, there was a second difficulty. If Dunne had shot young Brandon on the ground at the top of the sunk fence, the body must have fallen there and been found at that spot by Laxford and Hay. In that case, why had they told a deliberate lie about the corpse being at the foot of the ha-ha? There would be no point in a yarn of that sort. But, again, if Dunne had shot young Brandon at the edge of the ha-ha and the body had toppled down on to the grass below, why had Hinton failed to discover any trace of blood at the spot where it landed?

"This'll stand looking into," the inspector reflected in no little exasperation. "It doesn't make sense, no matter which way one looks at it."

CHAPTER 10 FROM INFORMATION RECEIVED

A day or two after his visit to Edgehill, Inspector Hinton ran out of tobacco; and as he was passing up the village street he turned into a shop which bore over its door the legend: "I. Copdock, General Dealer." The shopkeeper, a stout affable little man in shirt-sleeves, was arranging some goods at the moment, but he left his work at the sight of the customer and came forward dusting his hands mechanically.

"The usual," Hinton grunted, as he flung his pouch on the counter and began to count out the necessary coins.

Like many other smokers, the inspector held tight to the illusion that he possessed the secret of the ideal smoking mixture. "Brains will tell, even in small things," he would say, with a sigh of satisfaction, as he filled his pipe. After swearing Copdock to secrecy, he had supplied him with a written recipe for half a pound of the mixture, thus saving time when fresh supplies were needed. He was blissfully unaware that half the village had tried his special blend, by courtesy of Mr Copdock; and had rejected it with outspoken contempt.

The shopkeeper spread a sheet of paper on the counter and took down from his shelves various jars. Then, under the critical eye of the inspector, he busied himself with his scales, compounding the mixture according to his memorised formula.

"Nice weather we're having," he declared, to open conversation.

"Fair," the inspector admitted in an unbiased tone. "Watch the Latakia this time. You must have undershot the mark with it in the last lot. So I found, when I came to smoke it."

"I'm sure it was right, Mr Hinton," the dealer protested in an injured voice. "You know how partic'lar I am. Just you keep an eye on it now, when I come to weigh it out."

"I mean to," Hinton retorted. "Well, Copdock, what's all the news of the Great Metrollops of Talgarth?"

Copdock had once mispronounced the word 'metropolis' in the inspector's hearing; and Hinton, with all the mercilessness of his kind, never allowed the wretched man to forget it. Copdock winced slightly under the dig; but it was his policy never to quarrel with any customer, so he ignored it when he spoke.

"Oh, so-so. You'll know more than me, I expect, Mr Hinton. I haven't seen you since the inquest on young Mr Brandon, have I?"

"You have not," the inspector assured him gravely.

"I was on the jury," Copdock reminded him. "A sad affair, that. A nice young fellow he was. Used to be quite a good customer, one way and another, what with cartridges, cigarettes, tobacco, and such like. Very pleasant, too. He always had time for a little chat when he dropped in here."

"Yes, yes," said Hinton, with unfeigned indifference.

"His brother gave his evidence very well, I thought," Copdock pursued, quite undamped. "So did Mr Laxford, too, though he seemed a bit nervous-like. It was funny, though, that Mr Hay didn't turn up, wasn't it? Some of us was a bit surprised at that. He left by the afternoon train, didn't he, on the day of the accident? The summons didn't get there till after he'd gone, I heard."

"Oh, you did, did you?" said the inspector ruminatively. "Beauty, I suppose?"

Miss Jane Ann Tugby—'Beauty' to ironically minded intimates—became attached to the domestic staff of the Laxfords after their arrival at Edgehill. Her rather indeterminate function was to do any work which the other servants regarded as beneath them; but since this brought her into contact with both the cook and the housemaid. Miss Tugby preferred to describe herself as a between-maid, for she had a proper sense of values.

She had also a long sharply pointed nose which, according to unkind critics, she was for ever poking into affairs which were no concern of hers. It cannot be denied that she habitually listened at doors, and that no letter escaped her perusal if its owner left it within her reach. But these practices were not dictated by any hope of personal advantage. Indeed, much that she overheard through the keyhole of the servants' hall was greatly to her disadvantage, for the cook held decided views about her efficiency.

Miss Tugby, in fact, like many a distinguished scientist, 'wanted to know about things.' The pursuit of knowledge for its own sake, without ulterior design, was her object. And since the field of her researches was human nature, it would ill become the most eminent student of mere atoms and molecules to disclaim spiritual kinship with so zealous an investigator.

In most scientists the thirst of knowledge is accompanied by a desire to publish to the world the results which they have acquired. Hence these innumerable *Transactions, Zeitschriften, Bulletins, Rendiconti*, and what not, the stately and ever-lengthening ranks of which form the nightmare of university librarians in Europe, America, and the westernised portions of the Far East. Here the orthodox scientist had a decided advantage over Miss Tugby, who had no *Journal* or *Transactions* in which to record her discoveries.

But Nature ever finds a way. In addition to her sharp nose and receptive ears, Miss Tugby had a mouth and a mother. Mrs Tugby edited the raw material and then passed on to her sister-in-law the choicer morsels gleaned by her industrious daughter; and they thus, rather the worse for wear, came to the ears of the sister-in-law's husband, Mr Copdock, who put them into public circulation in the form of gossip across his counter, for he aimed to please his customers to the best of his ability.

Thus along this devious channel there came to Inspector Hinton some news which his methodical mind immediately docketed under the heading: "Information Received."

"Oh, no, it wasn't Beauty as told me about it," Mr Copdock asserted with the virtuous air of a man telling the literal truth. Then, with marked disingenuousness he added: "I don't just remember how it happened to come to my notice. It's no matter, anyhow. But I did hear that the summons missed him."

Quite unconsciously, Copdock had repaid the inspector for the gibe about 'Metropolis.' Hinton winced in his turn, for to his mind the dealer's remark was a reflection on his efficiency.

"I warned Hay that morning that he'd get a subpoena served on him. If he chose to clear out after that . . ." he said darkly. "Here! Go easy with that stuff! You're putting too much in."

Copdock had blundered on to a sore point on the inspector's skin. Hay's disappearance had completely surprised him; and he had been staggered when Laxford coolly disclaimed all knowledge of Hay's permanent address.

"He was a friend of young Brandon's," Laxford had assured Hinton. "I haven't the slightest idea where he lives. Young Brandon invited him down. It's my house, of course, and nominally he was my guest; but I know nothing about him. You didn't ask him his address yourself, did you?"

And thus the inspector had found his teeth drawn. In these circumstances it was impossible to pretend that Edgehill was Hay's 'last permanent address.' The fellow had simply vanished into thin air, so far as immediate affairs were concerned. Hinton had consoled himself with the thought that Hay's evidence was of no great value. The coroner could get on without it well enough. Still, the affair had rankled, and he had no wish to hear Copdock—the most notorious gossip in the village—enlarging upon the subject. Better let him think it was all right.

Copdock's attention had been diverted by the inspector's criticism of his skill as a compounder. He picked up a few shreds of tobacco from the scale-pan and dribbled them out one by one until the pointer showed exact equilibrium.

"There! You can't say that ain't right this time, Mr Hinton. And there's all the difference it'd have made," he added, exhibiting the wisp of tobacco still left between his finger and thumb. "By the way, you didn't put Mr Dunne up for to give his bit of a story."

The inspector tapped his forehead meaningly.

"Can't call that sort of testimony."

"No? Is that so? Well, I s'pose that's right enough," Copdock agreed, though his tone was rather dubious. "Still, he's none so loony as all that, by my way of thinking. I've seen him up there when the Fairlawns lot were playing the village eleven, this last summer or two, and he seemed as sane as what you and me are, in a manner of speaking."

"That's the law," the inspector assured him in a superior tone.

"Well, the verdict was all right," Copdock declared with something of an author's pride in his handiwork. "'Accidental death.' That seemed to put the thing in a nutshell, I thought. No words wasted, as one might say."

"Quite so," concurred the inspector drily. "And what's the rest of the Stop Press News?"

It would have taken much more than the dryness of Hinton's tone to discourage the dealer. He prided himself on being thoroughly up to date in local affairs. Still, he resented the inspector's superior airs, just then, and by way of retaliation he produced a piece of stale news to begin with.

"Speaking about Mr Laxford," he said, "that's a funny business, how he and the Brandon's seem to have had a split, lately. A regular dust-up they had, so I heard. And then the whole Laxford family bar the governess was just bundled out of Edgehill and told to camp in the Cottage till they'd got time to look around and find somewhere else to go to. So I'm told."

"I seem to have come across that before," said Hinton caustically. "In the Sunday papers last week, perhaps. Haven't you got something with fewer whiskers on it?"

Copdock considered for a moment before answering, then he

leaned forward across the counter in a confidential attitude.

"I don't give this to the general public," he pointed out cautiously. "Least said, soonest mended, in some things. But as it's you, Mr Hinton, I know it'll go no farther. I've just heard some more about that row, and it seems it was all about money. At least they were talking loud and angry between themselves all about money, and 'bankrupt,' and 'influence' and 'estates' or 'estate' and things of that sort. Mr John Brandon's name came into it, some way, it seems, too. Not very easy understood by an outsider, I'm told; but that was the way it went. And of course the governess was on the winning side."

"Anyone can guess that, seeing that she's stayed on at Edgehill instead of going with the Laxfords," grunted the inspector. "It'll be news to you, I expect, that she's engaged to one of the Brandons. And what side did Beauty favour?"

Mr Copdock did not quite relish the crude manner in which the inspector coupled Miss Tugby's name with the gossip which he had just retailed. One preferred a semblance of decency in such matters. This sort of information, one pretended, came to one from the air. It was bad taste to trace it to a definite source.

"Beauty was engaged by Mrs Laxford," he pointed out with dignity, "so nat'rally she stayed in Mrs Laxford's service. The rest of 'em weren't so partic'lar, it seems. They stayed on at Edgehill."

"Quite so," Hinton said, though from his tone it was hard to discover which policy met with his approval. Then he made another blunder in tact from Mr Copdock's point of view by asking, "And what's the latest about the Laxfords?"

The dealer momentarily shrugged his shoulders as if the stream of his information was exhausted; but the inspector knew his man and waited confidently. Copdock could never resist a chance of displaying inside knowledge of things.

"The Laxfords were in a queer hole, it seems," he said after a moment or two, stopping his weighing to lend emphasis to his tale. "It seems some people were coming to Edgehill to shoot. They'd have landed here the day after the accident, a whole bunch of them. Terrible, isn't it? to think of them expecting to come down on a visit to that young fellow; and then, just as they were on the edge of starting, to get a wire saying he was dead. Tragic, almost, as one might say."

"Almost," said the inspector sympathetically.

"There's another set of visitors instead, now," Copdock said cautiously as he began mixing the various ingredients together on the paper. "Some insurance people, come down about young Mr Brandon's death, it seems."

The inspector pricked up his ears, but outwardly he maintained an air of indifference.

"Indeed?"

"Yes. I heard a day or two ago that they'd be coming."

The inspector had no difficulty in guessing the source of this news. Evidently Laxford had been leaving his letters about after reading them, and Beauty had managed to get a glimpse of this one from an insurance company.

"They're at the Talgarth Arms," Copdock pursued. "Leastways they had lunch there and then went on to see Mr Laxford. They're catching the night train up to town, I'm told. They've ordered dinner at the Arms, but they haven't booked any rooms for tonight."

"I suppose they've got a car to take them into Ambledown?" Hinton said in a speculative tone, as though the matter hardly interested him. "They've been at Edgehill, too, I suppose?"

"No," Copdock asserted confidently. "Not unless they've been there within the last hour or so. The housemaid from Edgehill was in here just before you, and no one of their description had called at Edgehill up to the time she left the house. So she told me. No, their job has nothing to do with the Brandons, I gather. It's Mrs Laxford that's interested. Or so I'm told."

"Well, it's their business and I expect they know what they want," the inspector opined, reaching for the packet of tobacco which Copdock had finished tying up. "Time I was moving along."

He went out of the shop, outwardly alert, but actually in a

brown study. As he passed the gate of the coach-yard of the Talgarth Arms, he caught sight of a car with the two plates which showed it plied for hire. The registration number was a local one. In the gateway of the yard lounged the inn's handy-man; and the inspector paused as though merely to pass the time of day.

"Got some visitors at last, Fred?" he inquired jocularly, with a gesture towards the car. "Hope they're staying for a while."

Fred shook his head gloomily and spat on the ground before answering.

"Not staying long enough to need their shoes shined," he said in a disgusted tone. "No tips out of them, not even for carrying in their luggage. 'Cause why? 'Cause they ain't brought any. Not as much as a suitcase."

"Off tonight again, then," Hinton interpreted. "Hard lines on you, Fred. Are they staying to enjoy our celebrated table d'hôte dinner?"

Fred nodded again, a gloomy affirmative. Hinton made a rapid mental calculation. If the visitors dined at the usual time, they would have an hour in hand after dinner, before they needed to start out to catch the quick train at Ambledown. That would suit his purpose very nicely. He gave Fred a parting nod, which went unacknowledged, and moved slowly up the street again, deep in his brown study once more.

All the inspector's hunting instinct had been roused by a single piece of information which Copdock had given him. Insurance! That was a new factor in the Brandon affair. Insurance in itself was nothing to get suspicious about. If the Brandon family had stood to gain, the inspector would not have given the thing a second thought. But Laxford? Or, still more surprising, Mrs Laxford? What insurable interest could she have in young Brandon?

Hinton dismissed that detail from his mind at the moment, since he expected to get full information very shortly; but he held tight to the main fact that the Laxfords evidently had something to gain—whether much or little, he did not know as yet—from young Brandon's death. Fishy? Not necessarily, he admitted frankly to himself. It might be quite all right. But if it wasn't?... And at that thought Hinton felt a queer premonitory thrill which he strove bravely to disregard. Suppose, just suppose, that at last the long-awaited 'big case' had come his way: the case that was to win him his step and transmute Inspector Hinton into a Superintendent Hinton with the aura of high success about him.

The more he pondered over the Edgehill affair, the more tangled it seemed and the more sceptical he grew about the correctness of the jury's verdict. There were facts enough and to spare; but there was a lack of cohesion between them. It was like fitting a jigsaw puzzle together and discovering that instead of a single picture they would make fragments of three independent pictures.

He went over his data again, point by point. First of all, he had found no blood on the grass where blood might well have been expected from Laxford's evidence, tacitly corroborated by Hay. Next, there was Dunne's appearance on the scene, with a discharged gun in his hands and in a state which pointed to an attack of *petit mal*. Then, bearing upon that, came Dr Barreman's very evident desire to hush up the nature of Dunne's trouble; and the reason for this reticence was plain enough from the passage in the book on Forensic Medicine. After that, there was Hay's precipitate departure in the teeth of the warning that he might be called to give evidence. And, coupled with that, there was Laxford's denial that Hay was an intimate of his, and his professed ignorance of the man's permanent address. That, Hinton knew from other 'information received,' did not tally with the gossip of the Edgehill servants' hall; nor did it account for the fact that Laxford—and not young Brandon—had gone to the station to meet Hay on his arrival. Curious, too, that young Brandon had died just before the arrival of this shooting-party on 1st September. And then, after the tragedy, there was this quarrel between the Brandons and Laxford, ending in the ignominious expulsion of the Laxfords from Edgehill—an affair which puzzled the inspector more than a little. Finally, there was this sudden descent of insurance officials in connection with young Brandon's death; and Copdock's hint that Mrs Laxford was the interested party in that side of the business.

"There's something damned queer about the whole affair," the inspector assured himself hopefully. "At the least of it, there's enough to justify me bluffing these insurance fellows, if I can. And perhaps they won't need much bluffing after all. It's to their interest to get some excuse for not paying, I should think."

CHAPTER 11 THE INSURANCE POLICY

Inspector Hinton timed his arrival at the Talgarth Arms so that it coincided with the serving of the last course in the hotel's modest table d'hôte dinner. He watched the waiter take in the visitors' coffee; and then, with his eye on his watch, he made conversation with the landlord until he judged that his victims had reached a stage when they would be most tractable in his hands. He was a hearty trencherman himself, and he knew from experience the lenitive effect of a good dinner.

"Thanks," he said to the landlord. "That's the very thing. And you'll see we aren't disturbed in there? It won't take long."

The landlord nodded, and Hinton turned to the waiter who was near by.

"You go in now, Joe, and say that Inspector Hinton—mind you say Inspector Hinton; don't say just 'a gentleman'—say that Inspector Hinton presents his compliments and would be glad of the favour of a few minutes' conversation with them on important business. Now just repeat that, to make sure you've got it right."

It was not mere vanity which dictated this emphasis on his official status. If this interview was to start in the proper atmosphere, it was essential that these people should realise at once that they were dealing with a man in authority and not with some mere village constable. It was a similar idea which had led him to borrow the landlord's own sitting-room for the interview. As there were no other guests in the hotel, one of the public rooms would have been free enough from intrusion; but in that case Hinton would have had to present himself to the strangers. It was better to receive them on his own ground, as it were, in a private room.

"I understand well enough. I'm to say you're Inspector Hinton and not a gentleman," Joe assured him rather ambiguously. "And suppose they say they'll see you?"

"Then ask them to be so good as to step into the private sitting-room here. I'll be waiting for them," Hinton ordered.

As Joe set off on his errand, the inspector turned back to the landlord.

"What are they like, to look at?" he asked.

"One of them's a little reddish-haired Scotchman with a close-clipped moustache. His name's Templand. The other one's clean-shaven and thin, in a grey suit, name of Kirkstall. Templand's the boss. He gives the orders and the other man agrees or says nothing."

"All right. Send 'em in," said the inspector, going towards the sitting-room.

Hinton had evidently gauged his time accurately, for in a few moments the waiter ushered the two officials into the room. Hinton came forward as they entered.

"Mr Templand, I think? And Mr Kirkstall? Will you sit down?"

He busied himself with chairs to emphasise that he was taking the position of host. When they were seated, he glanced at his watch, estimated how much time he had in hand, and plunged at once into business.

"I think you gentlemen represent an insurance company?"

"The Mersey and Midland," Templand explained in a pleasant voice. His faint Scots burr and a peculiar running up and down from note to note during a sentence betrayed his nationality beyond any doubt, but neither characteristic was marked enough to be jarring to southern ears.

"Quite so." Hinton's nod suggested that he already knew the identity of the company. "And I believe you're down here in connection with the death of Mr John Brandon? Exactly."

He paused for a moment or two, and then went on in a deliberate tone:

"I'm looking into that affair myself."

It had been on the tip of his tongue to add: 'So we might join forces,' but he refrained at the last moment. His game was to make the offer come from their side. That would make it easier to get information from them. He noted a momentary lifting of Templand's eyebrows, then a swift exchange of glances between the two officials, and he congratulated himself on having won the first trick.

Templand leaned his elbow on the arm of his chair, took his chin between finger and thumb, and seemed to reflect for a second or two. The other man, evidently subordinate, waited with obvious interest for his chief's pronouncement.

"Then you think the coroner's jury brought in a wrong verdict?" Templand demanded with a sharp glance at the inspector's impassive face.

"No," Hinton said grudgingly, "they brought in a verdict in accordance with the evidence given before them. But they hadn't all the evidence before them."

Templand's attitude remained unchanged, but his eyes suddenly became alert.

"What evidence was there that didn't come out?" he demanded. "You understand, of course, that this may be a matter of some importance to my company?"

The offhand tone in the last sentence did not deceive the inspector. For a policy to be "a matter of some importance" to an insurance company, it must run into thousands and not mere hundreds. And when sums of such magnitude crop up in connection with a death by shooting...

"One bit of evidence that didn't come out before the jury was this very policy of yours," Hinton pointed out quietly.

Templand admitted this with a gesture. As though to give himself time for consideration, he produced a cigarette-case, offered it to the inspector, then with studied deliberation lit a cigarette himself and drew a few puffs before speaking again.

"We don't want to pay any claim where there's a doubt," he said at last in a judicial tone. "A big claim least of all. Now in this Brandon case, there's the verdict of the coroner's jury—'Accidental death.' If that stands, we may have to pay."

The inspector noted the 'may' in the last sentence. Evidently there was a catch somewhere, apart altogether from the manner in which young Brandon came by his death. He forebore to interrupt, however. Templand studied the coil of smoke rising from his cigarette and paused for a few moments before continuing.

"We're not wholly satisfied about this claim. I may tell you in confidence. There's a technical point. . . . But that can wait till later. If we had any reason to suppose that this death was still a subject of inquiry, we have the means of staving off payment for the time being. It's a mere matter of dilatory correspondence, consulting the head office at every turn, and so forth. We can play for time easily enough, provided that it's worth our while to do so."

He threw a quizzical glance at his subordinate, who suppressed a smile. Evidently, Hinton inferred, they already had their plans cut and dried for this part of the campaign, if it came to the pinch.

"Now *you* turn up," Templand pursued. "*You're* not satisfied in your own mind, evidently, or you wouldn't be here. That means there's something fishy, to put it bluntly, in the affair. Common sense, that, and nothing more. Very well, then, let's see if we can't arrange something to the advantage of both parties. Tell us what's made you suspicious about the affair, and I'll give you the story of this claim, which is . . . well, curious in some ways. Neither of us stands to gain by giving anything away in public at this stage. My company wouldn't thank me for any scandal until we're sure of our ground. That's common sense. So you can see for yourself that anything you tell us now will go no farther. You're quite safe there. Up to a point, our interests are identical. That's obvious. Now is it a bargain?"

Inspector Hinton paused before answering, but his hesitation had nothing to do with the acceptance or rejection of Templand's proposal. He was making a swift mental survey of the evidence and picking out those particular pieces which had a bearing on the insurance problem. The rest he intended to keep to himself. Finally he gave the insurance officials the points about the missing blood-stain, Hay's precipitate departure, and Laxford's professed ignorance of his guest's address.

"And I gather, from information received," he concluded, "that other people at Edgehill—not the Laxfords—were under the impression that Hay came down to visit Laxford himself and not young Brandon. It was Laxford who met Hay at the station. Young Brandon didn't turn up till lunch—he'd been out shooting all morning—and one of the maids, who saw them meet, says that Laxford introduced the two of them as if they were total strangers."

Templand listened intently to the inspector's account, and when it was complete he gave Hinton a shrewd glance.

"I think I see what's in your mind," he said, choosing his phrases with obvious care. "We needn't put it into words, need we? That's common sense, at this stage. Now I'll give you our side of the affair. Mr Kirkstall has copies of the documents with him, so I can give you chapter and verse. Of course," he added, "I'm depending on your discretion in the matter."

"I must be able to use the main facts if it comes to a pinch," Hinton pointed out, "otherwise the stuff's no use to me."

Templand considered this carefully.

"You can use the *facts*, so long as you don't quote me as your authority. But *opinions* are a different story. I don't want mine quoted in any shape or form. That's agreed?"

Hinton nodded his acceptance of the conditions, and Kirkstall took from a despatch-case some sheets of paper which he handed over to Templand.

"I'll begin right at the beginning," Templand said, putting on a pair of reading-glasses and selecting one of the papers from the bundle. "This is the first communication we had from Mr

Laxford. It's dated 23rd July, and it's addressed to our head office in Liverpool. Most of our business is done in the Midlands, you understand. My office in London is merely a branch office dealing with southern business. Under our system, this letter of Mr Laxford's was sent on to me, with instructions to take the matter up as it was in my district. As you can see"—he handed the copy to the inspector—"it's an inquiry as to the terms for an insurance on the life of John Brandon for the sum of £50,000."

"Phew!" ejaculated the inspector, his eyebrows rising despite himself at the magnitude of the figure. If anything came of this Edgehill affair, that £50,000 would make a fine headline in the newspapers. That, in itself, would make it a 'big case,' sure enough. He controlled his features, but underneath the surface he was all exultation. This, if it came to anything, would be a chance in a thousand for him.

"I needn't bother you with the routine part of the correspondence," Templand went on, turning over one or two sheets on the table before him. "We—the London office, that is—wrote to Mr Laxford on 25th July, quoting terms for this proposed policy; and on 27th July Mr Laxford wrote to me, making an appointment at my office on the following day."

"That's for 28th July?"

"Yes. On the morning of 28th July, Mr Laxford called at my office. I've no notes of the conversation between us. It was rather long and a bit involved, I may say; but I can give you the gist of it as it struck me. The first point that cropped up was the form of the insurance. It turned out that Mr Laxford wanted a policy for £50,000 on John Brandon's life, in the name of Mrs Laxford."

"Wait a minute," interrupted Hinton. "You mean that Mrs Laxford was to pay the premiums and that if Brandon died she was to get £50,000 from you?"

"Precisely," Templand agreed. "Now in a case of that sort, there must be what we call an 'insurable interest.'"

"Wait a moment," Hinton interrupted again. "I want to be quite clear about this. Do you mind explaining exactly what the point is?"

"Take a concrete case," Templand replied. "Suppose you came to me and wanted a £50,000 policy on the life of Mr Kirkstall here. The first question we'd ask you would be this: 'If Mr Kirkstall dies tomorrow, what do you stand to lose by his death?' You couldn't prove that you stood to lose anything, either financially or in your prospects. So we'd turn down your proposal without more ado. You've got no insurable interest in Mr Kirkstall's life."

"Quite so," the inspector agreed. "I suppose that's intended to block out the chance of X insuring Y's life and then cutting Y's throat so as to collect the insurance money."

Templand refused to rise to this bait. He glanced at his watch like a man pressed for time, and continued his narrative.

"When the proposal was put to me in that form, the first thing I had to ascertain was whether an insurable interest existed or not. If there was none, then the matter was done with. I put this to Mr Laxford. What was Mrs Laxford's interest in young Brandon's life? He gave me a very long and involved story about the Brandon estate, which wasn't much to the point, I thought. It seemed that the estate was entailed so that the present tenant, young Brandon's father, couldn't sell it to pay his debts. An insurance company, the Osprey, had taken a mortgage on old Brandon's life-interest and had been driven to foreclose, so that the old man was left without any income except what they allowed him, more or less out of charity. Mr Laxford left me with the impression that he was a trustee for young John Brandon and that negotiations were afoot to regularise the whole position. Mrs Laxford had an estate of her own and she was going to advance money to pay off the Osprey people and get control of the Brandon estate on behalf of young Brandon; and in some way or other she was to be recouped for her outlay later on. In the meanwhile, this policy of £50,000 was needed to safeguard her in the case of John Brandon dying before the negotiations came to a head. That was the gist of the business, so far as I was concerned, and I paid little attention to the details of Mr Laxford's story except in so far as they concerned this question of insurable interest."

"Laxford told you he was a trustee?" the inspector inquired, merely to show that he was following closely.

"He left that impression on my mind," Templand replied in a rather puzzled tone, "but I can't recall his exact words. He certainly gave me the idea that he was a trustee, and I gathered also that he was acting as guardian to young Brandon. 'In charge of him' was perhaps the way he put it. I can't remember the actual words, but it amounted to that. He must have said something of the sort, for that was the first inkling I had that young Brandon was under age then. It hardly concerned me at the moment. All this, you understand, was a mere preliminary canter. We had no proposal before us in black and white. I gave him the proposal form, and he went away."

"That finished the interview on the 28th July?" Hinton asked, looking up from the notebook in which he had been scribbling industriously.

"Yes. Next day we received by post the completed form, signed by Diana Laxford—Mrs Laxford—making a proposal for a policy of £50,000 on John Brandon's life. In our form there is a demand: 'State the nature of the interest in the life proposed to be insured.' The answer given by Mrs Laxford was simply: 'For value received, and to cover advances made and liabilities incurred in connection with the Brandon estate.'"

"Ah!" said the inspector.

He had only the vaguest idea whither all this was tending; but the bank manager's manner made it clear that there was more to come.

"On the same day, 29th July," Templand continued, turning over another sheet, "we wrote to Mr Laxford pointing out that this statement in the proposal form was far too vague to enable us to decide whether or not Mrs Laxford had any insurable interest in John Brandon's life; and we asked for full details under the three heads mentioned in the proposal form."

Templand paused to light a fresh cigarette before continuing.

"Mr Laxford evidently took time to think over the matter. We got his reply on August 3rd. Here's a copy of it. Instead of giving the information we asked for, he simply withdraws the proposal in his wife's name. That finished the first transaction, and I was rather glad to see the end of it, personally. One gets these ideas," he added, as though anxious to minimise his half-involuntary confession.

"We had another letter from Mr Laxford on August 5th," he continued. "It's merely a request for a blank proposal form for the case of a man insuring his own life. That was sent on to him; and on August 7th it was returned completed, signed by John Brandon. The policy in this case was to be a £25,000 one. I had to consult my head office about that. I'm not supposed to take as big a risk as that on my own responsibility. That caused some delay, but on August 7th I wrote Mr Laxford saying we were prepared to accept the proposal, subject to having Mr Brandon passed by two doctors, since the insurance was a big one. There was a day or two more delay. Mr Brandon had sprained his ankle and couldn't come up to London for his medical examination. Eventually he and Mr Laxford came by appointment on August 15th. Two doctors examined him and found no fault except the effects of the sprain, which were pretty obvious. In fact, one of the doctors mentioned that to me afterwards and said young Brandon should never have been up in town with a sprain like that. He might have got caught in the traffic and not been quick enough on his feet. However, so far as we were concerned, everything was in order."

"You saw them together on that day," the inspector asked. "What sort of terms were they on, did you notice?"

"Oh, very friendly, so far as one could see. You're thinking of some compulsion or other? I saw nothing to suggest it. Young Brandon seemed in high spirits, and I gathered that they were going to some show or other before they went home again."

"I see, I see," said Hinton. "Please go on."

"One thing I remember," Templand continued. "While John Brandon was being examined by the doctors, Mr Laxford spent the time with me. He asked me when I could arrange to hand over the policy. Would there be any delay? My recollection is that he was specially anxious to have everything in order as soon as possible. If I'm not mistaken he wanted it before the end of August. I'm pretty sure about that point. Then he wanted to know when the risk would be on, apart from the actual preparation of the policy. I told him that our risk begins as soon as the first premium is actually paid. He seemed quite satisfied with this. Then he began to discuss the premium. John Brandon had filled in a form for an insurance 'with profits' and Mr Laxford wanted to know what the corresponding premium would be 'without profits.' I explained that 'with profits' the premium was £1 19s. 4d. per cent, whilst 'without profits' it would be £1 11s. 2d. per cent. We worked out the total premium for the two cases and it came to £491 13s. 4d. on the policy 'with profits' and £389 11s. 8d. on the 'without profits' policy. He considered the figures for a moment or two. I remember. Then he said he thought John Brandon had made a slip. What was wanted was a policy 'without profits.' I said that could be rectified easily enough. It only meant filling in the proper form and tearing up the other one. He said he thought that was the best thing to do, and Brandon could fill in the fresh form when he came back from the doctor. Then he said he thought that the premium was pretty big. Would we take it in half-yearly instalments? There was no objection to that."

"Wait a minute," Hinton interjected. "What all this amounts to is that he got you to accept a £25,000 risk by a first payment of . . . let's see . . . Yes, a first payment of £194 15s. 10d. Is that right?"

"Quite correct," Templand admitted. "But it was a normal risk, you know. However, to continue. After the medical examination, John Brandon filled up the fresh form and I tore up his original proposal."

"He didn't make any fuss about the change?"

"Oh, no. Mr Laxford told him there had been a mistake made in the original form and that he'd have to fill in a fresh one for a 'without profits' policy. I gave him the form and helped him to fill it up. He didn't strike me as particularly bright, but he understood what he was doing, if that's what you're after."

"And after that?"

"They went away. Mr Laxford said that he would call next day and pay the first premium. I made an appointment with him."

"Do you usually receive premiums personally?" Hinton demanded.

Templand shook his head with a smile.

"I did in this case, though," he explained. "The fact is, we'd made some inquiries. Of course we made the usual inquiries about John Brandon's health from friends whose names we'd asked for. But we'd made other inquiries, and we found that Mr Laxford was an undischarged bankrupt. Naturally I didn't propose to take his cheque for the premium payment. But that's the sort of thing best settled by the man at the top without dragging the cashier into it, you understand?"

"Quite so," Hinton agreed.

"Next day, Mr Laxford turned up to pay the first premium. I glanced at the cheque and found it wasn't his. It was signed by Diana Laxford—Mrs Laxford. I took it, and gave him a receipt. He asked again if that meant that our risk was now on. I said that we accepted the risk from that moment. He seemed quite satisfied. Then he handed over a letter signed by young Brandon. I read it at the time. Here's a copy.

'EDGEHILL,
15*th August,* 1924.

DEAR SIR, I have assigned my insurance policy for £25,000 to Mrs Diana Laxford in return for value received. Be so good as to hand over this policy to her, as she will be the person to whom the money should be paid in the event of my death.

Yours faithfully, JOHN BRANDON.'"

"But that landed you just where you were, didn't it?" the inspector demanded. "In the event of Brandon's death, Mrs Laxford got the money. That was what you rejected in the first case."

Templand shook his head.

"No; there's a very big difference. A man can insure his own life if he likes. By a fiction, he's assumed to have an insurable interest in himself. And he can assign his life policy to anyone if he wants to, provided he's of age."

"Yes, but young Brandon wasn't of age at that time," Hinton objected.

"Of course not. But what difference did that make to us at the moment? We didn't expect him to die within a year. If he did, then it was up to his trustees to go into the matter and get a ruling as to the validity of the assignment. We'd have to pay the money in any case, and it didn't matter two straws to us who got it. We'd take care not to have to pay twice over. That's the only point so far as we're concerned. I knew quite well that this letter had no value in a court of law. Whether Laxford knew that or not was his own affair. No concern of mine."

"Naturally," Hinton agreed.

"Just as a precaution," Templand went on, with a shrewd glance, "I made immediate inquiry as to that cheque signed by Mrs Laxford. The reply I got was that, at the moment, there wasn't a penny in her account. The cheque went through eventually. Evidently some cash came into her account from somewhere, not long afterwards. But at the moment when Laxford handed me that cheque, it was a worthless bit of paper. In other words, he got us to take on the risk without paying any premium. I'm no legal expert; but it seems a pretty problem. Suppose we chose to make a fuss and say he'd induced us to take the risk under false pretences and for no consideration. There's enough point in it to form a basis for a spun-out correspondence, if we have any real grounds for delaying payment."

Hinton shook his head sceptically, but made no comment.

"Well, young Brandon dies, quite unexpectedly," Templand went on. "On behalf of his wife, Laxford writes to us and demands the payment of this £25,000 to her under the policy. Naturally we refuse, on the ground that the assignment was invalid because young Brandon was under age when he made it. There was some more correspondence, formal merely; and the result was our visit today."

Templand paused, with evident dramatic intention, as he felt for his cigarette-case. Then he continued:

"When Mr Kirkstall and I called on Laxford this afternoon, he put a new face on things. He produced a new assignment. I've a copy of it here.

'28*th August*, 1924.

In consideration of value received and hereby acknowledged, I assign to Mrs Diana Laxford the policy of insurance for £25,000 which I hold from the Mersey and Midland Insurance Company. She is to pay the premium on it on my behalf, and in the event of my death she is to be the sole beneficiary under that policy. I have given notice to the Mersey and Midland Company to this effect, and they have accepted this notice.

JOHN BRANDON.
Witnesses to the signature
of John Brandon
JOSEPH HAY
THOMAS LAXFORD.'

"That was written with pen and ink by young Brandon himself, Mr Laxford told me," Templand explained. "You notice the date, of course; it's the date on which young Brandon came of age, and therefore this new assignment is a valid document. Quite on a different footing from the one he mentioned in his letter to us. And of course you notice"—he made an almost imperceptible pause—"that on that morning he died."

"Yes, I remember that," Hinton returned thoughtfully. Then with a cynical smile he added: "Curious, isn't it?"

But there was no cynicism in the inspector's inner consciousness. Behind his emotionless facade, a flame of excitement had been rising higher and higher as Templand unfolded his narrative. Now, with that sinister coincidence before him, his last doubts were dispersed. This was 'the big case' at last, unmistakable, made for him.

"I'd be obliged for a copy of that correspondence," he said, closing his notebook. "It'll bear looking into a bit closer than I've been able to do just now."

"Certainly," Templand assured him. "So we're making common cause? My company certainly won't want to pay. . . . You mean to go on investigating, I take it?"

"You can put your shirt on that!" the inspector declared in vulgar exultation. "And the longer you can spin things out on your side, the better."

CHAPTER 12 THE LAXFORD FINANCES

Fortified by several pipefuls of his special smoking-mixture, Inspector Hinton devoted the rest of that evening to a full reconsideration of the Edgehill problem. Templand's evidence had thrown a flood of light upon it from a fresh quarter. What was even more satisfactory, the insurance transactions furnished a sound motive—hitherto missing—for the elimination of young Brandon. On the solid basis of that £25,000 policy it seemed, at the first glance, a simple enough matter to build up the remainder of the evidence into a coherent and convincing structure of argument.

How would it look to a jury? That was the ultimate test, from Hinton's point of view. Well, first of all, there was Laxford's attempt to insure the boy's life for £50,000 in favour of Mrs Laxford. Why Mrs Laxford? Obviously because Laxford himself was an undischarged bankrupt who would have difficulty in entering into the transaction in his own name. That attempt failed. No insurable interest. Still, it would influence the jury when it was dragged out before them.

Just as he was dismissing this episode from his mind, another idea struck Inspector Hinton; and he reached for his notebook to make a jotting. The pretext for that business had been that Mrs Laxford, out of her personal estate, was going to advance money in order to buy out an insurance company's claim and get control of an estate on behalf of young Brandon. But if she were rolling in cash to this extent, why didn't she pay off her husband's debts and clear him of the slur of bankruptcy? And if she had all this pile in hand, why had her current account sunk so low that she had no assets to meet that cheque she drew for the first premium payment? Further, how did this Brandon estate business actually stand? That might be worth looking into. Hinton scribbled some memoranda in his notebook before turning to the next phase of the case.

The second insurance transaction was quite above-board, so far as the company went. But how would it look to a jury? Again it was Mrs Laxford who was to profit ultimately, though this time it was under an assignment of the £25,000 policy taken out by young Brandon himself. But in this assignment there was no mention of the Brandon estate. Instead, there was that curious phrase about 'value received and hereby acknowledged.' A jury would want to know what 'value' was received. But it would be Laxford's job to tell them that, not Hinton's.

Then there was the business of the two assignments. The first of them had been made on or before 15th August, when young Brandon was a minor. The second one, dated 28th August, must have been signed on the very morning of the boy's death—at the earliest moment when he could make a valid assignment after coming of age. Templand had not been able to say whether Laxford knew that a minor could not make a valid assignment; but on the face of the transaction it was plain enough that he did not know that on August 15th, but that later, having found out the fact, he had got the boy to make a fresh and valid assignment on the 28th. And immediately after signing that, he had come to grief. That would be a bit of a fish-bone in the jury's throat, if Hinton knew much about juries. So far, so good. Even at that stage of the case the prosecutor would manage to instil something stronger than doubts into the minds of the jurymen.

And that wouldn't stand alone. One could follow it up with an awkward point or two. The youngster signs the assignment. Then they go out shooting. What sort of morning was it? The inspector remembered it well enough: a blustering, squally day, with rain beating in torrents at intervals. Hardly the weather to choose specially, seeing they could go out rabbit-shooting at any time they liked. But the next thing on the bill would be the arrival of this shooting-party that had been invited. If Laxford meant to remove young Brandon, he could hardly afford to wait until all that pack came on the scene. The jury would appreciate the bearing of that point, without having it explained in big type.

Then a fresh argument occurred to him. Laxford had taken out that £25,000 policy on the 'without profits' basis. Well, if the boy wasn't expected to live for even six months, then there would be no profits accruing and there was no point in paying the higher rate of premium. The same argument fitted the fact that the cheque covered only the first half-year's premium. Nothing much in it, perhaps, but it would help to build up an impression in the minds of the fellows in the jury-box.

The next thing was the distance from which the shooting had been done. That would have to be tried out with the gun itself. Hinton jotted down a reminder to procure the guns from Edgehill. That could be done without setting Laxford on the alert, thanks to this row between the Laxfords and the Brandons.

Then, with something of a shock, the inspector recalled that Laxford's gun had been in the hands of Dunne at the moment of the tragedy.

He laid down his pencil and puffed at his pipe for some time before seeing his way through the tangle of possibilities which this fact suggested.

"Well," he said aloud in an irritable tone, "there were only four guns out that morning—his own, his brother's, Laxford's, and Hay's. He must have been shot by one of them, whichever it was. It may have been his own gun, by accident. But then where's the blood in the ditch? It may have been his brother's gun—no, that's bosh, on the face of it. Far too far off, for one thing; the charge would have spread, at that distance. Of course it might have been Dunne, with Laxford's gun. Or it might even have been Hay. That would fit in with his vamoosing so slick, instead of turning up to give evidence at the inquest. Holy blue smoke! A cross-word puzzle's a fool to this business. Still, so far as any traceable motive's concerned, Laxford must have been at the back of the business somewhere. O Lord! If only that damned lunatic could get his memory back for five minutes, I'd have the whole thing cut and dried, even if we couldn't call him as a witness. But there's no chance of that, I suppose. Or if I could only lay my hands on Hay . . ."

By the time Inspector Hinton knocked the ashes from his last pipe that night, he had lost a good deal of his initial confidence. Wherever he turned, he was met by one elusive figure, a thing that was by turns a normal human being and a mere sentient machine without control of its actions or memory of its deeds. That, his cooler judgment told him, was the weak spot in the affair, unless he could build up an absolutely cast-iron case against Laxford. With that in their hands, it was easy enough to forecast what line the defence would adopt. They would find some more or less plausible excuse to account for the insurance transactions, and then they would turn the spot-light upon the sinister figure of the epileptic coming quietly out from among the bushes with Laxford's gun in its hand. That puppet could find no legal place in court. Barred alike from witness-box and dock, it would none the less dominate the whole trial. "Can you be sure," the defending barrister would ask, "Can you be *sure*, gentlemen of the jury, that this is not the killer of John Brandon?" And, on the face of things, no jury could be *sure*. They would give Laxford the benefit of the doubt. In a hanging case, almost any jury would be glad to escape from "Guilty" if they could honestly convince themselves that there was an alternative explanation. And here was the alternative, ready-made, with no rope for Dunne, no matter what happened. Of course the jury would take that line, unless one could prove the case against Laxford up to the very hilt.

"Damn that lunatic!" the inspector growled to himself as he glanced once more over his notes before going to bed. "He's the rock my case'll split on, if I don't manage to steer round him."

Next morning, at the earliest convenient hour, he presented himself at Edgehill.

"Can I see Mr Brandon?" he asked the maid who came to the door.

"Mr Brandon's not well today. He's keeping his room, and Miss Menteith's sent for Dr Brinkworth. He had a bad night..."

"Oh, you mean old Mr Brandon?" the inspector interrupted rather unsympathetically. "I don't want to see him. It's Mr James Brandon I mean."

"He's in London."

"Then his brother will do instead."

"He's not here, either."

At these answers, the inspector's hopes of picking up information about the Brandon estate diminished uncomfortably.

"Ask if old Mr Brandon will see me for a moment or two," he proposed.

The maid shook her head without hesitation.

"I'm sure he wouldn't. He's not well at all."

Hinton seemed to have reached a blank end. All he would get for his visit now would be the guns, and he might have sent a constable to fetch them. Then a fresh idea crossed his mind.

"Ask Miss Menteith if she'll speak to me, just for a moment or two," he ordered.

The ex-governess might know nothing useful, but at least he could try her, since he had come all this length.

"She's with Mr Brandon just now; but I'll ask her, if you'll come in and wait," the maid explained, stepping aside to allow Hinton to enter. "If you'll go into the drawing-room, there. I'll run upstairs and tell her."

When Hinton's message was delivered to her, Una Menteith was taken aback, though she did not show it. She had watched the inquest with anxiety, always with the fear at the back of her mind that some scrap of evidence might put the coroner on the alert and open up the whole sordid business which they had taken such pains to hide. With the announcement of the verdict, her anxiety had vanished. The affair seemed closed for good. That miserable scandal need never be dragged into public view to throw discredit on the Brandon name.

And now, while they were relaxing in their fancied security, came this inspector, like some bird of ill-omen, to show that the danger was still alive.

Obviously he must have come to Edgehill in connection with Johnnie's death. Obviously he must suspect that something still remained to be cleared up, despite the verdict of the jury. Obviously, too, he was pertinacious: his successive demands for one person after another showed that plainly enough.

Una swiftly reviewed the situation as it presented itself to her. If she refused to see Hinton, he would not be permanently baulked; he would merely return later, with increased suspicion, to renew his inquiries. There was nothing to be gained by that policy. On the other hand, by speaking to him now, she might get some hint of his purpose and thus be able to fore-warn the Brandons ere it came to their turn to be questioned. Incontinently she decided on her course of action. She would see Hinton, give nothing away, and discover, if possible, what he had in his mind.

The inspector rose to his feet as she entered the room; but she invited him, with a gesture, to sit down again. Now that the plunge had been taken, she meant to see the thing through; and quite probably she would need time to elicit what she wanted from him. Besides, by sitting down she gained a weapon. By rising from her chair she could tacitly hint that the interview had lasted long enough. Cool and collected, she chose a chair which gave Hinton no advantage of light; and then, turning to him, she waited for him to make the first move.

"Sorry to trouble you, Miss Menteith," the inspector began. "I've called to ask for the loan—only temporary, of course—of the guns that were used on the morning of that shooting-accident."

Una saw her fears realised, but she managed to feign surprise in her reply.

"I thought all that was over and done with."

"It's just a formal matter," the inspector lied glibly. "We need particulars of them for record purposes."

"Oh? Is that so? Well, they're in the gun-room, if you want them," Una answered with well-assumed indifference.

But here Hinton had over-reached himself by despising his opponent. Una knew nothing of police procedure, but the inspector had under-rated her intelligence when he coined that feeble excuse. A request for Johnnie's gun alone, she could have understood, although it had already been produced and examined at the inquest. But at the inquest there had been no question of the other guns. Why were they wanted now? What had they to do with the 'accident'? She could make neither head nor tail of it at the moment. One thought occupied the foreground of her mind just then: the whole affair was going to be raked up afresh, evidently, and it behoved her to walk cautiously.

The inspector seemed in no hurry to take possession of the guns. In a casual tone, as though merely making conversation, he put a new question which surprised Una by its apparent irrelevance.

"You were staying with Mrs Laxford, weren't you?"

"I was employed by Mrs Laxford," Una corrected him. "I'm engaged to Mr Oswald Brandon. I'm staying here for the present to look after old Mr Brandon while his sons are away on business."

Inspector Hinton did not quite like the dry tone in which these particulars were volunteered. "What business is it of yours?" was the tacit query underlying the frankness of her response to his question.

"Yes, yes," he acknowledged. "I see, quite. The point is this, Miss Menteith. A Mr Hay was staying here, not long ago, you remember. We can't get his address. As you were on the spot at the time, perhaps you know it?"

At Hay's name, Una had difficulty in restraining a start. How much did this man know about Hay and his doings? But at least this question presented no difficulties. She shook her head decidedly.

"Mr Laxford could give you it, surely," she suggested. "Mr Hay was a friend of his."

"Mr Hay wasn't a friend of Mr John Brandon's, by any chance?"

"Oh, no! They were complete strangers. Mr John Brandon told me so before Mr Hay arrived. He said something about Mr Hay having business with Mr Laxford."

Una congratulated herself that this, while truthful, would put the inspector off the dangerous track. Her main object was to keep Johnnie's name out of the talk and to prevent Hinton from thinking that Hay and Johnnie had anything in common.

"Business," the inspector echoed ruminatively. "What sort of business, I wonder?"

"Something about timber, I gathered," Una volunteered, after a moment's reflection.

"What makes you say that?"

Una could not restrain her natural irony, now that she had steered him away from the dangerous subject.

"Another formal inquiry?" she asked. "For record purposes?"

"Just so," Hinton assured her stolidly.

He hardly took the trouble to pretend, now. The girl's looks and tone betrayed that his half-truth about formalities had not deceived her in the slightest. Still, he had no desire to show his hand just then. Until he knew where she stood, it was safer to keep up the thin fiction that he was merely following out a prescribed routine. Una ignored his last words. She knitted her brows in an evident effort to recall something which eluded her memory for a few moments. Then it came back to her suddenly.

"Yes, I remember now," she declared with assurance. "I happened to be in the room with Mr Laxford and Mr Hay. They were talking low, and naturally I paid no attention. Then Mr Hay raised his voice for a moment. Rather pleased with himself over something, I thought. And he said"—she imitated Hay's accent —"'Ain't I a workman? There ain't another lumberer could do it as neat as that.' Mr Laxford glanced across at me and seemed annoyed about something. He said a word or two about timber and felling trees—lumber, you know. I paid no more attention to what they said. It was obviously a bit of private talk and no affair of mine."

The inspector's face betrayed nothing except a certain dull interest; but behind his mask he was jubilant. Miss Menteith might be content with Laxford's gloss about timber, but Hinton had a different interpretation for the word 'lumberer.' With this information, there was a chance that Scotland Yard might solve the mystery of Hay's identity without much trouble.

"Felling timber?" he said doubtfully. "But a tenant can't fell timber, surely?"

"There was some talk of buying Edgehill," Una explained.

"How did you hear that?" Hinton inquired ponderously.

Una now saw that she had blundered in making that admission.

"Mr John Brandon told me," she confessed reluctantly.

"Oh, so Mr Laxford thought of buying the estate?"

Una saw that she was getting deeper and deeper. Johnnie's name was drifting into the centre of the field again.

"No, the idea was to buy the estate on behalf of Mr John Brandon I believe. It was to be done in his name, anyhow. You see, Mr Laxford couldn't manage it in his own name. He's an undischarged bankrupt."

There! That carrot might lead this ass off on a fresh track and let her get Johnnie's name out of the picture. To her delight, Hinton seemed to rise to the bait.

"An undischarged bankrupt, is he? Well, well. But perhaps his wife has means of her own?"

Una hastened to take full advantage of this opportunity. She owed nothing to the Laxfords and had not the slightest scruple in telling what she knew about them.

"I hardly think so," she said ironically. "People with large private incomes are not usually in debt to their governesses."

"I'm not so sure about that," the inspector commented with a laugh. "Having money and parting with it aren't the same thing."

He seemed rather pleased with his feeble joke. Una smiled, but not at the jest.

"That may be. Still, would a woman with large private means let her husband pawn her personal jewellery—rings and trinkets—to raise money to pay the railway fares of the family and square off the milk account?"

"They did that, did they?"

"Yes, when they were coming to Edgehill from the last place we lived at. As to my salary, it's months in arrear. I didn't press for it. I don't need the money urgently."

"How do you know all this about pawning?" Hinton demanded, dropping his pretences completely.

"I saw Mr Laxford hand over the tickets to his wife, telling her how much he'd raised. They made no concealment about it. In fact, it was rather a family joke."

"Of course they redeemed the jewellery later?"

Una shook her head.

"Not so far as I know. The pawn-tickets were in a drawer of a writing bureau. I saw them not long ago, just before the Laxfords left here."

The inspector's evident interest in the Laxford finances surprised Una more than a little; but her main feeling was one of relief that she had led him away from the subject of Johnnie. His next question, however, brought her back on to dangerous ground.

"Was Mr Laxford in the position of guardian or trustee to Mr John Brandon, do you know?"

"Not so far as I know. It's hardly likely, is it? with old Mr Brandon still alive."

Hinton reflected for a moment before putting his next question.

"You lived with the family, Miss Menteith. Did you see anything to suggest that Mr Laxford had any power over young Mr Brandon?"

Una thought swiftly before answering. This was the most dangerous subject of all, from her point of view.

"You mean, had he much influence with Mr John Brandon?" she asked, adroitly shifting the ground. "Well, in a way, yes. Mr

Brandon admired him, you see, and took a lot of ideas from him. He had very considerable trust in Mr Laxford's judgment, I could see. If Mr Laxford had advised him, I think he'd have taken the advice."

"Quite so. And did the rest of the Brandon family approve of that state of affairs?"

Una evaded this blunt question.

"I think the rest of the Brandon family could answer that much better than I can. If you don't mind, let's stick to what I know myself. I can't speak for other people's opinions."

"Yes, yes, of course," the inspector agreed. "Now from your own knowledge, can you tell me if Mr Laxford was interested in the Brandon estate?"

"There was some friction between him and the rest of the Brandon family, I believe," Una admitted with some reluctance.

"Quite so. Now, Miss Menteith, from your own knowledge have you the impression that Mr John Brandon was, putting it figuratively, a pawn in some game?"

Una could have ground her teeth with vexation. This man with his polite noises, his "Quite so," and "Yes, yes, of course," had driven her into a comer. Then a possible line of escape opened up before her.

"A pawn in some game? In connection with the Brandon estate?" she asked, changing the bearing of the question by her qualification. "Well, I can't speak for the Brandon family. As a mere looker-on, I certainly got the impression that they were anxious to get Mr John Brandon away from Mr Laxford. Natural enough, isn't it?"

"Oh, quite. But why was Mr Laxford so anxious to retain him?" asked the inspector shrewdly.

Una saw that she had been out-manoeuvred and that once again the inquiry was bringing her on to thin ice.

"I don't understand much about the Brandon estate," she said candidly. "You'll have to see Mr James Brandon about that, if you want details. He has it all at his finger ends. It's got something to do with a custom called 'borough English,' if that's the right name for it. All I know about it is that before they could do anything about the estate they had to wait till Mr John Brandon came of age and gave his consent to some arrangement or other."

"Ah! And so Mr Laxford's influence with the boy might be a factor in the business when they got to that stage?"

"You can form your own opinion about that," Una retorted rather tartly, as though she felt that she was being trapped into going further than she intended.

"Just so, just so," Hinton admitted, as though he recognised that he was asking an unfair question. Then, to Una's relief, he changed the subject.

"You were on the spot when Edgehill was leased, weren't you, Miss Menteith? It wasn't taken in Mr Laxford's name, I suppose, since he's an undischarged bankrupt?"

Una pondered for a moment or two before replying.

"I'm trying to remember," she explained. Then after a further pause she added, "I believe it was taken on behalf of Mr John Brandon. The first payment was made by a cheque drawn on Mrs Laxford's account. I know that because Mr John Brandon mentioned it to me at the time."

"But she had no money, you told me," the inspector countered swiftly.

Una looked puzzled for a moment.

"She hadn't, shortly after that," she said. "But perhaps she ran herself short by drawing that cheque. It may have taken the whole of her balance to meet it."

"Something in that, perhaps," the inspector admitted, though in a grudging tone.

Much to Una's relief, he rose to his feet.

"I think I'll take those guns, now, Miss Menteith, if you'll let me borrow them. They'll be returned in due course. I'll give you a receipt for them, to keep things shipshape."

Una led the way to the gun-room, where Hinton picked out the guns and gave her a receipt for them. As he turned to go, a fresh idea seemed to strike him.

"I'd better take some of the cartridges also, perhaps," he suggested. "Number Fives, they were."

"They're in this drawer," Una explained.

Hinton helped himself to a double handful which he slipped into his pocket.

"That's all I need trouble you with, Miss Menteith," he said, courteously enough, as he stood aside to let her pass out first. "It's very good of you to spare the time to give me this information."

Una accompanied him to the front door and watched him stow the guns in the rear seats of a car which waited there in charge of a constable. The inspector took the wheel, and she noticed that he turned into the back road by the Long Plantation.

That interview had left an uncomfortable feeling in her mind. Una Menteith liked to understand things; and in this affair there had been several points which puzzled her. Why were all three guns wanted? Not for 'record purposes'; that excuse had been much too thin. And why this sudden interest in Hay, who had played no part at the inquest? Again, what lay behind the inspector's evident curiosity about the Laxford finances? What had they to do with Johnnie's death. But the crucial thing was this sinister suggestion that Johnnie might have been 'a pawn in a game.' The inspector was no fool, evidently, since he had seen as far into the affair as that. If he persisted along that line, the whole scandal might be unearthed, just when they had begun to hope that it was dead and buried.

Her thoughts were so much concentrated on this single aspect of the case that she missed the main object of Hinton's investigation at the moment.

Meanwhile the inspector had stopped his car by the Long Plantation, got out, and given the constable instructions to take the guns to the police station, and return later on. Hinton cut through the Plantation to the spot where a little pile of stones marked the position where Johnnie's body had lain at the top of the sunk fence.

Hinton began by making a minute examination of the trees

on the north side of the glade. Here and there he seemed to find something: withered leaves, snapped twigs, or marks on the bark of branches or trunks. At each of these, he affixed scraps of paper; and soon a dozen or more white patches stood out against the foliage. One spot in particular, where there was a localised shattering of twigs, appeared to interest him particularly; and he fixed there a half-sheet from his notebook, as a conspicuous sign.

Taking a prismatic compass from his pocket, the inspector then retired to the southern side of the glade; and from two points among the bushes he examined the positions of his white scraps. He took a number of bearings with his compass, jotted the figures down in his notebook, and then, advancing to the tiny cairn, he took some further measurements which he entered up in turn. The results, evidently, were not what he had hoped for; and he spent some time in making rough sketches in his book and examining the half-sheet of paper on the tree from various points in the glade and along the line of the sunk fence.

Finally, with a somewhat puzzled air, he returned his compass to his pocket, removed his paper indicators from the trees, and fell to making a minute search of the glade and its immediate neighbourhood. He persisted in this until interrupted by the appearance of the constable among the trees.

"You can take on this job," Hinton ordered. "Hunt about all around here and see if you find anything out of the common among the grass or in the bushes."

"What sort of thing, sir?" the constable inquired.

"I don't know what sort of thing," Hinton retorted, rather irritably. "Anything you can find. I want to be able to say that this place has been thoroughly searched, so see you don't miss anything."

The constable set to work with a somewhat rueful face. Hinton watched him sardonically for a moment or two.

"Don't spare the knees of your trousers," he suggested. "Get down to it. We can't all have brains, but everybody's got a pair of eyes. And bending your back's good for rheumatism, they say."

He walked off through the Plantation to where the car was waiting on the back road. The morning's work had resulted in a very mixed bag, but his researches in the wood had not been one of its successes. He got into the car and drove slowly back towards Talgarth, still puzzling over his results.

His luck served him at the last, however, for just as he was about to enter the village he saw in front of him a rather ungainly girl with a market-basket on her arm, evidently on her way to the village shops. The inspector's face brightened as he caught sight of her; and as he drew level with her he stopped his car and leaned over to speak.

"Hullo, Beauty! Going to buy your trousseau?"

"As soon as you ask me," Miss Tugby retorted impudently.

"No use putting your money on a non-starter," advised the inspector. "But if you want me to talk business, I'll oblige you. It would be worth a matter of ten bob to me if Mr Copdock, by a slip of somebody's tongue, was able to tell me who pays cheques to Mrs Laxford. But of course if everybody had the same bit of information, it wouldn't be worth anything to me, because I could get it for nothing. See?"

Miss Tugby's small eyes twinkled. Ten shillings meant a good deal to her; but to be put on the track of some scandal meant much more.

"I'll get it for you," she said eagerly.

"Oh, no, you won't," rejoined the inspector, who preferred a roundabout method when handling dirty tools. "If Mr Copdock happens to drop me that information next time I see him, he'll get a present of a ten-bob note in an envelope with no name on it. *And*, if I hear about it in the bar at the Arms, I shouldn't be surprised if you got the push from your job. Queer affair, this cause-and-effect business, ain't it? So you be careful, Beauty, or you'll be caught in the larder with cream on your whiskers, one of these days. And then the trouble'll start."

"Well, see there's no mistake about the envelope," Miss Tugby warned him, quite unabashed. "It'd be a nice little surprise for me if I found a quid in it, wouldn't it? You think that over."

"It'd surprise me more than you, even," said the inspector as he let in his clutch. "By-by, Beauty. People might get talking if I gave you a lift."

CHAPTER 13
HINTON'S BALLISTICS

Inspector Hinton was, as he himself put it, "no great hand with a gun." The modest phraseology did him no injustice. Not having served in the War, he had only the vaguest ideas about the mechanism of a rifle; and as he was no sportsman, his acquaintance with shot-guns was of the very sketchiest kind.

That, however, need have been no handicap to him; for in that country-side there were plenty of people who could have lent him expert assistance willingly enough. To go no farther afield, Wendover of the Grange would have been only too pleased to help, had he been asked. But Hinton preferred to work entirely on his own. His implicit belief in his own cleverness, coupled with his selfish desire for the whole credit of the affair, deterred him from taking any advice which would have to be acknowledged in his reports. 'Alone I did it!' was to be his watchword in the 'big case.'

"It only needs a bit of common sense," he assured himself confidently, as he began an examination of the four guns from Edgehill.

He had taken the precaution to get each weapon identified, and a tiny label indicated who had used it on the morning of the tragedy in the Long Plantation.

Johnnie's 12-bore was the first to which the inspector turned. He had already seen it at the inquest, but had made no close examination of it then. Now, as he held it in his hand, he was rather in doubt as to how he should begin. He put the tip of his little finger into the muzzle, twisted it about, and then, withdrawing it, examined the black smudge on the skin.

In his inexperience, it did not occur to him that he was fortunate in finding the gun just as it had been left after the disaster. In the disturbance at Edgehill consequent upon Johnnie's death all the guns had been overlooked, and no one had remembered to clean them after the firing, except Jim Brandon, who had taken his own one to pieces and stowed it away in its case. Johnnie's gun had been returned to Edgehill when the two Brandon brothers were away, and it had simply been put back in the rack by Una exactly as it was.

Hinton stared at his blackened finger-tip, which suggested nothing to him beyond the fact that the gun had been fired. He made a jotting in his notebook, stating the mere fact, and then opened the breech. The left barrel contained a live cartridge which the inspector gingerly withdrew and placed in an envelope on which he wrote: "Unused cartridge from left barrel of John Brandon's gun." The right barrel also contained a cartridge-case; but the indentation made on the cap by the striker showed that it had been fired. The inspector extracted it in its turn and placed it also in an envelope with a written description of the contents. Then, turning the muzzle toward the window, he peered into the barrels without even discovering that he had a choke-bore in his hands.

What should he do next? The idea of finger-prints crossed his mind; but a remembrance of the narratives of the doings on that fatal morning convinced him that very little could be got from evidence of that sort. The guns had changed hands too often to make anything important out of that. And so far as this gun went, it had been handled by all and sundry at the inquest.

The inspector could think of nothing further, so he put down Johnnie's gun and picked up the one with the label "Hay" on it. This also gave a positive result with the finger-tip test, and the inspector solemnly noted down his result. Both barrels were empty; but this suggested nothing to Hinton, not even the possibility that Hay had unloaded his gun on entering the house. A glance down the barrels yielded nothing, not even that this, like Johnnie's gun, was a choke-bore.

Laxford's weapon gave the black smudge like the others. In the breech were two empty cases which the inspector meticulously placed in labelled envelopes. His perfunctory glance into the barrels failed to inform him that this also was a choke-bore gun.

Finally he unstrapped the leg-of-mutton case and extracted Jim's old smooth-bore. After a little inexpert fumbling, he managed to get it assembled; but since it had been cleaned and contained no cartridges, live or otherwise, Hinton found himself hard put to it to concoct any note about it for his report.

He had to admit to himself that so far he had not secured any data throwing light on his problem. The state of the guns tallied with the oral evidence, so far as he could see. He glanced at the weapons in turn, but they suggested nothing fresh to his mind. He had got everything from them that mattered; and he could now proceed to what he described to himself as "the real business."

Inspector Hinton had no intention of carrying out the next stage of his investigation under the public eye. He pretended to himself that secrecy was essential; but his real reason was a distaste for displaying his marksmanship under the eyes of his subordinates. One never knew what sort of fist one might make of a thing like that; and he recoiled from the idea of conducting his tests in the little garden behind the police station. He knew a quiet spinney not far off which would serve his turn.

He took down a broad roll of white paper from a cupboard, and then, laden in addition with cartridges, the guns, and a long surveyor's tape-measure, he went out to his car. A drive of some twenty minutes brought him to the spinney; and in a very short time he had selected a suitable spot and made his preparations. An almost perpendicular bank of earth served him as a convenient butt on which to fasten his paper sheets. With the help of his surveyor's tape he measured off distances of ten, fifteen, and twenty yards from his target and marked the spots by means of sticks thrust into the ground. Then, beginning at the closest range, he set to work.

The inspector was even less of a marksman than he had suspected, and it was well for him that he had brought several packets of ammunition with him, similar to the cartridges which he had picked up at Edgehill. Even at the ten yards range he expended a number of rounds before he obtained a pellet-pattern which satisfied him. True to his policy of "Thorough," he repeated his experiment with all four guns in turn; then, retiring successively to the fifteen and twenty yard marks, he persisted doggedly with his firing until he had secured results sufficient for his purpose. After each trial he noted the details of range and gun on the actual sheet used in that test, to avoid any possible mistakes. Finally he put up a fresh paper, approached to within six feet, and under these conditions blew a ragged hole through the paper with the massed charge.

Once more back in his headquarters, he set to work with a tape-measure on his various sheets, making a rough estimate of the circles covered by the shot-patterns in his several experiments. If the fatal shot had been fired from Laxford's gun in the hands of Dunne, the range from the body's position to the spot where Dunne could have concealed himself in the bushes was fifteen yards. The range from the point where Hay and Laxford had emerged from the undergrowth was about ten yards. As for Jim Brandon, he could never have been nearer than twenty yards from his brother, since the Carron cut him off from the glade.

Hinton, taking these figures along with those he had obtained from his experiments, jotted down a table which he examined with no great satisfaction.

Shooter.		Range.	Diameter of Circle containing Pellets.
Laxford or Hay	.	10 yards	9 inches
Dunne	. . .	15 yards	16 inches
Brandon	. . .	20 yards	32 inches

Hinton seemed to find little satisfaction in this result. From a drawer he took the records of the affair: papers in a folder and a little packet containing the fragment of the skull which he had secured as a rather gruesome relic. He turned over the sheets in the folder until he reached his shorthand notes of Dr Brinkworth's evidence at the inquest, and then began to read:

"The wound was roughly triangular, the apex being toward the rear. It was about three and a half inches long and two and a half inches broad at the base of the triangle. . . . I found only seven pellets in the brain. . . . The ear was severely lacerated, as though the shot had gone through it, carrying away the middle part of the external ear. . . . My impression is that the shot struck the bone almost *en masse* and after causing the wound, was deflected through the ear flap, scattering as it went. . . . I did not observe the numerous wounds which I should have expected if the shot had scattered much before impact."

The inspector put the papers back into the drawer and spread out the sheet at which he had fired with young Brandon's gun at a couple of yards range. That punched-out hole certainly fitted Brinkworth's report; and undoubtedly none of the other results agreed with the post-mortem results. He leaned back in his chair, staring at the torn paper and cudgelling his brains to find some way of harmonising his preconceived ideas with these hard facts.

At last a possible solution dawned upon him. Suppose the shot had been fired by someone concealed behind the drop of the ha-ha. A man thus hidden might have been able to get within close range of young Brandon and shoot him from behind, just after he had passed.

Hinton produced his sketch of the ground and studied the position of the mass of shattered twigs on the north side of the glade. So far as the line went, that might be fitted into his hypothesis without too much of a strain. But then his rising hopes were dashed by the remembrance that the broken twigs were hardly higher than his own eye-level. If the shot had been fired from low down, behind the ha-ha, the trajectory would have been a rising one, and the shot would have struck the trees at a level much higher: some twenty feet from the ground, probably. Either his hypothesis would have to go, or else he would have to drop the shattered twigs out of his argument. And if he did that, a sharp barrister would want to know where the charge had actually gone after striking young Brandon and glancing off.

And a little further consideration deepened his doubts about the value of his idea. If the evidence counted for anything, young Brandon was walking up the line of the ha-ha itself and was in a position to see the ground below him on the right. There were no bushes there behind which an assailant could find concealment, as the inspector clearly remembered. No, that cock wouldn't fight.

But suddenly a fresh idea altered the whole business in Hinton's mind; an idea so simple that he wondered he had not thought of it immediately. If Laxford was the assailant—or Hay, for that matter—why should he trouble to conceal himself at all? Young Brandon would suspect nothing if he had seen Laxford on the ground below the ha-ha. In fact, why assume that he had got down the ha-ha at all? If he had come up behind the youngster, young Brandon would never have suspected foul play, and he could have been shot from behind at close range and with the gun held level.

"That's a winner!" the inspector commented to himself with some pride. "It accounts for that yarn of Laxford's about finding the body at the foot of the ha-ha. Of course they had to cook up some yarn to account for his gun going off and a fall off the dyke was the obvious thing to try. But they forgot the blood, like fools!"

Little by little, however, doubts began to creep in. How would it look to a jury? And on applying that criterion, he was forced to admit that his hypothesis had some awkward points in it. Why, with all the line of the ha-ha to choose from, would any murderer pick out that glade for his work, when at other points he could have kept under cover? The other Brandon brother was across the stream and might well have been in such a position—for all Laxford could tell—that he could overlook the whole affair. And if Laxford fired the shot, it must have been with Hay's gun. That meant making Hay an accessory either before or after the fact. And what motive could one produce to show that Hay was implicated, either as principal—if he fired the shot himself—or as an accessory? That would be the trouble with a jury. Bring in Laxford and you drag in Hay, whether you like it or not. And when the jury asks: 'What does Hay stand to gain by it?' there's no answer. And if Hay gets off, Laxford drops out of the picture too, on this basis.

"Damn!" said the inspector fervently as he surveyed the shortcomings of his hypothesis from this angle.

Shaking himself free from these ideas, he turned to another aspect of the case. What about Dunne? On the face of things, Dunne could not possibly have fired the fatal shot from among the bushes. At that range his gun scattered far too much to have inflicted the fatal wound in young Brandon's head. Could he have got nearer? His case was not like that of Laxford. Dunne was a total stranger to young Brandon. In that Plantation, with a gun in his hand, he was no better than a poacher; and young Brandon would have wanted to know what he was doing there. He would have ordered him off the premises and, the inspector surmised, he would have seen him go. That precluded any likelihood of Dunne having been able to creep up behind young Brandon unsuspected.

"No, that puts that little skunk Dunne out of the picture," Hinton decided. "He's beside the mark."

When he was puzzled, Inspector Hinton had a habit of going back to first principles—"Getting a thing down to dots," as he expressed it. And now in his perplexity, he resorted to this method.

"There are six ways of dying in this country, and only six," he reflected. "Natural death, accident, manslaughter, murder, execution, and suicide: that's the lot. This isn't natural death and it isn't execution. That leaves four. And if Dunne's out of the business, it isn't manslaughter. So it's accident, or murder, or suicide."

He scribbled the three words on a piece of paper as an aid to concentration, and sat for a while staring at them in the hope of stimulating his brain. After awhile he drew his pencil through the first word.

"No, that won't wash. If it was an accident, how did his gun go off on a level with his head? It must have done, judging by the direction of the wound; and that fits in with the height where I found these smashed twigs. If he dropped his gun over the ha-ha and it went off when it hit the ground and shot him, the charge would have gone sky-high after glancing off his skull. And there was no blood at the foot of the ha-ha, either. No, it wasn't an accident, I'll bet."

He sat gazing absently at the two remaining words on the paper: MURDER and SUICIDE, looking from one to the other and allowing his brain to work without conscious direction. Before long, an unsought memory surged up in his mind. A year or two before, he had dealt with a case of attempted suicide. It was a common enough business: some poor devil had tried to finish himself by putting his head into an oven and turning on the gas. But he had made a muddle of it and had been rescued before he was quite dead. He'd been tried for attempted suicide, of course, and then a sordid little story had come out. A not very important moral side-slip, then blackmail, then more blackmail, then a final turn of the screw which had driven him almost out of his mind. And so to the gas-oven. Hinton recalled his own pleasure in sending the blackmailer to gaol for a lengthy term.

As this case drifted up in his memory, it threw fresh light upon the Brandon affair. What about suicide? Why had he been so blind as to leave that glaring possibility out of his calculations? Suicide with a firearm would require a shot at close range, just such a shot as had killed young Brandon. On the face of it, young Brandon had no motive for suicide; but the inspector remembered the big financial schemes in the background, the sinister manoeuvres of Laxford in the insurance field. Not an ordinary suicide, but a forced suicide due to hidden pressure—that would cover the case. And then, suddenly, the inspector realised that he had left a gap in his investigations. He knew nothing about young Brandon's personality and very little indeed about his relations with Laxford. All the way through, he had been treating young Brandon as a lay figure —"the corpse" or "the body" or "the deceased." He had overlooked the plain fact that what was shot was not a "body" or a "corpse" but a living man with ordinary human passions and emotions.

So illuminating was this thought to him that he dismissed the technical side of the affair from his mind for the time being, in order to concentrate all his energy on this new field of inquiry. Where could he get the information he needed? Not from Laxford, certainly; and Beauty Tugby was hardly likely to be of much help either, in a matter of this sort. The Menteith girl might have seen something, but he had already had a taste of her quality. If he began to ask questions, she'd refer him to the Brandons, just as she did before. There was no help to be got in that quarter, he felt sure. That left the Brandon brothers. The younger one came down for week-ends, the inspector knew. He could be got at the next time he came.

Inspector Hinton picked up his desk telephone and asked to be put through to Edgehill.

CHAPTER 14 THE SIGNATURE

The inspector had fixed his appointment at Edgehill for Saturday evening, and when he arrived he was shown immediately into the familiar drawing-room. Jim Brandon was alone, and he greeted Hinton with the curtest of nods.

"Well, what do you want?" he demanded ungraciously, without any polite preamble.

The inspector was somewhat taken aback by this bluntness.

"I came across in the hope that you might be able to answer one or two questions, Mr Brandon."

"One or two questions!" Jim repeated angrily. "Now, look here, Inspector. I'm not satisfied with all this. You came up here on the day of my brother's death and you got all the information I had to give you. The next thing I hear is that you're back again asking more questions, trying to get something out of Miss Menteith. And here you are again, with another batch! The inquest's over long ago. The jury brought in their verdict. The affair's dead and done with, isn't it? Then what do you mean by coming nosing round, asking questions about the private concerns of my family? It's my turn to ask questions, I think; and I'll begin with that one, if you please."

Inspector Hinton's temper, according to his subordinates, was none of the best; and this rudeness tried it sorely. But evidently his only course was to pocket his pride and gain his ends by diplomacy. Still, he entered up in his mental ledger a black mark against Jim Brandon, for his feelings had been severely rasped by this reception.

"I assure you, Mr Brandon," he declared suavely, "it's no pleasure to me to have to trouble people. I like it as little as they do. But I'm paid to do certain work, and I have to earn my salary honestly, just as you'd have to do if you were in my shoes. The coroner's not my master. What he does, and what the jury think, that's their own concern. But I'm responsible to the Chief Constable in matters of this kind, and my duty is to collect all the information that he might want in certain contingencies. Mostly," he went on quickly, "these contingencies never turn up. Still, one has to be prepared. It's part of the routine. We've files and files of information that has never been used and never will be; but we've had to collect it. It's part of the system, and I can't change the system, even if I wanted to."

The inspector had purposely made his explanation lengthy, so as to allow Jim's temper to cool, before he had a chance of breaking in. The tremor of vexation in Jim's voice when he replied was enough to show that Hinton's attempt had not been wholly successful.

"It comes to this, then. People are badgered by all sorts of aimless questions, merely so that you can write up a lot of useless stuff to show how zealous you are. And suppose I refuse to take a hand? Suppose I say: 'Nothing doing.' What then?"

The inspector reflected for a moment or two before replying.

"Well, sir," he answered in the tone of one giving friendly advice, "if you ask me, I don't think that would be a sound course. Look at it this way. I have to make my reports to my superintendent. Suppose I write: 'Mr Brandon refuses all information.' The superintendent doesn't know you as I do; he's never met you personally. All he sees is that sentence. Now put yourself in his place. Wouldn't you say to yourself: 'Ah! Refuses information, does he? Then he must have something he wants to hide. What is it?' And down would come instructions for me to find out all about this mare's nest. I don't want that; and you don't, either, I'm sure."

Jim Brandon seemed to give the matter careful consideration before he answered.

"Something in what you say, perhaps," he agreed with less asperity than he had hitherto shown. "I hadn't looked at it in that light."

He pondered for a few more seconds and then added:

"I think Miss Menteith had better be here. She might perhaps be able to throw some light on these points of yours, whatever they are. Any objection?"

Hinton had a preference for taking his witnesses singly. One got more out of a man if he was alone. But he could adduce no valid argument for excluding Una, and to object to her presence might set off Brandon's hair-trigger temper again. He consented, therefore; and Jim, going to the bell, summoned a maid and gave instructions which brought Una to the drawing-room almost immediately. Jim briefly explained the situation to her. She gave an understanding nod and, seating herself, made a gesture inviting Hinton to take a chair.

"Well, what is it you want?" Jim demanded as he followed their example.

Hinton had carefully considered his opening move beforehand, so that he was ready with a question which sounded innocent enough.

"During your brother's minority, who was his guardian or trustee, Mr Brandon?"

Jim looked slightly puzzled.

"Guardian? I'm not sure about the legal meaning. Is a parent a guardian according to law? What it amounted to in practice was that my father was responsible for him."

"I see. But he was in Mr Laxford's charge, wasn't he?"

Jim frowned momentarily. This touched a sore spot.

"Mr Laxford was engaged as my brother's tutor, purely for educational purposes."

"Yes, yes. He wasn't a trustee? He hadn't any power to act as one?"

Jim shook his head decidedly.

"No. Laxford was employed as a tutor to my brother. That was his position."

"I believe," Hinton glanced aside at Una, "that this Edgehill estate was leased in the name of your brother. Was that done with your father's consent?"

"No, he was never consulted about it."

"There was some talk of buying the estate, I believe?"

Una interposed swiftly before Jim began to answer:

"Mr John Brandon told me about that."

"So you mentioned before," the inspector reminded her politely. "Can you remember when he told you?"

"It was about the time he and Mr Laxford went up to London, I think. I can't remember exactly. It didn't interest me much and I paid no attention, no particular attention, I mean."

"Quite so. And now, Mr Brandon, can you tell me this. What led to the . . . h'm . . . disagreement between you and Mr Laxford which ended in his leaving this house?"

Jim considered this question for ten or fifteen seconds before answering.

"We disapproved of Mr Laxford."

"We?" queried the inspector with a glance towards Una.

"By 'we,' I mean my brother and myself—and my father also," Jim replied stiffly.

"I see. Now, Mr Brandon, on what account did you disapprove of Mr Laxford?"

"We thought he had a bad influence over my brother," Jim answered frankly.

"Ah? A bad influence? Just so." Hinton paused for a moment and then demanded: "Do you think your brother had anything on his mind lately?"

With the tail of his eye, the inspector surprised a piece of by-play between his two witnesses. Evidently his question had taken them both aback, and by an interchange of glances they were making silent efforts to agree on some policy. Una's brows showed her disapproval of some course which Jim seemed to be urging; but she gave way, finally, with a tiny shrug, as though leaving him to take the responsibility if he chose. The whole thing was over almost before Hinton noticed it, but he had no difficulty in seeing that this particular point had been discussed between them beforehand. That was the worst of making appointments; it gave people a chance of putting their heads together before they were questioned.

Jim Brandon brought a pair of steady eyes round to the inspector's face.

"Anything on his mind?" he echoed, as though not quite sure of Hinton's meaning. "That's a bit vague, isn't it? Can't you say what you mean, exactly?"

But this was precisely what the inspector could not do. He was surer than ever that he was on the track of something. That mute exchange of glances showed divided councils; and divided councils mean, in a case like this, that somebody wants to hold something back. He decided to try another cast.

"You spoke of Mr Laxford having an influence over your brother. A strong influence, was it?"

"Too strong for my liking."

The inspector made up his mind to play his biggest trump now. He leaned forward slightly in his chair and spoke with studied deliberation so that no word should be lost.

"Do you think this influence might account for your brother assigning that insurance policy to Mrs Laxford?"

There was no mistaking the surprise on both the faces before him. Evidently his bombshell had done its work. Jim was the first to recover.

"I'm afraid I don't quite follow you," he said, with a marked change in his tone. "Do you mind explaining this?"

"Oh, I supposed you knew about it," Hinton declared disingenuously. "Your brother took out a policy on his own life for £25,000 a few weeks ago and assigned it to Mrs Laxford 'for value received.' Your brother didn't mention it to you?"

"Twenty-five thousand!" Jim repeated, as though the figure made a profound impression on him. Then, in a harsh tone, he went on jerkily, "And he made it over to that . . .? You hear, Una?

196

He made it over to her!"

Una made no reply in words, but she moved slightly in her chair as though freeing herself from something physically repellent.

"She doesn't like it, any more than he does," the inspector inferred, "but she's got a better grip on herself. And it's plain enough that I'm on to something here."

Jim Brandon repeated "Twenty-five thousand!" under his breath as though it were a curse; then he seemed to recover his balance, though with a visible effort.

"There's something far wrong here," he said in a troubled voice. "Would you mind explaining it? A bit more detail, please."

Hinton gave them only the minimum of facts: the issue of the final insurance policy, Johnnie's letter to the insurance company, and Laxford's production of the assignment witnessed by himself and Hay. Jim listened intently with a frown on his face.

"There's something very fishy about this," he commented in a graver tone than he had used up to that moment. "That assignment can't be worth the paper it's written on. My brother only came of age on the morning of his death. Before that, he could make no legal assignment."

Inspector Hinton verified something in his notebook before answering.

"The actual assignment which Mr Laxford showed to the insurance people was dated 28th August," he said. "He came of age that morning, Mr Brandon, didn't he? So it's quite a valid document."

"Then," Jim demanded, "how do you square that with the fact that I asked my brother, just before we went out to shoot, if he had signed any document? He denied it, flat."

Inspector Hinton, though not so clever as he imagined himself, was no fool. Jim had exposed the joint in his harness for which Hinton had been searching; and he seized his chance.

"How did you come to put *that* question to him?" he demanded. "Rather a funny one, wasn't it? in the circumstances."

Jim was obviously taken aback by this riposte; and a glance at Una's face showed the inspector that he had scored heavily. He noted a quick exchange of glances between the two. Una seemed to be reproaching Jim for a blunder, whilst he was trying to reassure her. After a pause of a few seconds, Jim explained:

"I told you already that we distrusted Laxford's influence over my brother."

"That doesn't explain why you put your question at that particular moment, though," Hinton persisted.

Jim kept his eyes on the inspector's face, as though wilfully avoiding Una's warning look.

"I'll be quite plain with you," he said deliberately, "for purely official purposes only. I don't want this sort of thing made public, naturally."

Una made a sound of protest, but Jim went on.

"It's all right, Una. I see where this is moving and it's bound to come out, sooner or later. We've nothing to suppress. The inspector won't gossip, we can be sure of that. Here are the plain facts, Inspector. The night before my brother's death, I learned with my own ears that Laxford and Hay had trapped him in a false position. It was a planned affair."

He gave the inspector an outline of the plot which he had unearthed, without mentioning Una's share in the matter.

"That was the state of affairs," he concluded. "Do you think it funny that I should ask my brother if he'd signed anything?"

"No, it was a very wise precaution," the inspector admitted. "And your brother denied that he'd signed anything? H'm! I don't want to be offensive, Mr Brandon, but could you rely on your brother telling you the truth about it?"

"Johnnie never lied in his life," Una broke in hotly. "He was absolutely truthful."

"He was perfectly truthful, as Miss Menteith says," Jim said bluntly. "You can rule that out."

The inspector accepted their statements with a little gesture. Inwardly, he was congratulating himself on his clairvoyance. Here was the very case he had foretold: blackmail with suicide as its sequel.

"You could testify on oath to all you've told me?" he asked in a very serious tone.

"Of course I could," Jim answered at once.

"I'm not doubting your recollections for a moment," Hinton went on, "but it's established by documentary evidence that your brother had the intention of making this assignment—in fact, he'd signed an invalid assignment of the same kind—as far back as 15th August. He wrote that letter to the insurance company on that date. You can see how the existence of that letter might tell with a jury."

Jim rubbed his chin with his hand, like a man who sees a difficulty but has not found its solution.

"Facts are facts," he asserted stoutly after a moment or two. "My brother signed nothing that morning."

The inspector was looking at the matter from another viewpoint as his next words showed.

"This man Hay is one of our difficulties," he admitted with a show of frankness. "We can't put our hands on him. Now his name's on that assignment as a witness, along with Mr Laxford. If the executors of your brother chose to contest that assignment, Mr Laxford would have to produce his witness, I think."

"Oh, we'll contest the assignment all right," said Jim with a snarl. "Don't you be afraid of that. Twenty-five thousand's worth making a fight for."

"Yes, yes," Hinton agreed. "And in the course of that business something might come out which would be of use to us, of course. Now there's another point. What was your brother's state of mind before his death?"

"Perfectly normal, I should say," Jim said with some assurance. "Just wait a moment."

He left the room and came back in a minute or two with a quarto exercise book which he handed to the inspector.

"That's a diary my brother kept. Just glance through it and you'll see the sort of thing."

Hinton opened the book, which was an ordinary ruled volume and not a specially prepared diary. The first entry that met his eye was perfectly commonplace: a bald note of hours spent in study, a record of a rabbit and two wood-pigeons shot, the route of a country walk. He turned over to the date 'August 15th,' where, in the same characteristic sprawling hand, he found a colourless account of a visit to London: lunch, some shopping, dinner, and the name of a music-hall. Hinton marked the place with his finger and showed the book to Jim.

"There's no mention of his being overhauled by the insurance doctors. That happened on August 15th."

"Oh, so that was what he went up to town for?" Jim exclaimed in enlightenment. "I knew there was something fishy, then! He wouldn't tell me what he'd been doing, barring this sort of stuff"—he pointed to the diary. "Laxford had told him to keep his jaw shut, I saw, and my brother wasn't the kind that breaks its word. He's left it out of his diary, even. Doesn't that prove what I said about Laxford having too much influence over him?"

"Of course, of course," Hinton agreed, rather indifferently as he continued to glance through the pages of the book. "Well, I admit that up to August 27th, this diary seems to show nothing out of the common. But ... it stops there, Mr Brandon. It doesn't even mention your arrival here. There's no entry at all for the day before his death, and that's rather significant, isn't it?"

"He had no time to write up anything, that day," Jim pointed out, in an attempt to put a better face on the matter. "He was with me most of the time, and he went to bed very late."

"I dare say," Hinton answered, quite unconvinced. "Let's leave that, Mr Brandon. There's this question of the illegal assignment your brother made on 15th August, which was replaced later by the assignment dated on the morning of his death, evidently. What was at the back of that, in your opinion?"

Jim did not answer immediately. Evidently he had not thought out this matter. But in a very short time he made a suggestion.

"Assume the Laxfords didn't know then that it was an invalid document. Take it that they thought it constituted a legal transfer. My brother, when he came of age, would have been in a position to drive a bargain in connection with our family estate and if Laxford had been his adviser, my brother might have been induced to drive a very hard bargain. Now suppose they went to a moneylender and tried to raise cash on the strength of my brother's expectations when he came of age. The moneylender would say: 'Yes, but suppose you die in the meanwhile? Then your expectations are a wash-out and I might whistle for my cash.' The counter to that would be to insure my brother's life until he came of age, and use that policy as security for a loan. You see, it isn't like an ordinary policy which is only worth its surrender value if you try to borrow on it. This policy makes a perfectly sound asset. If my brother died before coming of age, then there's the £25,000 cash to indemnify the moneylender. If my brother lived till he was twenty-one, then his rights in our family estate could be realised so as to bring in enough to pay off the loan. That would leave the moneylender safe, either way. You see that?"

"I see that," the inspector echoed thoughtfully. "And your idea is that this . . . h'm! . . . trap that your brother was led into was a means of ensuring that he followed Mr Laxford's advice when the time came to bargain over your family estate? By the way, what is the exact position of the estate affair, Mr Brandon?"

"It's entailed according to what's called the custom of 'borough English,' which gives the youngest son the powers that usually fall to the eldest son in the case of entails."

"And if your brother had driven the hardest bargain he could, would he have got £25,000 out of the estate, do you think?"

Jim reflected for a few moments.

"I haven't got the figures at my finger ends," he said in a tone of some uncertainty. "I should doubt, though, if his share would have come to that figure, if he had taken the course I've sketched out."

The inspector tapped his fingers on the arm of his chair as though thinking deeply.

"What it comes to is this, then," he said at last. "I'm sorry to put it crudely, Mr Brandon, but your statement boils down to this, doesn't it? If your brother died, it was worth £25,000 in hard cash to the holder of the policy; whereas if he lived, he might secure a sum round about £25,000, and that sum would go into his own pocket, to do what he liked with?"

"I hadn't looked at it in that way, quite," Jim admitted reluctantly, "but that's what it amounts to in fact."

The inspector nodded, and put another question.

"Suppose this assignment turns out to be invalid, where will the £25,000 go?"

"I suppose my father gets it. My brother died intestate, of course, and my father would be his next of kin, I expect. I don't know definitely, but I believe that's correct."

"I see," said Hinton. "That's right, I think."

He pushed his notebook over for Jim to initial, after reading the notes. Then, putting the book in his pocket, he picked up the diary.

"You've no objection to my borrowing this?" he asked. "And keeping these guns a little longer? Thanks. And, Mr Brandon, about that assignment . . ."

"The executors will contest it, you may be sure of that," Jim assured him with a rather ugly smile.

Inspector Hinton took his leave without further ado. When he had left the room, Una turned a strained face to Jim.

"What's he thinking, Jim? He didn't *say* anything, but . . ."

"Thinking!" Jim retorted savagely. "He's thinking just what I think myself, and what I'd have thought straight away if I'd known about that insurance policy before. He's thinking what you're thinking yourself, Una. You needn't deny it! It's too plain for that pretence. Hinton thinks that swine Laxford was responsible for Johnnie's death, and I hope he proves it! Once I heard of that policy, I saw through the whole game. A child could grasp it. Poor Johnnie! And that was the hound he trusted so much."

As a mind-reader, Jim was unusually successful in this case. Inspector Hinton left Edgehill in higher spirits than he expected. That intuition of his about blackmail had brought in a far better harvest than he had hoped for. The trapping of Johnnie accounted neatly for the hurried completion of the valid assignment on that fatal morning. That would be a nasty bit of evidence to set before the jury; and the defence wouldn't be able to shake it. Brandon was a good witness, from what the inspector had seen of him. And there was no saying what Hay and Laxford's wife might not let out under cross-examination. Against that, the only snag in the affair was Brandon's insistence that his brother had denied signing anything that morning. But the inspector brushed that aside in his mind. Let the defence dig it out for themselves, if they could; he wasn't going to help them. And besides, he had an idea that what a dead man said wasn't evidence. Nothing in it, nothing whatever.

Pushing his good luck, he dropped into Copdock's shop on his way back. It chanced to be empty at the moment, and the dealer, with a mysterious air which annoyed Hinton intensely, produced a dirty piece of paper and handed it across the counter. The inspector opened it and read a single name: "P.J. Pluscarden." He fumbled in his pocket, produced an envelope and handed it over to Copdock, who, not to be outdone in caution, held it up to the light to see that it really contained a Treasury note.

"P.J. Pluscarden." The name conveyed nothing to the inspector at the moment, but he had means of enlightenment. He turned into the village post office, secured the telephone booth, rang up the public library in Ambledown, and within a few minutes the librarian had consulted the London Directory and informed him that P.J. Pluscarden described himself as a financial agent.

"A moneylender! I thought as much," Hinton said to himself as he hung up the receiver. "This affair's shaping better than I thought, a day or two ago."

But even then the inspector's run of luck persisted. At the police station, he found a communication from Scotland Yard in answer to a letter which he had written. He tore it open and muttered some of its phrases as he glanced through it.

"Joseph Hay, *alias* Flash Joe, *alias* Deal-'em-out Hay . . . confidence trick . . . card-sharper . . . twice charged, no convictions . . . ostensible occupation, agent for a moneylending firm. . ."

Hinton smiled in a satisfied way as he filed this letter.

"Lives by his wits, does Mr Hay," he commented to himself. "What we used to call a 'lumberer' or a 'workman.' Just so. And if he's a tout for a moneylender, really, then that moneylender's name's Pluscarden, or you can dye me green."

Putting the file back on the shelf, he consulted the telephone directory and gave a number to the exchange. In a very short time he had ascertained from the agents for the Edgehill estate that Laxford had actually approached them. But all he had done was to ask over the telephone what price they wanted for Edgehill. When he heard the figure he had said he would think over the matter. They had not heard from him since. His telephone call had been made on 29th July.

"And on 16th August, neither Laxford nor his missus had a stiver in the bank," Hinton recalled, as he hung up the receiver. "That inquiry was a flam. But what did he make it for?"

CHAPTER 15 THE CARTRIDGE-CASE

Inspector Hinton was not afraid of the Chief Constable, yet he never felt entirely at his ease with him. He had an uncomfortable suspicion that Sir Clinton looked on him much as he himself looked upon the common run of humanity; and it rankled with him that his chief showed no sign that he regarded Inspector Hinton as a particularly bright star. Like many cynical people, the inspector had a strong dislike of cynicism in others; and he took no pleasure in Sir Clinton's occasional exercises in the sardonic.

The Chief Constable's eye roved round the inspector's dingy little office, resting momentarily in turn on the guns in one corner of the room, the shot-torn papers which Hinton had pinned on the wall, the minor exhibits on the desk, and the folder which lay before him. He handed a couple of sheets of notes back to the inspector for replacement in the file and glanced at Wendover who, much to Hinton's annoyance, had been a silent spectator at this interview.

"That brings me up to date," he said as Hinton closed the file. "I've read all your previous reports. Very good, inspector. You put things clearly."

Hinton accepted this tribute without undue gratification.

"And now you propose to take out a warrant and arrest Laxford?" the Chief Constable pursued.

"Well, sir, I think it advisable to act at once." Hinton's 'official' vocabulary was a shade stilted. "Laxford is leaving this district next week, I learn. It'll save trouble if we lay our hands on him before he vanishes."

"I agree with you," Sir Clinton said, rather to the inspector's relief. "You'll get your warrant. Mr Wendover's a J.P. and can give us one. I prefer that Mr Wendover should issue it, you understand?" he added with just enough emphasis to make his statement a veiled order.

Hinton nodded. Of course, he reflected sulkily, Driffield would want to flatter this dilettante crime-monger by giving him a finger in the pie, just because he happened to be staying at Wendover's house. The inspector had no use for these would-be-wise amateurs.

"Another thing," Sir Clinton went on. "Better get into touch with the London people and ask them to pick up this fellow Hay. If they can't manage it any other way, they can detain him on suspicion and hand him on to us. Give them a couple of days' grace. So long as we have him here before Laxford's arrested, it's quite sufficient. I may want to ask him a question or two myself."

"Very good, sir," Hinton concurred morosely.

Of course! he reflected angrily. Just when all the hard work had been done, Driffield proposed to step in, ask a question or two, and take all the credit. Bad luck that he should have landed in the neighbourhood at this juncture. Worse luck that he should be putting his finger into 'the big case' that was to make Hinton's name. These fellows higher up were all like that. Grabbers, every man jack of them!

The Chief Constable seemed to be something of a thought-reader, or else he knew his subordinate thoroughly.

"This is your case, Inspector," he said in a studiedly 'official' tone. "The credit will be entirely yours—and the responsibility."

Sir Clinton had a penchant for helping subordinates in their difficult cases, but he never took the slightest public credit for the assistance which he gave. His reward in the matter was the intellectual pleasure of pitting his wits against those of a criminal, a slight recompense for the hours spent in the dull routine of his office. But in return for his help, he expected a certain amount of friendly co-operation on the part of the man he was assisting. Reading Inspector Hinton like a book, he saw that little co-operation could be expected from him. That would make things less pleasant. Wendover would be the chief sufferer. There would be none of these friendly confabulations *à trois* which the Squire had enjoyed in some earlier cases. A pity, that, but apparently unavoidable.

Sir Clinton pulled out his cigarette-case and offered it to the inspector, who rejected it with very thinly veiled scorn.

"No, thanks, sir. I never touch them. I'm a pipe-smoker," he explained with an air which suggested that cigarettes were fit only for children.

"Ah," said Sir Clinton interestedly. "Mr Wendover smokes cigars. It takes all sorts to make a world. Have a cigar, Wendover? You'll find one in your own case. Light your pipe, Inspector. I don't mind the odour."

Hinton, vaguely suspicious that he was being 'got at,' declined with a grunt and a nod.

"Now about this case of yours," Sir Clinton went on briskly. "There's a little bit of doggerel I've found useful sometimes. There's a Latin original, but I'll give you an English version...."

"I can construe Latin," Hinton interrupted.

He hated those university fellows with their assumption that they were the only educated people in the country. They thought nobody knew Latin unless he'd been birched at their old school. He'd been at a secondary school himself and was as well educated as they were.

"Oh, very well, if you'd rather have the original," Sir Clinton concurred blandly, "here it is: '*Quis, quid, ubi, quibus auxiliis, cur, quomodo, quando?*'"

"Who, what, where ..." the inspector translated. "It doesn't make sense, sir. There isn't a verb in it."

"Oh, it's sensible enough," Sir Clinton assured him, tactfully ignoring Hinton's obvious discomfiture. "Here's an English version. It's easier to remember, because it rhymes:

'What was the crime? Who did it? When was it done and where?
How done, and with what motive? Who in the deed did share?'

Now, Inspector, let's test your case by putting these seven questions in turn. 'What was the crime?'"

"The murder of young Brandon," Hinton declared boldly.

"Murder?" Sir Clinton queried in a doubtful tone. "The *shooting* of young Brandon's beyond dispute, I admit. But what makes you so sure it's murder? Why not suicide, or accident?"

"It couldn't have been either," Hinton declared bluntly, as he had thought over these possibilities a good deal and felt sure of his ground. "The position and the direction of the wound, sir, absolutely preclude either accident or suicide. I've gone into it carefully. He was shot standing up, with the gun almost horizontal. Now look here, sir."

He picked up one of the guns from the comer of the room and illustrated the difficulty, if not the impossibility, of anyone holding and firing a gun in the required direction.

"Yes, suicide would be difficult," Sir Clinton admitted without ado, "I'm merely testing all sides of your case. "But what about accident?"

"If his gun had slipped out of his hand and fallen, the shot from it would have had to go upwards to hit him. The wound's horizontal. Therefore it wasn't accident," Hinton declared positively.

Sir Clinton looked at him with a faintly quizzical smile.

"Not if he was shot with his own gun," he said drily. "But somebody else's gun might have gone off by accident and killed him. Your reasoning doesn't rule that out. It fits it, in fact."

The inspector had difficulty in repressing a movement of vexation. This was a mere quibble, he felt; and yet he had never taken that possibility into account and he had no reply ready.

"All the evidence tells against it," he said sullenly.

"You mean the verbal evidence," Sir Clinton corrected him. "The evidence of Mr Laxford who's such a stickler for truth, and the evidence of Mr Dunne whose testimony is so reliable that you can't put him into the witness-box. No good, Inspector."

Hinton's attitude betrayed clearly enough that he had not foreseen this line of attack, and it was several seconds before he found a counter-suggestion.

"But if Laxford shot him by accident, sir, why didn't he say so?"

"Put yourself in his place," advised the Chief Constable. "Laxford stood to gain £25,000 by young Brandon's death. A bit awkward to come forward and say: 'I shot him, but it was a pure accident?' I shouldn't care to be in that position myself. People are so sceptical about affairs of that sort."

He flicked the ash from his cigarette and then continued in a slightly different tone:

"Well, apparently you're determined to call it 'Murder' and not 'Manslaughter' or 'Accident.' Pass that, then, and let's go on to the next question: 'Who did it?'"

"Laxford, sir."

"Laxford was the only one of the three who had no gun," Sir Clinton pointed out.

"He must have used Hay's gun," Hinton declared.

"Or borrowed young Brandon's own gun for a moment and shot him with that. Or perhaps he had his own gun all the time and handed it to Dunne after the shooting. That's a possibility, if Laxford knew what Dunne's mental trouble was. Dunne would remember nothing about it when he woke up and found the gun in his hands."

The inspector had difficulty in concealing his vexation. Why had he not thought of Laxford borrowing young Brandon's gun? Now that it was put to him, he could see how neatly it covered the case, and yet he had missed it completely. A less self-centred man might have said: "That's clever," but Hinton's mental comment was merely: "That's damned annoying."

"Oh, if you think it likely, sir," he said aloud in a tone which disparaged the Chief Constable's suggestions without being exactly rude.

"You pin yourself down to Laxford?" Sir Clinton continued, ignoring the inspector's manner. "But why not Hay? Or Dunne?"

"No motive, sir," Hinton retorted tartly.

"None needed in Dunne's case, I imagine."

"I suppose not," Hinton admitted in a sullen tone.

"Then that question's still an open one," the Chief Constable pointed out. "Try the next one: 'When was it done?' Suppose we say, 'On the morning of August 28th, 1924' and let it go at that. 'Where?' is the next query."

"In the glade in the Long Plantation," said the inspector, with the air of an adult consenting to join in a child's game. "Where else could it have been done?"

"Well, they might have shot him in some secluded place farther down the wood, wrapped his head in their handkerchiefs to keep the blood from leaving traces, and carried him to the glade. Then when they took off the handkerchiefs, the blood would have made a pool and the little bit of bone would naturally fall out. That's a possibility. Still, I'm inclined to agree with you that he was shot in the glade. But the glade's of some size. Where, precisely, do you claim that he was shot?"

"Where his brother saw the body when he arrived," Hinton said quite assuredly. "Nothing else'll fit."

"That hinges conveniently on to the next query: 'How done?'" Sir Clinton pursued. "What have you to say about that?"

"He was shot from behind at fairly close quarters, sir, in my opinion. Nothing else fits in with these shot-patterns," the inspector declared, with a wave of his hand towards the sheets of paper pinned to the wall.

"H'm!" said the Chief Constable doubtfully. "If the shot came from behind and glanced off his skull, then surely these smashed twigs should have been farther east. In fact, from your little map I'd have assumed that a glancing shot would have gone off up the line of the ha-ha if not still farther to the right of the shooter. However, I haven't seen the ground yet. Pass that for the present."

"If young Brandon had been standing on the edge of the ha-ha, then it makes it worse, on your argument, sir. That's why I assume he was shot on the spot where his brother found his body."

"And that implies that Laxford told a lie when he said they found the body at the foot of the ha-ha?"

"Of course, sir. There was no blood there. I searched carefully for any trace, but there wasn't a sign of blood."

Sir Clinton nodded without comment.

"And now: 'With what motive?' It meant £25,000 into Mrs Laxford's bank account. A good many people would commit murder for much less than that, I admit. If you're putting Laxford in the dock, then your motive would pass muster. Now the final question: 'Who in the deed did share?'"

"Hay must have had a hand in it," the inspector declared without hesitation. "My view is that he lent Laxford his gun to do the job, which would bring him in as an accessory before the fact. Anyway, he backed up Laxford afterwards in his lies, so he's an accessory after the fact for certain."

"He had a hand in part of the affair undoubtedly," Sir Clinton admitted without demur.

He smoked for almost a minute in silence, evidently thinking over the points which Hinton had laid down. Then he threw the end of his cigarette into the fireplace and took a fresh one from his case.

"The weak spot in your whole case," he said abruptly, "is the fact that you can't prove definitely which of the guns fired the fatal shot. If I were for the defence, I'd adopt the accident hypothesis I sketched for you. Laxford shot the boy by accident and in the flurry of realising how bad it looked, with this £25,000 in the wind, he told a lot of lies which he'll retract in the witness-box. You can't disprove that except by establishing beyond a doubt which gun the shot was fired from—and keeping your thumb on that until he brings the wrong gun into his tale. He must say whether the accident happened with young Brandon's gun or the one Hay was carrying. If you can prove the boy wasn't killed with the one he chooses for his story, you'd prove your case. Otherwise, the worst Laxford has to fear is a few years for manslaughter, and perhaps not even that."

"It can't be done from finger-prints, sir, if you're thinking of that," the inspector pointed out in a slightly superior tone. "About everybody at Edgehill had handled these guns just before and after the business. It wasn't even worth looking for prints on them."

"I wasn't thinking of finger-prints," Sir Clinton assured him blandly. "By the way, Inspector, when you searched the ground you didn't notice a small piece of wire-gauze, did you? A little bit about a couple of inches square, or thereby?"

The inspector evidently suspected that the Chief Constable was pulling his leg.

"I saw nothing of the sort," he said surlily. "I couldn't have missed it if it had been on the grass. And after I'd gone over the place myself, a constable searched it for hours. There was nothing of that sort there, sir."

"I hardly expected it," Sir Clinton admitted. "I don't think the thing was done quite in that way."

The inspector happened to glance at Wendover and saw from his expression that the mention of wire-gauze had touched some chord in his memory. But despite this, Wendover seemed not much wiser than Hinton, so far as his features showed.

Sir Clinton rose from his chair.

"Just send these guns up to me at the Grange," he said, indicating the weapons stacked against the wall. "And that fragment of bone. Wrap it up carefully and seal it. And . . . oh, yes, send up young Brandon's diary also."

Outside the police station, a big car was waiting. Wendover took the wheel.

"Where away now?" he asked as Sir Clinton got in beside him.

"As near that glade in the Long Plantation as you can manage," the Chief Constable directed. Then he reconsidered his proposal. "No, make it Edgehill—the house. Squire. Brother Brandon will be up in town, I expect, so we needn't bother about him. But if we can pick up that gardener—Stoke is his name—he may be useful. You'd better do the talking. I don't want to advertise myself too much."

Wendover agreed with a nod and drove on. He seemed slightly ruffled, and the cause of this appeared when he spoke.

"That inspector of yours didn't like my being there."

"Hinton? Oh, he's new to the district, Squire, and hasn't had time to fall under your charm," the Chief Constable replied soothingly. "These zealous beggars don't like interference. In fact, I've got a feeling that he's wishing me at the other end of the county."

"I had a suspicion of the sort myself, from his manner," Wendover commented drily.

"I have a suspicion that you think he's a bonehead," Sir Clinton retorted with a grin. "He's not that. I should say that he has the knack of seeing the obvious just a shade quicker than most people."

Wendover smiled in his turn.

"That compliment would please him, no doubt, though it's a bit restricted. By the way, Clinton, what made you ask about wire-gauze? I've used it myself in shooting, sometimes, but I haven't your friend's knack of seeing the obvious. And now I think of it, he didn't seem to grasp the great idea immediately either."

"That was just to make sure of stopping every burrow. Wire-gauze didn't come into the thing, I was sure. Still, one has to ask, just to be on the safe side. That was all."

Their arrival at Edgehill interrupted the conversation. Wendover successfully obtained the services of the gardener by sending a message to Una through the maid who answered the door. They picked up Stoke, and under his direction, drove down the back road towards the glade.

"That heap of stones is where young Mr Brandon was lying when I saw the body," Stoke explained when they reached the scene of the tragedy. "He was lying with his head *that* way, with his gun beside him in the grass and a pool of blood just at his head. He'd slipped his foot when he was walking up the sunk fence, you see, sir, and fallen over the edge, just here. Then the gun went off and killed him, and they lifted him up on to the grass where the stones are."

"You didn't see them lift him?" Sir Clinton asked.

"No, sir. That was done before I came. He was lying on the grass when I saw him first."

Sir Clinton walked to the north side of the glade and examined the spot where the twigs had been broken by the shot. He faced about and took a prismatic compass from his pocket.

"Just stand at that heap of stones, for a moment, Wendover," he directed. "And you, Stoke, please stand on the top of the ha-ha at the place where you said Mr Brandon stumbled. Thanks. Just a moment. . . . You might turn your head a bit to your left, Stoke. . . . That'll do, thanks. By the way, you're facing a bit to the left of me now, aren't you? I mean when you look straight in front of you, I'm a shade to the right of the bull's eye. . . . Thanks. That's all."

He jotted down the bearings of Wendover and Stoke from his own position. Then, coming down to the sunk fence, he took Stoke's place as exactly as he could.

"What did you see in front of you when I told you to stand fast?" he asked.

"That silver birch trunk, sir, as near as might be."

Sir Clinton made a slight turn to the left until his eyes came full on the birch, then with evident accuracy, he made a right turn and took a further bearing which he jotted down. After a moment's calculation, he turned slowly to his right and looked through his compass, though without putting any figures in his notebook.

"Just point out the places where Mr Dunne and Mr Laxford were said to have got into the glade," he said to Stoke. "Go to them in turn, please."

Stoke did so, and Sir Clinton took the bearing of each position from the little cairn and the point on the ha-ha where the slip was supposed to have occurred.

214

"What makes you so sure about these places, Stoke?"

"Well, sir, they're both places where paths lead into this little bit of a clearing."

Sir Clinton nodded and put his compass back into his pocket.

"I think that finishes us here. I only wanted to see the place with my own eyes. We can get home now."

As they were making their way through the wood towards the car. Stoke betrayed signs of some suppressed desire; and after some preliminary fidgeting and false starts, he summoned up his courage to make a suggestion.

"Do you think, sir," he asked Wendover, "that Sir Clinton would care for to look at my little museum? It might interest him, perhaps. You'll be passing the door."

Sir Clinton caught the eagerness, diffidence, and modest pride which somehow managed to express themselves in Stoke's face; and he good-naturedly fell in with the proposal. Kindness costs little, and the man was so evidently anxious to exhibit his treasures that it would be hard-hearted to refuse.

"We've a while yet, before lunch," he said glancing at his watch. "If it won't take too long, I'd be very glad to see it. We do a little collecting ourselves, you know, in our Black Museum at Headquarters."

Stoke's obvious pleasure was a reward in itself.

"I'd be very proud if you'd give mine a look-over, sir. Some people like it very much. I was trying to get Inspector Hinton to come and see it, one day he was up here, but he didn't seem much interested. He wouldn't look at it."

"Well, you can tell him you've had a visit from the Chief Constable," Wendover pointed out. "Perhaps he won't find it beneath his notice then."

The car took them to Stoke's cottage in a few moments, and the gardener ushered them into a room which he had set apart for his 'museum.' Wendover had seen it all before, and Stoke attached himself to Sir Clinton in the capacity of cicerone, keeping up a running commentary as they passed from object to object.

"That's a white starling, sir. You won't see a thing like that twice in a blue moon. I stuffed it myself. . . . Yes, these are flint arrow-heads. They came from a friend; he found them on the South Downs. . . . That duck's egg with the coloured design on it, sir? Yes, I did that myself. I drew the design in grease and then boiled the shell in water with cochineal in it; that was how it was done. . . . That's a curious candle-extinguisher, sir. You won't see a thing like that often, nowadays. You see you dig that spike into the candle, and when it burns down to that height the trigger works and the extinguisher pops on and puts out the candle. Very ingenious, I've always thought, sir. . . . This pear inside the lemonade bottle, sir? You put the pear in when its small enough to go through the neck and tie the bottle to the branch. The pear goes on growing and you cut off the twig and fill the bottle with methylated spirits. It puzzles a lot of people, sir. . . . So does this ship in the bottle. I made that myself, sir. The masts and rigging are hinged so that they lie flat while you slip the ship into the bottle. Then you pull a thread and bring the masts upright, and it's too big to come out through the neck. Very few people guess how it's done, sir. . . . That picture of Napoleon III, sir? Take it down from the nail and turn it upside down, and you'll see it makes a donkey. . . . These are Norwegian wedding spoons; wooden they are and the chain between them's wooden, too. At the wedding breakfast the bride and bridegroom take a spoon each and eat out of the same dish, sir. A sailor friend brought me those. . . . Here's a robin's nest in a tin can, sir, very curious. I found it quite near here. . . . Yes, I stuffed them myself. . . . And this is a very good collection of huntsmen's buttons, sir. My father had that. He came from a hunting county, sir. . . . That's a German note for a million marks, sir. Fifty thousand pounds it would be worth if it was its right value, sir. . . . I made that snake out of postage stamps, as you can see, sir. It's six feet long, and when you hold it by the tail it moves about very lifelike. I'll just show you. . . ."

But that demonstration was never given. Sir Clinton's eye, roaming along the shelf, had fallen upon a little object which riveted his attention: an empty cartridge-case propped against a label with the lettering: "CARTRIDGE THAT KILLED JOHN BRANDON, ESQ. 28th Aug., 1924."

"Where did you get that?" the Chief Constable demanded, with extended forefinger.

Stoke was completely taken aback. He had forgotten the existence of that particular exhibit when he invited Sir Clinton to his museum.

"I took it out of his gun, that morning, sir," he confessed guiltily.

Much to his relief, the Chief Constable seemed more interested than angry.

"How did you come to get hold of it?" he asked, picking up the case and eyeing it curiously.

Stoke, rather relieved at not being severely blamed, made a clean breast of the whole affair.

"And you replaced it in Mr Brandon's gun by another cartridge case, from Mr Hay's gun, you say?"

"Yes, sir, that's it."

Sir Clinton turned the little object about in his fingers and examined the brass end.

"I don't think the Brandon family would be very well pleased if they knew you were exhibiting this. Stoke," he pointed out. "It might lose you your job, quite likely."

Stoke was evidently full of contrition.

"I'm downright sorry, sir. I never gave a thought to that side of it; but I see now it wasn't the thing at all."

"Well, you can't go on exhibiting it, that's plain. I'll take charge of it. You'd recognise it again? Just write your initials on it—here's a pen—to make sure."

Stoke, who moment by moment was becoming more conscious of the bad taste of his proceedings, was glad enough to comply. Sir Clinton let the ink dry, and then put the case into his pocket.

"We'll say no more about it, Stoke. Just thoughtlessness, wasn't it? 'Of course, of course,' as a friend of mine would say.

And thanks for letting me see the rest of your collection. It's been well worth a visit." He glanced at his watch. "Time we thought of moving, isn't it, Wendover?"

Stoke showed them out, his heart full of gratitude for the kindly way in which Sir Clinton had dealt with the matter. He was beginning to realise what might have happened had Inspector Hinton been in the Chief Constable's place.

"Stoke's a decent fellow," Wendover said defensively as they drove off. "These people have no imagination, you know, Clinton. He didn't realise in the least what annoyance that exhibit of his might have given to the Brandons."

"I'm not blaming him," Sir Clinton assured him. "In fact, it's on the cards that he's done us a good turn without knowing it."

"If your inspector hadn't turned up his nose at Stoke's invitation, he'd have got ahead of you there," Wendover pointed out with a spice of malice. "With his talent for noting the obvious, he couldn't have missed seeing that exhibit."

"Hinton is a little lacking in human sympathy," the Chief Constable admitted. "Anyone could see how proud that gardener is of his grotesque collection, and it didn't cost much to pay it a visit. See how virtue is rewarded! Still, Hinton writes a first-class report, you know."

"I don't quite see what you expect to get out of that cartridge-case," Wendover mused. "It came out of young Brandon's gun, apparently. But you've got the gun itself, and you could fire a shot from it yourself any time."

"Just what I'm going to do, Squire. Your appreciation of the obvious runs Hinton neck and neck, if I may say so."

They were running into the village, and before Wendover could reply, Sir Clinton gave a sudden exclamation:

"Here! Stop, Squire. I want to buy a bottle of Milton. Where can I get it?"

"At Copdock's, I expect," Wendover answered, drawing up the car before the door of the shop.

Sir Clinton went in and returned again in a few moments with a little parcel.

"Get it?" Wendover inquired, as he let in the clutch.

"Yes," Sir Clinton said as he stowed the bottle in his pocket.

"What do you want it for?" demanded Wendover inquisitively.

"Eye-wash."

"Eye-wash?" Wendover exclaimed incredulously. "You aren't going to put hypochlorite in your eye, are you?"

"A slip of the tongue," Sir Clinton apologised gravely. "I'm going to see if it will take out a stain, really. And I can always use the rest as a mouthwash. Waste not, want not."

"Brilliant idea!" said Wendover crossly, as he recognised that his friend had given the facts without the explanation.

When they reached the Grange it was still early for luncheon. Sir Clinton went to his room and came back with a slim volume, in which he at once became engrossed. A casual glance showed Wendover that the dust-cover bore an arresting picture of a brown-faced individual with green eyes, holding a talisman.

"A thriller?" he inquired.

Sir Clinton shook his head impatiently at the interruption and shifted his hand so that Wendover could read the lettering: "THE PROPHECIES OF THE BRAHAN SEER."

"Oh, that thing?" he said, enlightened. "There was a copy of it knocking about the house when I was a boy. I remember reading it then. But it was a pamphlet bound in dull green with a white label. Nothing so flamboyant as this affair you've got."

"This is a new edition, Squire. Came out this year, luckily, or I might have had a devil of a hunt for a second-hand copy. I'm going to Fairlawns this afternoon, and I'm refreshing my memory to make sure of getting on the right side of friend Dunne. Damn this stone of Coinneach's! Sometimes they say it was white, sometimes they say it was blue."

"It's green, according to the picture on the jacket," Wendover pointed out helpfully. "That gives you plenty of choice."

"So far as I'm concerned, it'll have to be just 'a stone' until I get a look at friend Dunne's talisman and see what colour it ought to be. And kindly remember, Squire, if you come along with me, you'll have to be a true believer. I want none of this nasty sceptical atmosphere about, when I'm dealing with a re-incarnation of Coinneach Odhar Fiosaiche. Take your cue from me and be surprised, but not too much surprised, at anything he gives us. And now, just shut up, please, and let me get on with my lithomantic studies."

CHAPTER 16
THE STONE AND
THE BONE

"I've heard it objected, Mr Dunne, that some of Coinneach's prophecies could have been made by an exceptionally shrewd man without any supernatural insight to help him. Take that one about full-rigged ships sailing round the back of Tomnahurich Hill, for instance. Admittedly it was made a century and a half before the Caledonian Canal was cut. Still, there were the three lochs in a straight line between the Inverness Firth at one end and Loch Linnhe at the other. A clever man might easily have foreseen that a little cutting would make the whole system into one water-way."

The Chief Constable spoke in the tone of one who would like to believe if he could, but who was still hampered by some last doubts. Mr Dunne rose to the bait.

"But would any 'natural shrewdness' cover the other prophecy about Tomnahurich?" he demanded. "Dun Kenneth foretold that it would be put under lock and key, and the spirits would be secured within. Could anyone in his day have guessed that, a couple of centuries later, Tomnahurich would be a cemetery, enclosed and locked and with the spirits of the dead within its bounds?"

"Very remarkable," Wendover commented, playing the part which Sir Clinton had assigned to him. "Difficult to get over that, I think."

Dunne evidently felt that Sir Clinton was on the brink of conversion, if only these last few doubts could be dispelled.

"To my mind," he said, "the most convincing thing is this. Some of the prophecies have been fulfilled by inventions which were undreamed-of in Dun Kenneth's day. He had no way of describing clearly what he saw in his vision. The underlying ideas were outside his scope completely. He had to make shift with words as best he could. Now take the case of that prediction, 'The day will come when fire and water shall run through all the streets and lanes of Inverness.' That represents his attempt to describe the gas-pipes and water-mains, of course. Lighting by gas wasn't dreamed of in his day. He had no words to fit his vision, and yet he made a recognisable attempt to tell us what he saw. Then again, 'The day will come when long strings of carriages without horses shall run between Dingwall and Inverness.' Just imagine a man in the early sixteen hundreds being shown a railway train. What would he have made of it? Would he not have described the railway in just those very terms?"

He glanced triumphantly at Sir Clinton, who nodded his head as though admitting the force of the argument.

"I give in," said the Chief Constable, with a smile. "In any case, no natural shrewdness could have predicted the Doom of the Seaforths so accurately. Tell Mr Wendover about that, Mr Dunne."

Dunne was nothing loath.

"Dun Kenneth was put to death by Lady Seaforth," he explained, "and when he was about to die, he prophesied that the last chief of the clan would be both deaf and dumb. He would have four sons, all of whom would die before their father. And in that day there would be four great lairds—Gairloch, Chisholm, Grant, and Ramsay—who would be neighbours of the last Seaforth. And one would be buck-toothed, another would be hare-lipped, a third half-witted, and the last a stammerer. That prophecy was fulfilled to the very letter, Mr Wendover, when the last of the Seaforth chiefs died in 1815—more than two centuries after Dun Kenneth had spoken."

"That's amazing," Wendover ejaculated, without the need to feign astonishment. "There's no explaining that away by guesswork or chance coincidence. Marvellous!"

"And now, Mr Dunne, you promised to show us Coinneach's talisman, you remember," Sir Clinton reminded him.

Dunne was nothing loath. He opened a drawer and produced the stone which Inspector Hinton had seen at an earlier date.

"This is Coinneach Odhar Fiosaiche's talisman," he said solemnly, as he handed it to Sir Clinton. "I found it on the shore of the loch into which he cast it on the day of his death. When he threw it away, he prophesied that its finder would be gifted as he himself was."

Sir Clinton took the stone and seemed to muse for a moment.

"Coinneach Odhar—Dun Kenneth," he said absently. And your name is Kenneth also, isn't it, Mr Dunne? That's a very curious coincidence—if it *is* a coincidence."

He turned the stone over in his hand.

"And have you inherited Coinneach's gifts?" he asked.

Dunne shook his head despondently.

"Sometimes I see vague . . . it's hard to find a word for them . . . not quite pictures, they are," he said in a half-doubting tone. "Nothing really clear," he added honestly.

Sir Clinton's attention seemed to be caught by the little tube of pasteboard inserted into the hollow of the stone.

"What's this?" he inquired curiously.

"I thought perhaps the hole had been widened by wear, during all these centuries," Mr Dunne explained, "and I pushed that tube into the cavity to bring it back to its original size or near it. I thought it might make all the difference. But the visions are still too vague for me to understand them," he concluded in a disheartened tone which touched Wendover's feelings.

"I think I might help you," Sir Clinton said slowly. "By the way, Mr Dunne, where did you pick up this bit of cardboard?"

"In a wood, on the edge of a stream. There was a dead body near by," Mr Dunne explained in the most matter-of-fact way.

Sir Clinton exchanged a glance with Wendover. Evidently Dunne's memory of events after the crucial moment was fairly clear.

The Chief Constable turned the stone in his hand as though not quite sure of his ground.

"It occurs to me," he said to Dunne in a half-hesitating voice, "that perhaps you've done more harm than good by inserting this thing into the talisman. You're an expert in such things. I'm the merest amateur. Still, one hears of natural sympathies and antipathies, doesn't one? Suppose this had been a loadstone and you inserted an iron tube into it, wouldn't that have a bad effect on the magnetic properties of the loadstone?"

"I believe it might," Dunne concurred with a gleam of hope in his face. "And you think . . .?"

"My impression is that if you're going to put anything into that cavity, it ought to be of the same nature as the stone itself. This is quartz, isn't it?"

"Yes, it's quartz," Dunne assured him with almost painful eagerness.

Sir Clinton seemed to reflect for some seconds.

"These things are beyond me," he admitted at last. "One can but try, and luckily trying can do no harm. They make silica tubes now out of fused quartz. Now if I get you a tube of silica to fit that hole, will you give it a trial, Mr Dunne? It might help. It might be no good. Still, it's worth trying, I think."

Dunne's depression seemed to pass off in a pathetic wave of hope.

"If you could, Sir Clinton!"

"We must have it made to the exact size," the Chief Constable pointed out. "This cardboard affair would serve as a model. It's no use to you. I'll take it, and get a duplicate made in quartz for you. It's no trouble. I know where these things can be done."

Dunne, evidently excited by a renewal of his hopes, made no objection. In fact, he pressed the tiny object on Sir Clinton with a flood of warm thanks.

When they had taken their leave of him and were back in the

car, Wendover turned to his guest with an air of disapproval.

"You're rather a beast, Clinton, deluding that poor devil as you did."

Sir Clinton shrugged his shoulders.

"He's no worse off than before," he said. "In fact, he's happier, owing to my kindness. For a week at least, until he gets this quartz tube, he'll be living in a pipe-dream of expectancy, gloating over the coming visions. I've given him that, and he wouldn't have had it without me."

"I hadn't thought of it in that way," Wendover acknowledged.

"Besides," Sir Clinton continued, "I had to get hold of that bit of cardboard. If I'd insisted on taking it from him, he'd have been terribly upset, I expect. But with a little tact, one can get what one wants without ruffling people's feelings, as you see."

"What is it?" Wendover inquired. "I didn't get much of a look at it before you slipped it into your pocket."

Sir Clinton took out the little object, and Wendover stopped the car to examine it. He saw a ring of greencovered paste-board which seemed faintly familiar. Then as he turned it round in his fingers he read

BRI
SMOK
CART

Above this was a printed ring with part of some animal's head in the centre and the inscription: "KYN . . . Trad . . ." round about. The rest of the printing had been cut away. Wendover had no difficulty in filling the blanks: "BRITISH SMOKELESS CART-RIDGE. KYNOCH. Trade Mark." His memory told him that this little ring had been cut from the shot-filled end of a sporting cartridge; and a closer inspection showed the knife-mark where the cut had been made. The other end of the ring had a rough edge, where the turn-over had been blown out in the discharge of the shot. Apparently the ring had fitted neatly into the cavity of the stone, for there was no sign of crushing or abrasion on the smooth paper surface.

"How did you know to look for this?" Wendover asked, as he returned it to Sir Clinton.

"I told you that Hinton writes excellent reports," the Chief Constable answered as he stowed the little object in his pocket. "He saw this thing—Dunne forced it on his notice, in fact. He knew where it came from, for Dunne made no secret of it. The finding of it was a check on Dunne's memory, so Hinton entered it up in his report. That's how I knew. Quite simple."

"It's a bit cut off the top of an exploded cartridge?"

"The cartridge it came from is the same make as the ones they were using that morning," Sir Clinton pointed out. "I haven't got the covering-disk; but I've no doubt it had Number Five shot in it, like the others."

"What do you make of it?" Wendover demanded.

"It's more fun to work out a puzzle than to look up the answer," Sir Clinton pointed out. "I'd hate to deprive you of that pleasure, Squire. Excellent practice for the rural brain, especially for a sporting man like yourself. Think away. It's plain enough, since you've got all the facts from Hinton's reports. And while you're cogitating, suppose you buzz along to Dr Aloysius Brinkworth's. I made an appointment with him this afternoon, and we're just about due."

They found Dr Brinkworth in his consulting-room awaiting them, and the Chief Constable plunged at once into the business in hand.

"I shan't detain you long, Dr Brinkworth," he explained. "I merely wish to ask one or two questions. You carried out the post-mortem on Mr John Brandon's body?"

"Yes," Dr Brinkworth acknowledged. "I have my notes here . . . er . . . if you wish to see them."

"Hardly worth while, unless you wish to refer to them yourself," Sir Clinton assured him. "Now what did you give as the

226

cause of his death?"

"Er . . . I put it down that he died from shock resulting from a gunshot injury to the skull and brain, with subsequent loss of blood."

"Shock, one can understand. The points I wish to be clear about are the injury and the haemorrhage. Never mind about the surface injuries, the skin, and so forth. I've read about these. A bone was injured, wasn't it?"

"Er . . . yes . . . the right temporal bone. It lies here," Dr Brinkworth explained, passing his fingers to and fro from his eye to the top of his ear on the right side. "That bone was badly damaged by the shot and part of it was broken off."

"This part?" Sir Clinton asked, taking out a little box and showing the piece of bone he had got from the inspector.

"Yes . . . er . . . that part, that is a bit of the so-called petrous part of the temporal bone. It's one of the hardest bones in the skeleton."

Sir Clinton seemed to think for a moment before putting his next question.

"If this petrous fragment got detached by the force of the shot on the outer part of the temporal bone, it might be driven inward, mightn't it?"

"Er . . . I think that's correct. It might be forced forward and inward, possibly."

"So that it would be bedded on soft tissue?"

"Yes, that is so."

Sir Clinton seemed satisfied with this.

"Now, Dr Brinkworth, I'm no anatomist, so you must help me to understand. In the case of a gun-shot like that, where would the blood come from?"

Dr Brinkworth considered for a few moments.

"Er . . . Mainly, I think, from the principal vein there, the lateral sinus."

"Does that run in the neighbourhood of where this petrous bone would land among the tissues after its detachment from the main block of the temporal bone?"

Dr Brinkworth closed his eyes and seemed to be visualising the relative positions of the objects.

"Yes," he admitted, "the bone fragment would be lying near the vein. I think one might ... er ... go a step further and assume that the rupture of the vein was due to the action of this bit of the petrous bone."

"Now this is what I want to get at," Sir Clinton explained. "Suppose that state of affairs, is it not just on the cards that this petrous fragment, after rupturing the vein, remained *in situ* and plugged the wound in the vein so as to prevent an immediate haemorrhage?"

"I hadn't ... er ... thought of that point; but you're quite right, Sir Clinton. Undoubtedly the bone fragment might block the tear it had made and prevent any effusion—any marked effusion, at any rate."

"But if there was a second shock of any sort, the bone might be slightly displaced and a flow of blood might occur?"

"Yes. Assuming, of course, that the second shock was not too long delayed."

"A good shake, or anything of that sort, would do it? And this fragment of the bone might be loosened from its temporary bed and might drop out of the main wound, or it might be carried out by a heavy flow of blood if there was one, owing to the position of the body?"

"That might quite well happen," Dr Brinkworth agreed. "How did you come to think of this, Sir Clinton? It's very ... er ... ingenious."

"But not to my credit," Sir Clinton said with a smile. "The defence pleaded it in one of the most famous shooting cases when I was in my cradle. I've read about it, and it struck me that something of the same sort might have happened here."

He returned the bone fragment to its box and rose from his chair.

"Thanks for your help, Dr Brinkworth. You could, of course, give evidence on this point, if necessary?"

Dr Brinkworth concurred without ado, though with the

qualification that the matter was one of opinion rather than of fact. Sir Clinton and Wendover took their leave and went back to the car.

"So that puts a blue pencil through Hinton's notion about Laxford's evidence," Wendover remarked with a trace of *Schadenfreude*, as they drove off towards the Grange. "The boy was shot on the edge of the ha-ha and fell on to the ground below, just as Laxford said. But there was no blood on the grass there because this bit of bone plugged the big vein. Then when they shifted the body, the jolt loosened the bone. Out it came, and the vein began to bleed. That's it, isn't it?"

"It's mostly hypothetical," Sir Clinton pointed out. "But it wouldn't surprise me if it had happened. And now, Squire, let's get home quick. I've got young Brandon's diary to read over. To judge from what one's heard, he seems to have been a simple soul, poor cub. We'll see if the diary bears that out."

CHAPTER 17 THE ASSIGNMENT

"Here we are, then," said the Chief Constable cheerfully, as the car pulled up before The Cottage. "A yard or two farther on, I think, Wendover. Leave room for Hinton. He's just coming."

As Jim Brandon stepped out of the big saloon, the inspector's car drew up immediately behind, so that in moving towards The Cottage gate, Jim had to pass its windows. He halted momentarily as his eye lighted upon Hay, sitting in the back seat between two impassive uniformed constables. Jim's glance seemed to make him uneasy, for after an attempt to brazen things out, he turned his head and stared sullenly through the farther window.

The inspector got down from his driving-seat and went up to Sir Clinton, who was standing at the gate with a small attaché-case in his hand.

"What about *him*, sir?" Hinton inquired in a low tone as he made a covert gesture towards Hay.

"We don't need him immediately," Sir Clinton answered. "Leave him in charge of your men for the present, in the car."

"And about a warrant, sir?"

From the inspector's intonation, it was clear that he was nursing a grievance. He had received his orders, but no explanation of them had been vouchsafed to him, and his dignity had been offended by this procedure. He guessed, from the Chief Constable's preparations, that the case was coming to a crisis, and the failure to provide a warrant seemed to him a gross oversight on the part of his superior.

"I'm not sure we shall need a warrant," Sir Clinton replied cautiously. "I haven't heard what Hay has to say for himself yet. You've told him nothing? Asked no questions that might put him on the alert?"

"No, sir. I've done exactly as you ordered," Hinton explained, with an air of throwing all responsibility on his superior.

"Very well. Then we'd better go in, now. I got Mr Wendover to ring up and make an appointment with Mr Laxford, to make sure he'd be on the spot; but I don't suppose he's expecting half the local police force to drop in on him. It'll be a pleasant surprise, no doubt."

The inspector grudgingly admitted to himself that Wendover had his uses. That move would enable them to descend on Laxford like a bolt from the blue. Much better than ringing up officially and giving him time to prepare himself for the interview. Very much better than swooping down in force, only to find that Laxford was not on the premises.

The Cottage was built on much less generous lines than Edgehill, and when the four of them were ushered into its sitting-room they made it seem almost crowded.

"My friend, Sir Clinton Driffield," said Wendover in an easy tone, as Laxford rose to his feet. "He wants to see you about something or other, Mr Laxford, so I came across to introduce him. You know the inspector, of course, and Mr Brandon also."

Laxford's glance flitted from one to another of his undesired guests as he mechanically acknowledged Wendover's introduction. He seemed doubtful of Sir Clinton, distrustful of the inspector, and resentful of Jim Brandon's presence. His face was pale, and it was clear that this invasion in force had come as a most unpleasant shock.

"You won't mind answering a question or two, Mr Laxford?" Sir Clinton said briskly, as though he took consent for granted and was anxious to get through some purely formal business as quickly as possible.

Laxford glanced again round the group: at Wendover who had effaced himself when his part was played, at the inspector's hard eyes in the official mask, at Jim Brandon's lowering face, and at Sir Clinton awaiting his answer with an encouraging smile.

"Am I bound to answer questions?" he demanded with a touch of sullenness.

The encouraging smile vanished.

"You're not bound to; but it might be awkward if you didn't," the Chief Constable answered coldly.

Laxford studied the carpet at his feet for some seconds while he considered his course. At last he seemed to see a way.

"Perhaps if you put your questions . . .?" he suggested tentatively.

"Very well. It's come to our knowledge that John Brandon's life was insured for £25,000, and that just before his death he assigned the policy to your wife. Is that correct?"

Wendover saw Laxford wince. He had the look of a man who finds that an expected blow has got home at last, and despite his efforts fear showed in his eyes. He did not answer immediately, and Sir Clinton, with unusual testiness, broke in.

"That's merely a formal question, Mr Laxford. We have all the facts. You may as well answer."

Laxford made a nervous gesture.

"There was an assignment of the sort," he admitted in a low voice.

"You have it here, I suppose? Kindly let me see it." Sir Clinton directed. Then, as Laxford appeared to demur, he added sharply, "It's not a confidential document, Mr Laxford. You'll have to produce it to claim the money. And we can always insist on seeing it, if necessary, through the insurance company. There's no need to put difficulties in our way since it's bound to come out in the end."

Laxford recognised that Sir Clinton had the whip hand. Procrastination would serve no purpose. He rose from his chair, went to a little cupboard, searched among some papers, and produced the required document. Sir Clinton unfolded it and, after a casual glance through it, handed it over to the inspector. Opening his attaché-case he took out some sheets of quarto paper.

"Make a copy of that assignment," he directed, passing the blank paper to Hinton. "You can use that table over there to write on. And, by the way," he added, "copy it line for line, just as it is."

"Very good, sir," Hinton said, as he set to work.

Sir Clinton closed his attaché-case again and made no effort to continue his examination of Laxford until the inspector had completed his task. Then he took back the original assignment and turned to Laxford.

"I notice a phrase here, 'for value received.' Would you be good enough to explain its precies meaning?"

Laxford had evidently not expected this question, but he made an attempt to side-track it.

"Isn't a contract void, unless it mentions some 'valuable consideration'? One has to put that in, or else there's no contract at all."

"Do you mean that in this case 'for value received' was merely eye-wash?" Sir Clinton inquired.

"Oh, no," Laxford protested. "My wife had been at considerable expense in providing him with food, lodging, clothes, and so forth. The Brandon family"—he shot a malicious glance at Jim—"had made promises which were never implemented, and my wife had to foot the bill."

"Hardly to the extent of £25,000, though, surely." Sir Clinton pointed out. "But in any case, past services are not a 'valuable consideration' in a contract, I believe. I'm not a lawyer, and I may be wrong. But that's my impression."

"I only mentioned these things as examples," Laxford declared, but it was evident that Sir Clinton's dictum had disturbed him. "It was arranged that my wife was to find a large sum of money for him when he came of age, in connection with the Brandon estate."

"Then her promise to do this was the 'valuable consideration'?"

"It was," said Laxford, with the air of a man who has got well out of a tight corner.

Sir Clinton turned to Jim Brandon.

"Was any document to that effect among your brother's papers?"

Jim shook his head contemptuously.

"Curious," Sir Clinton said musingly. "However, that's your affair, I suppose, Mr Laxford, if Mr Brandon's executors contest the validity of this document. And, by the way, there's another thing that invalidates this kind of contract. They call it 'undue influence.'"

"I never brought any pressure to bear on him to sign that," Laxford declared boldly, with a curious ring in his voice.

"You needn't tell lies," Jim Brandon interrupted savagely. "I know all about your games—you, and your wife, and that Hay fellow. You put the screw on Johnnie and made him sign that thing. It's not worth denying it. I can believe my own ears and I was out in the garden that night, I may tell you."

"That'll do, Mr Brandon," said Sir Clinton sharply. You're not here for that sort of thing."

He turned back to Laxford and put a plain question.

"You didn't exercise any moral pressure to obtain John Brandon's signature to this document?"

"No, I did not," said Laxford with equal bluntness, and Wendover was surprised to find that his tone gave the impression that he was telling the literal truth.

Sir Clinton seemed in no way surprised.

"I think I see your point," he said quietly.

Wendover was again surprised, for Laxford did not seem pleased by this. Rather the reverse, it appeared, from his looks. He glanced suspiciously at the Chief Constable, as though that last sentence had made him more uneasy than Jim Brandon's outburst. And then came a third surprise; for Sir Clinton, with the game apparently in his hands, dropped the subject and turned to a fresh aspect of the affair. He picked up the assignment and passed it across to Jim Brandon.

"That's in your brother's handwriting, isn't it?"

Jim studied it for some minutes with almost meticulous care, scanning it word by word and occasionally going back to an earlier line to make comparisons. It was plain that he meant to find a flaw in it if that were possible. But as time passed, his face showed disappointment more and more plainly. At last he gave it up, with something that sounded like a sigh of disappointment, and handed back the paper to the Chief Constable.

"It seems to be my brother's writing," he admitted, though with the most obvious reluctance.

"So I expected," Sir Clinton said, with a rather bleak smile. "A document of this sort is more convincing when it's a holograph. I suppose you saw him write it, Mr Laxford?"

"Yes, that's so," Laxford admitted.

"You didn't dictate it, of course?"

"Oh, no," Laxford declared flatly, and again Wendover was impressed by the ring of truth in the tone.

"My brother never wrote that off his own bat," Jim Brandon broke in. "It's not his style, even if it's his writing."

"We may come to that in a moment," Sir Clinton said, with a gesture which silenced Jim. "Just one more question, Mr Laxford. You signed this as a witness, didn't you? Did you put your signature to it when it was written?"

"Yes," Laxford asserted.

"You're quite sure about that? Your memory isn't playing you a trick?"

"I'm quite sure."

Jim Brandon made a movement as though about to say something, then, apparently, he thought better of it and leaned back in his chair. Evidently he felt he was trying the Chief Constable's patience too highly by his repeated interruptions. Sir Clinton, after a glance at him, opened his attaché-case again and took out the volume which Wendover recognised as Johnnie's diary.

"You recognise this, I think, Mr Laxford? And you, Mr Brandon? It's your brother's diary, isn't it? It's not a confidential affair like Pepys's Diary, and I suppose he didn't keep it under lock and key."

"Miss Menteith told me it lay about the house, anywhere," Jim confirmed. "I found it myself in the smoking-room after his death."

Sir Clinton opened the volume and turned over some pages.

"Anyone might read it," he commented. "For instance, here's an entry: 'August 7th. Read my books for two hours. Went into Ambledown with Una in car. She shopped and I got back my shoes re-soled. In afternoon, went fishing. Di came along. Caught three trout, biggest a half-pounder. Sprained my ankle jumping down bank. Di helped me home. Played bridge in evening. Ankle rather swollen.' Quite commonplace, evidently. Here's another: '28th July. Took a day off. Shot a brace of rabbits and one wood-pigeon. Helped Una to clean car. In afternoon, with Una to the Grange. She beat me 3 up and 2. Off my game. Took out boat on lake after that. After dinner, walk in garden with Di. Billiards later with Mr L.'"

Wendover, listening to these innocuous chronicles, was surprised to see the effect which they had upon Laxford. To him they seemed to convey some esoteric meaning which was completely veiled from the rest of the audience; and though he kept himself in hand, his dilated eyes betrayed his deepening uneasiness as Sir Clinton passed from the first entry to the second.

The Chief Constable picked up the assignment and seemed to compare something in its upper half with the two entries in the diary, while Laxford watched him with strained attention. Then he closed the volume and settled himself comfortably in his chair.

"This is a second edition, isn't it?" he asked Laxford, with a gesture towards the assignment on the table before him.

Laxford's lips seemed to have gone dry. He passed his tongue over them nervously before answering.

"I don't quite follow you."

"I'll put it plainer," Sir Clinton answered with a faint gesture of apology. "There was an earlier document assigning this £25,000 policy to Mrs Laxford, wasn't there?"

"I don't see the point," Laxford retorted huskily. "Why should there have been any other?"

"Well," Sir Clinton pointed out, "on 15th August Mr John Brandon wrote to the Mersey and Midland Insurance Company, saying that he had assigned his £25,000 policy to Mrs Laxford. Therefore, on 15th August, some assignment must have been in existence. It couldn't be this one, for this one's dated 28th August, a fortnight later than the date of his letter. Hence there must have been a previous assignment. Q.E.D."

"Yes," Laxford muttered. ""I remember now. There was an earlier document. It slipped my memory for the moment."

"That earlier assignment was, of course, invalid, since John Brandon was a minor on 15th August. I infer that the person who induced him to make the assignment learned a little more about the law between the middle of August and the end of the month. But that's mere surmise on my part. Don't let's discuss it. We've more important things to talk about."

The Chief Constable picked up the assignment and glanced over it casually.

"A holograph's much more convincing than a typewritten document in a case like this," he said reflectively. "And in this case we've had the handwriting vouched for by Mr James Brandon, who has no incentive to identify it, seeing that it tells against the financial interests of his father. The signature's all right, because it was witnessed by Mr Laxford and a Mr Joseph Hay. The body of the document's all right, for no ordinary person could forge such a long story well enough to deceive Mr Brandon. That leaves only the date . . . Do you find the room too hot, Mr Laxford? . . . No? then that's all right. I can go on."

A glance at Laxford's face showed Wendover that the Chief Constable had touched a sore point in his last few words.

"Ah, yes, the date, as I was saying," Sir Clinton continued blandly. "A date is a very short bit of writing; and a date makes a lot of difference, in some cases—in this case, for example, when a boy is coming of age."

Wendover saw Laxford's face lose its colour as though the blood were answering some call.

"Now here's a hypothetical case," Sir Clinton proceeded with a slight increase in suavity. "John Doe, a minor, makes a written assignment on or before August 15th. A few days later, Richard Roe, who has an indirect interest in the assignment, discovers that it is invalid, because John Doe is under age. Richard Roe persuades John Doe to make a fresh assignment, let us say on 24th August, when a visitor, Joseph Hoe, is available as a witness. Richard Roe sets John Doe down at a table with pen, ink, and paper, and proceeds to dictate from the existing assignment. But he begins his dictation with the words: 'In consideration of value received . . .' And John Doe obediently writes that down and continues under the dictation. Now John Doe is a simple youngster, not much versed in business, and he doesn't notice that no date was dictated to him. So the dictation continues to the end; John Doe signs; and Richard Roe and Joseph Hoe obligingly add their signatures as witnesses. That gives Richard Roe an assignment, undated.

"John Doe dies suddenly on 28th August, the morning when he came of age. Now if Richard Roe could put the date, 28th August, to the assignment, it would apparently be a valid assignment. I think you follow me?"

He lifted the document from the table and passed it to Wendover.

"I want you to read that over carefully, and then put your initials in the comer. Look at the date, specially."

Wendover scrutinised the assignment most minutely, but he detected nothing out of the common. After reading it through twice, he initialled it. Sir Clinton handed it to Jim Brandon with the same request. Jim, in his turn, pored over it, evidently in the hope of putting his finger on something amiss; but finally he initialled it and handed it back with a look of disappointment on his face.

"I'm not a skilled forger myself," Sir Clinton confessed, "so when I put myself into the position of the ordinary man who finds forgery essential to his comfort, I probably follow his line of reasoning more or less. Copying writing by freehand drawing would be beyond me. Tracing is as high as I could rise, if I had a model to trace from. Now in this case I put before you, all a forger needs in the way of a model is a date, and that date can be built up from the separate sections, '28th,' 'August,' and '1924.' Where can you get models for these in the original handwriting? Old letters, perhaps. Better still, a diary.

"But if the forgery is to be done in pen and ink, you come up against a practical difficulty. It's easy enough to cover a bit of manuscript with a sheet of plain paper, stick the combination up against the window-pane, and trace the thing in pencil. But you can't use ink in that position with satisfactory results, as you'll find if you try. You might trace in pencil that way, then write over the pencil tracing with ink, with the paper on a table. But pencil lines don't take ink over well; and besides, you'd have to use india-rubber later to remove the obvious pencil-marks; and that spoils the surface of the paper.

"A much sounder method is this. Put a sheet of carbon paper under your model, and your undated document under the carbon. Then trace over the model with a fine point—a pin fastened in a penholder does very well. That gives you a faint carbon tracing of your model, and you ink it in at leisure. Since the carbon ink is much the same colour as ordinary ink, you don't need to rub out anything; and if your model happens to be written in thick scrawly caligraphy, you can easily make your ink lines broad enough to cover the carbon tracing completely.

Sir Clinton reached over and picked up Johnnie's diary.

"Here we have a forger's model which gives all he wants. So I examined it with interest and a magnifying glass. It wasn't a long business. All I had to look at were the entries during 'August' and the '28th,' in each of the earlier months. When I came to the entry for August 7th—the one I read out to you first—the magnifying-glass showed up the trace of scratchings on the name of the month. The same thing occurred on the '28th' of

July. Now if we compare the '28th' and the 'August' of the assignment with these two entries in the diary, I think we'll find them identical. And it's only by the merest accident that a person writes a date twice in the same way, line for line."

He opened the diary at the entry for August 7th and spread out the assignment alongside. Wendover, Jim Brandon, and the inspector examined the two writings in turn. Laxford, crouching in his chair, had the look of a predatory creature brought to bay.

"All that's mere surmise, of course," Sir Clinton went on. "It needs something more to make it certain. You've no objection to my trying a little experiment, have you, Mr Laxford? It won't do any permanent damage to your assignment."

Laxford saw that he would have to go through it, and he pulled himself together sufficiently to give a husky permission. Sir Clinton re-opened his attaché-case and, to Wendover's surprise, took out the six-penny bottle of Milton which he had bought in the village. He also produced a small piece of cotton-wool.

"Now," he explained, as he spread the assignment on the table, "all I propose to do is to bleach one or two letters in this date. That doesn't destroy the ink, it merely decolorises it temporarily. The permanent record is still there and can be restored by another chemical. Let's try our luck."

He moistened the cotton-wool with some of the Milton solution and applied it carefully to the last four letters of "August" in the date. Swiftly the writing faded and, untouched by the chemical, a faint thin lettering stood out: "g u s t."

"The ink fades, as you see, but the Milton doesn't affect the carbon tracing, so it shows up clearly enough, doesn't it?"

Sir Clinton corked the bottle of Milton and put it back into his attaché-case.

"I think that converts the thing into proof," he said to Jim Brandon. "It's hardly likely that this assignment will make its appearance in court, now."

"We owe you one for that," Jim said cordially. "I'd never

have thought of it. And, of course, that fits in exactly with my brother telling me he had signed nothing, that morning."

"That was my starting-point when I began to think the thing out," Sir Clinton explained. "And now, Inspector, I think we might have Mr Joseph Hay, if you please."

At the sound of Hay's name, Laxford evidently recognised that the game was up. His face betrayed him, and Wendover was glad to look elsewhere. The inspector left the room, and in a minute or so returned, ushering Hay before him.

"Sit down, Mr Hay," Sir Clinton invited him. "Over there, beside Inspector Hinton. We want to ask you a question or two. Any objections?"

Hay glanced at Laxford. The game was up, evidently. His little piggish eyes took on a ruminative expression for a moment or two as he considered the course which would pay him best.

"What's it all about?" he demanded, obviously to gain time.

"This assignment, mainly. Let him see it, Inspector."

Hay glanced at the document, still thinking hard as his face showed.

"And what difference'll it make whether I answer or don't answer?" he demanded cautiously.

"Just the difference between a subpoena and a warrant," Sir Clinton assured him blandly. "Or, if you like it better, just the difference between the witness-box and the dock."

"Oh, I see," Hay replied with a shrewd look. "The witness-box suits me best. None o' this business about 'whatever you say will be taken down in writing and used as evidence against you,' eh?"

"All I promise you is a chance to make a clean breast of your share in the business of this assignment," Sir Clinton said bluntly. "You're not on oath, of course."

Hay reflected for a moment or two longer. Then he made up his mind.

"Well, I've nothin' to lose by it," he said confidently. "Ask away."

"Hurrying to the assistance of the victors," Sir Clinton commented with an ironic smile. "A sound policy, Mr Hay. Well, let's get to business. How long have you known Mr Laxford?"

"That's an easy one," Hay said impudently. "Three or four years is the tally. It was the year of Spion Kop's Derby."

"And when did you first meet Mr John Brandon?"

"Just before he came by his sad accident," Hay explained cheerfully. "Never set eyes on him before I came down here that time."

Wendover felt almost sorry for Laxford as his futile lies were thus exposed, one after another.

"Would you mind explaining, Mr Hay, what brought you down here. It was business, wasn't it?"

"Oh, I don't mind tellin' you," Hay assured him. "It's all plain and above-board, so far as I'm concerned. Quite straight. I've done nothin' I'm ashamed of."

"I quite believe that," Sir Clinton interrupted rather ambiguously. "But don't try to gain time by repeating yourself. The plain truth is all we want and you don't need to think before speaking it."

"Well, it was this way," Hay went on, quite unabashed. "I do a bit of business with Pluscarden the moneylender. Find him mugs with expectations and rake in a commission for introducin' them. See? Laxford put me wise about this young Brandon's expectations, and nat'rally I was on to it like tar. Cuttin' the story as short's a terrier's tail, Pluscarden's been financin' the Laxford lot for quite a while, payin' cheques to Mrs L on account o' Laxford here bein' an undischarged bankrupt. And all seemed as rosy as a pig's complexion with great hopes in the here-after, when young Brandon came of age and got his claws on some money. Nothin' wrong with that. All quite straight, and you can have my word for it.

"I suppose Laxford was standin' in with Pluscarden someways; but lately he began to think up a game on his own. I don't rightly know what it was. Somethin' to do with insurin' the boy and usin' the policy in some wangle or other over the estate. No business o' mine, so long's I stood in for a corner. The details were beyond me, and didn't matter a damn anyhow, so far's I was concerned. The bother was, Laxford hadn't a blue stiver and he needed bread-and-honey for the insurance premium. He got it out o' Pluscarden, with some yarn about buyin' this place and payin' a deposit. So poor old Pluscarden told me, and I never winked.

"Next move by Laxford was to get an assignment out o' young Brandon. He got it easy, for young Brandon was silly-simple, the kind o' mug you write with a capital M. But then Laxford found out it was no good because the youngster was under age; and by that time he'd paid the first premium. A most orkward state of affairs, wasn't it? Quite distressin', after all the bother he'd taken. That first assignment with its date on it was no better than . . . well, it was a good bit o' paper spoiled, and that was all it was.

"Laxford got a new notion, then, and asked me down here. He told the boy some yarn about a flaw in the first assignment—or so I suppose—and he dictated a new assignment, with me as a witness. Only, the new assignment hadn't a date on it."

"When was this done?" Sir Clinton inquired.

"It was the night I arrived here—Tuesday. That'd be the 24th of August."

"But Brandon was still a minor, then, and the new assignment was no more valid than the first one," Sir Clinton objected.

"That's so. But it had no date on it. That was the difference. You could fill in any date that suited you, later on; and if it was nobody's interest to ask questions, then that was all right."

"Why not simply have waited till Brandon came of age?"

Hay seemed to be enjoying his own revelations.

"Because we ain't got to the end yet," he explained. "There's another thrillin' instalment introducing that sex interest so necessary to the films. Laxford explained to me that he thought his young friend was gettin' a bit too fond of Mrs L. I was to keep my eye on 'em, if I didn't mind. I didn't, o' course. Always ready to help a friend, so long's there's something in it for me. And as it happened, I surprised the two o' them in compromising circumstances, as it says in the divorce reports. Shockin'! My modesty's hardly got over it yet."

"That was on August 27th?"

"It was. The reason for the hurry was that a shootin' party was arrivin' the next week and they'd have been all over the place and gettin' in the way, thus reducin' my chances of actin' as guardian of respectability. And I couldn't be stayin' on here indefinitely, waitin' till they'd finished their visit."

"In fact, you laid a trap for Brandon?"

"It's you that puts that interpretation on it, not me. Well, that, o' course, gave Laxford an extra hold on the boy if he wanted to use it. He could put any date he liked on the assignment and the boy wouldn't object. And yet Laxford could go into the box and swear that the boy hadn't been subject to any pressure when he wrote the assignment; and the boy would have to keep his mouth shut about the date."

"What was the point of all this manoeuvring?"

"Laxford was afraid that at the last moment young Brandon's family would get hold of him. As a matter of fact, Mr Brandon here"—he pointed to Jim—"turned up in the nick o' time, just as Laxford was anticipatin', and nearly bust the whole scheme."

"And what was this £25,000 policy to be used for?"

"Search me! I didn't inquire too closely. Some financial wangle in connection with young Brandon's estate, as I told you. But what it was all about, I didn't inquire."

Sir Clinton considered for some moments. Then he turned to the inspector.

"Mr Wendover will give you a warrant to arrest Thomas Laxford on a charge of attempting to obtain money on false pretences. You'd better go into another room and make a sworn declaration. Here's a Testament."

He took the little volume from his attaché-case and handed it to the inspector, who withdrew for a few minutes along with Wendover. When they returned, Hinton made his formal arrest and handed Laxford over to the constables who were waiting.

"Now, Inspector, you'll search these premises for any evidence you can get. Cheque-books, pass-books, and correspondence are what you'll need to look for, mainly. Take care of that assignment and John Brandon's diary."

He turned to Hay, who seemed to have taken Laxford's arrest as a matter of course.

"We're going to detain you for the present, Mr Hay. You'll spend your leisure in making a full statement—the fullest possible statement, please—in writing. The inspector will assist you with questions, I've no doubt. You gave us only an outline, just now. We want the details as well, you understand. Then I leave you to Inspector Hinton. He'll look after your comfort."

Hinton handed Hay over to the constables and followed Sir Clinton to the door, where he drew him aside from the others. The recent events had left the inspector a little crestfallen; for his judgment told him that, with all the evidence in his hands, he had failed to get as much out of it as the Chief Constable had done. Still, the main problem still faced them. All this business about the assignment was trifling in comparison with the issue of a capital charge.

"But what about the other business, sir?" he asked.

Sir Clinton's eyebrows lifted slightly.

"One can't expect to clear everything up at one swoop. You've got these two fellows under lock and key for the present, so that we can put our hands on them at any moment. That's something accomplished, isn't it? As to the other business, as you call it, the evidence isn't complete yet, and there's no need to hurry. Come up to the Grange tonight after dinner and we can talk it over."

"Very good, sir."

"And, by the way, Inspector, I congratulate you—quite unofficially—on the way you've collected the evidence in this affair. A very good bit of work. And your reports were admirable."

"Thank you, sir."

Hinton was not over-gratified by this praise, which he took to be merely his due. He saw his 'big case' eluding his grasp. The crucial thing in it was the assignment; and his fairness forced him to recognise that the Chief Constable was the man who had established the trickery of Laxford in that matter. All that Hinton had done was to reach the stage where Jim Brandon's oath would have been pitted against Laxford's evidence, and a jury might have believed one witness just as readily as the other. But that Milton experiment had gone to the root of the business and had exposed Laxford completely. And he acknowledged to himself that that experiment had been outside his scope.

Sir Clinton went out to the car and took his seat beside Jim Brandon.

"We'll drop you at Edgehill," he said.

Jim nodded his thanks for the courtesy.

"We owe you a good deal for that affair," he said gratefully. "If we'd had to fight a case against Laxford it would have cost a mint of money and we might have lost in the end. As it is, we get that £25,000 as a windfall; and it'll come in very useful. I always distrusted that fellow. He stuck at nothing."

CHAPTER 18 THE SOLUTION

When he presented himself at the Grange, late in the evening, Inspector Hinton hardly felt in his best form. At the back of his mind was the depressing conviction that, although he had ferreted out the main factors in the Edgehill drama, he had failed to score when it came to those finer details which may be all-important when placed before a jury. The Chief Constable had wiped his eye in that match; and while Hinton was honest enough to admit this to himself, still eye-wiping is not a pleasant process for the patient. Worst of all, he knew that he had not cleared up the actual shooting of young Brandon. On that crucial point, a sharp barrister might easily make hay of his case; for there was no denying that it did not hang together at all. Some of the facts seemed in flat contradiction with the rest.

When he was shown into the smoking-room where Wendover and his guest awaited him, it added to his annoyance to find that Sir Clinton was obviously in the best of spirits.

"Well, Inspector, you've got your men under lock and key," the Chief Constable greeted him. "And Mr Hay has made a clean breast of his share in the business? I was pretty sure he'd come across without difficulty."

"Oh, he squealed loud enough, sir. A pig with a knife in its throat couldn't have done more," Hinton declared coarsely. "I've got it all down in writing, signed and witnessed. So far as the minor charge goes, Laxford's number's up, sir. But . . ."

"But the shooting case is still about as clear as muddy water, you mean? Well, we can't afford to hang about till the mud settles. We'll have to filter it, metaphorically. The filtering apparatus is on the table over yonder. Perhaps we'd better bring it nearer to hand."

As they shifted the table into a more convenient position, Hinton noted the things which lay on it: the four guns, some empty cartridge-cases, and the little ring of pasteboard which he had last seen in Kenneth Dunne's talisman.

"You're not a shooting man, Inspector?" Sir Clinton asked, when they had settled down again. "No? Then in that case we'll take Mr Wendover's opinion."

He reached over and picked up one of the guns on the table.

"This is James Brandon's gun," he explained as he passed it to Wendover. "Have a look at the barrel and tell us what you make of it."

"It's a cylinder, apparently," Wendover pronounced, after a brief examination. "A fairly old gun, I should say, by the look of it."

"What Mr Wendover means is that the barrel has the same diameter all the way up from the chamber to the muzzle," Sir Clinton translated. "Now this is young Brandon's gun. What do you make of it?"

"A half-choke, by the look of it."

"And this one? It's the one Laxford started out with."

"Another half-choke," was Wendover's verdict.

"And now the last one, the one Hay went off with that morning."

"A full-choke."

"What Mr Wendover means is that in each of these last three guns there's a constriction in the barrel near the muzzle, so that the bore at the muzzle is smaller than the bore at the breech, where the cartridge-chamber is. I'm not going to give a lecture on ballistics, but the choke acts as a kind of mechanical 'shaker-up' of the column of moving shot, and tends to prevent the charge of shot from spreading as much as it does from a cylindrical barrel. You must have noticed that in your own experiments."

"I see, sir," the inspector hastened to declare, though in truth he could not make out what bearing this had upon the problem at issue.

"What we want to establish, if possible," Sir Clinton pointed out, "is simply this: which of these four guns actually killed young Brandon."

"Yes, sir, of course," the inspector agreed, "but I don't see that this gets us any nearer to it."

"Then we'll turn to the cartridge question next," Sir Clinton pursued. "Perhaps we may get some help there. When these guns came into your hands, you found—I'll take them in the same order as before—that James Brandon's gun was empty. It had been cleaned, dissembled, and packed away in its case, which is what one might have expected from a man who looked after his gun properly. So no cartridges were found in its barrels. In the barrels of young Brandon's gun, you found an empty case in the right barrel, and a live cartridge in the left barrel. Here they are, labelled. In Laxford's gun—which had been in Dunne's hands—you found two empty cases, these two which I've labelled like the others. In the gun that Hay used, you found no cartridges, used or unused. That's correct?"

"That's quite correct, sir," Hinton confirmed. He was thinking hard, but he could see no light in the affair at all. The Chief Constable, so far, had merely recapitulated the evidence which he himself had ferreted out.

"Now at this point," Sir Clinton went on, "you must take into account a little shuffle which occurred. Your friend Stoke, the gardener, has a passion for curiosities, as you'd have discovered if you'd accepted his invitation to inspect his museum. I strongly advise you to pay it a visit. Inspector. It's worth seeing."

Hinton had difficulty in repressing a snort of contempt. That miserable collection of rubbish! He'd heard about it. Nobody but a fool would waste time staring at trash of that sort. But the

Chief Constable's next words gave him a shock.

"To a man like Stoke any little curiosity is worth having, I should think. What would appeal to him more than the very cartridge which had killed a man? So, when he got an opportunity—as he very frankly explained to me—he pocketed the cartridge which was originally in the right barrel of young Brandon's gun after the tragedy. And to make sure that his larceny wasn't noticed, he replaced it. He took both the used cartridge-cases from Hay's gun, slipped one into the barrel from which he had taken the 'fatal' cartridge, pitched the second of Hay's empty cases out of the window. I found it when I looked for it, so that his tale's corroborated to that extent. And, further, you found Hay's two barrels empty yourself, which also fits in. So here"—he picked up one of the empty cases from the table —"is the actual empty case which was in the discharged barrel of young Brandon's gun when it got up to the gun-room at Edge-hill."

"How did you get on to this, sir?" Hinton asked, with a slight quiver in his voice.

He could not yet see what the Chief Constable was driving at, but he could guess from his tone that he regarded the empty case as important. And he, Inspector Hinton, had missed that bit of evidence. Damn!

"How did I get it?" Sir Clinton echoed. "I visited Stoke's museum and found it there, all neatly labelled and ready for me."

Hinton's feelings clamoured for unprintable expression, but with an effort he choked them down and maintained his official mask.

"Indeed, sir. Very interesting."

Sir Clinton busied himself with lighting a fresh cigarette and put the spent match in an ashtray before going on.

"Now we come to a rather interesting point. I've spent some minutes this evening in firing shots from young Brandon's gun, and also from the other guns, just in case there might have been any other little shuffles going on. Now here are the results."

He pointed to a number of spent cartridge-cases on the table.

"I don't see much use in that," Wendover interjected in a critical tone. "With a high-velocity firearm like an automatic, I'll admit, you get marks left by the breech-shield, the extractor, and the ejector on the soft brass of the cartridge-case. But the back-pressure in a shot-gun isn't big enough to leave any pattern of the breech-shield on the brass; and the extractor works far too gently to make a mark except by accident. You'll not get much out of that."

"Quite admitted," Sir Clinton agreed. "In fact, here are three cases got by firing from the right barrel of young Brandon's gun; and they're absolutely identical, with no marks on the brass. Still, there are variations, if one keeps one's eyes open for them."

He picked up two empty cases and handed them to Wendover who examined them side by side. The inspector leaned forward so that he also could see them.

"Just have a look at the ends," Sir Clinton suggested. "If you examine closely, you'll see that the indentation made by the striker on the cap isn't in the same place. In the one case, it's quite concentric with the rim of the cap—that's the cartridge I fired myself from the right barrel of young Brandon's gun. In the second case, the indentation's just a trifle off the centre. That's the cartridge-case that Stoke removed from the same barrel when the gun was back in the gun-room."

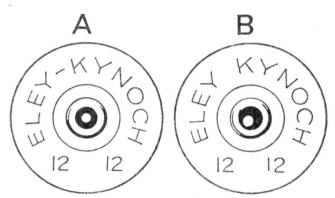

A is the cartridge fired by Sir Clinton.
B is the cartridge removed from the gun by Stoke.

"They're different," Wendover acknowledged after a careful scrutiny. "You fired several shots, and they all gave the same result?"

"Yes. The indentation of the striker's central in them all. You can see for yourself if you like; the cases are on the table, here."

The inspector rose and began to examine them sceptically; but Wendover's experience raised a further objection.

"What about the left barrel? Couldn't it come in?"

"I tested it, too," Sir Clinton rejoined. "Its striker gives a central indentation very like the right barrel's."

"Wait a moment till we think this out," Wendover requested. "It comes to this, doesn't it? The cartridge-case that Stoke found in young Brandon's right barrel hadn't been fired in young Brandon's gun at all, but had been fired in some other gun."

"That's correct," confirmed Sir Clinton.

"Therefore," Wendover pursued his argument, "someone must have slipped this spent cartridge into young Brandon's gun after the fatal shot was fired. But why should anybody do a thing like that? What was the point in hanky-panky of that sort?"

"This is where we leave sure ground and come to guess-work," Sir Clinton admitted cautiously, while the inspector pricked up his ears. "Now suppose young Brandon had reloaded after his last shot at a rabbit. He's found dead, with his head blown in. Accident with his own gun? Hardly, when both barrels have unfired cartridges in them. To make it look like an accident, you have to exchange one of these live rounds for a spent cartridge. They were all using the same make of cartridges, remember, so the exchange wouldn't be noticeable on a casual inspection. But on this hypothesis, that spent cartridge must have been fired in the gun of the murderer."

"Fits very neatly, that," Wendover admitted, while the inspector resumed his seat in glum silence. "And that gun must have been in the hands of one of the four people on the spot— Laxford, Hay, James Brandon, or Dunne. But wait a moment! It couldn't have been Dunne. He had two empty cases in his gun

252

and no other ammunition of any sort. So he hadn't a third case to put into young Brandon's barrel."

"And James Brandon's cleared as well," Hinton asserted. "He was on the other side of the stream—far too far off to shatter young Brandon's skull with a shot, the way it was shattered. I've proved that in these experiments of mine. So it comes down now to proving whether it was Hay or Laxford that fired the shot. Well, we've got 'em both under lock and key."

"I think we'd better get back on to the safe ground of hard fact," Sir Clinton suggested mildly. "That was mere hypothesis, you know. The crucial question is: 'Which gun fired the cartridge that Stoke found, empty, in young Brandon's gun?' I needn't beat about the bush and play the mystery man." He took a cartridge-case from his pocket and handed it to the inspector. "That's what I got when I fired a shot from James Brandon's gun. It's got the characteristic off-centre indentation, exactly the same as Stoke's one. There's no mistake possible. And none of the other guns gives anything like it."

The inspector compared the two brass ends in a fervid though unsuccessful effort to find some vital difference between them; but finally he gave in and handed them across to Wendover, who was waiting to examine them.

"I see no differences between 'em, sir, I admit," he conceded, though his tone suggested that very likely there might be a difference after all. "Still, you can't get over the fact that Brandon couldn't get to close range with his brother, and the boy was shot at close range."

"Young Brandon was shot on the right side of the head," Sir Clinton pointed out. "That is, on the side towards the stream."

"He might have turned his head to look towards his brother, sir, and Laxford or Hay, shooting from behind the bushes, could have hit him on the right side as he turned."

"And then how would the glancing charge have hit the twigs where you found the greatest breakage? It would have gone over the stream, on the line you're supposing."

Hinton gave up his objection, though not very graciously.

"You're quite right, sir. Still, the thing's impossible."

Sir Clinton cleared a space on the table and placed on it Jim Brandon's gun and the little ring which he had got from Dunne.

"I think we'll fall back on Mr Wendover's expert knowledge here," he said to the inspector. "Just tell us, Wendover, how one can alter the spread of shot from a sporting gun."

Wendover considered the problem for a few moments.

"Well, of course, if you use a smooth bore you get more spread than you do with a choke bore," he began. "That's one way of doing it. Or if you change the thickness of the felt wadding between the powder and shot, you can alter the spread. If you make the wadding thinner, you get more spread. Or you can get a bigger scattering by putting one or two thin card wads between layers of shot and using thin felt wads on top and bottom. Or else you can crimp your cartridge with an extra big turn-over. But that gives a nasty recoil and a poor shot-pattern."

"But suppose you want to doctor your cartridge to get *less* spread," Sir Clinton asked, "how would you go about it?"

"Some people make a little cage of wire-gauze to hold the shot," Wendover explained. "I've used that trick, but I'm not very keen on it. . . . By Jove! So that's why you asked the inspector if he'd seen any wire-gauze lying about. I ought to have tumbled to the point when you said that."

"Yes; but it wasn't done with wire-gauze," Sir Clinton rejoined. "It was done with this."

He held up the little ring of pasteboard with its broken inscription:

BRI

SMOK

CART

Wendover pored over it for awhile, then his eyes went to Jim

Brandon's gun, and his face lighted up with comprehension.

"Oh, I see! With a cylinder barrel, of course, it's possible. I'd forgotten his gun was a smooth bore. Is this how it was done? He cut into the pasteboard of the cartridge just at the powder end of the wad and left it hanging by a mere shred. When he fired, the shreds would give, and the whole mass of shot in this little tube, with a wad at top and bottom, would go out like a solid block. It would keep together for a fair distance and then the different momenta of the various components would begin to sift them out, and the thing would disintegrate. But for a fair distance the whole contraption would hang together as if it were a single projectile; and even after the ring dropped away, the shot would be lumped together and give the effect of a short-range normal shot. Of course it only works with smooth bores; a choke in the barrel would block the way and probably burst the gun. That's the general idea of the business, isn't it?"

"More or less," Sir Clinton agreed. "And that accounts for Dunne finding this ring of pasteboard casing on the slope between the ha-ha and the stream. One had to fit in that cut cartridge somehow, and you see it gives roughly the line of fire, for it must have lain somewhere between young Brandon and his brother's gun."

"Then where did James Brandon shoot from, sir?" the inspector inquired sceptically.

"As I work it out, roughly, he was hidden amongst the bushes a little down-stream from the elbow that the river makes just opposite the glade. We'll have to go there tomorrow and see if we can find any footprints. It was muddy weather and there may be some. Bring a quarter stone of plaster of Paris and a tin basin, on the off-chance that we may be lucky to get a cast."

"Well, sir," the inspector admitted grudgingly, "you seem to have an answer for everything. But there's one thing you haven't brought out," he added, fighting grimly to the last.

"And that is?"

"The motive, sir. You haven't produced any reason why James Brandon shot his brother."

Sir Clinton gave him a quizzical glance.

"Ever read Lewis Carroll's *Hunting of the Snark*? No? It's a pity to see the classics neglected. As the Snark says:

Let me tell you, my friends, the whole question depends
On an ancient manorial right.

A curious old custom, at least. I believe that in the course of this case you heard the phrase, 'borough English.' Do you remember what it means?"

The inspector shook his head gloomily. There seemed to be no end to the things he had overlooked in this infernal case.

"It's a system of inheritance still in vogue in the case of a few estates. A kind of survival, like gavel-kind. Instead of the estate going to the eldest son, as in the normal case, under 'borough English' it goes to the youngest surviving son. Young John Brandon was the heir to the Brandon estate, so long as no younger heir was born. I gather that no younger heir is likely to be born, owing to the particular disease that old Brandon suffers from. So when his father died, John Brandon would have come into the estate if he had survived. You can see how that made him so important, both to the Brandon family and to Laxford, who was manoeuvring to get a finger into the pie. But supposing young Brandon was out of the way, who came next in the succession? James Brandon, of course. And even in my short acquaintance with him, I got the idea that money bulked very large in James Brandon's cosmos. He talks as if it did, anyhow. There's your motive, Inspector; and a big enough one, too, for the Brandon estate isn't three acres and a cow, as you'll find if you look it up. That was what James Brandon stood to gain in this affair."

"Then you mean to arrest him, sir?"

"Immediately, of course. In fact, Mr Wendover will give you a warrant now, and you'd better take him at once. That gives you three people under lock and key, and if I were you, I'd keep them well apart. For one reason, they won't be friendly to one another."

"And Hay, sir? Is there anything against him? I mean, do I detain him after tomorrow?"

"We want him as a witness. Beyond that, he's no concern of ours. We can't prove that he was actually a cognisant partner in Laxford's insurance swindle, though I suspect he was. Laxford might try to implicate him, but a jury would hardly take Laxford's word against Hay's, and that's all there is in it. It will pay us better to make sure of Hay giving evidence against Laxford."

"Very good, sir. If Mr Wendover will give me the warrant, I'll execute it at once."

Inspector Hinton's dream had vanished. The 'big case' had actually come within his reach, and he had failed to clear it up. With his eyes fixed on the will-o'-the-wisp of Laxford's guilt, he had let himself be led away from the real trail and had landed himself in a bog. Just what an ordinary bungler might have done. More bitter still, to a man of Hinton's temperament, was the realisation that the Chief Constable had shown himself to be the cleverer man. He had used the very evidence that Hinton himself had collected so laboriously, and he had known how to interpret it correctly. That was what stung the inspector as he stood waiting for Wendover to complete the formalities and hand over the warrant for Jim Brandon's arrest.

"Here's your warrant," Sir Clinton said. "Now, Inspector, it's for you to get up this case. I've only given you the outline of it, and I trust you to make it lock-fast. You've got a free hand. It's your case. And I shouldn't wonder but it'll make something of a splash when it comes into court. Good luck!"

Inspector Hinton was not the sort of man to show gratitude. The feeling that he had been outstripped was too rankling to fade out under a favour. He received his warrant with some rather ungracious words of thanks and took himself off.

"Not a very grateful type," Wendover commented when he had gone.

"Oh, there's nothing wrong with him," Sir Clinton declared. "Not so clever as he thinks he is, probably. And you know, Squire, it must have been a bit vexing for him when he found the case being handled over his head, so to speak. He's a bit uncouth, I admit; but he dug out the evidence wonderfully well, and his reports are first-class."

Wendover sat down again in his arm-chair.

"To be honest," he admitted, "I've no reason to crow, myself. I missed the main point, just like Hinton. Laxford was a fellow I never could manage to like, somehow. Still, I ought to have seen the truth when 'borough English' came into the affair. And your talk about wire-gauze should have put me on the scent. Tell me how you piece the thing together, Clinton. I know your methods, Watson; but I'd like to have it reconstructed as you see it."

"If I do that," Sir Clinton retorted, "I'll have to copy the Snark's treatment of the evidence when it

> . . . 'Summed it so well that it came to far more
> Than the Witnesses ever had said!'

There's a lot of guess-work in it that Hinton will have to find chapter and verse for, before he's ready for the Crown Prosecutor. Still, here it is as I see it."

He helped himself to a cigarette, lit it, and sat down before opening his exposition.

"Start with the affairs of the Brandon estate," he began. "By the custom of 'borough English,' young Brandon—still a minor —is the heir, since his father can't have any more children who might oust Johnnie. When Johnnie comes of age, there are two courses before him. He can either stand pat and wait for his father's death, in which case he comes into the rent-roll for life; or else he can agree to bar the entail and drive a bargain with his father which will lose them the estate but will bring in a fair amount of hard cash. The first course is the sound one from Johnnie's point of view; the second is the one that appeals to the Brandon family, naturally.

"Now the Brandon family made a very bad blunder when they took on Laxford as tutor to Johnnie. One admits the difficulty of their position and the old man's desire to do his best for the boy. Still, in choosing Laxford they made a hash of things. Laxford saw his chance. If he could get the boy under his influence, he would be able to sway him to take either of the courses open when Johnnie came of age. Which would pay Laxford best? The first one, obviously. Old Brandon couldn't live long at the best, and by sitting tight and waiting till he died, Johnnie would come into an unencumbered income of thousands a year. And that would be very convenient for Laxford, if he had gained an ascendancy over the boy. Further, he could recommend that course as being in the boy's own best interest, as indeed it was. Naturally, Laxford set about gaining an influence over his pupil. And when the Brandons discovered how great that influence was, they naturally got the wind up.

"Now we come to these insurance transactions. If Tom, Dick, or Harry insures his life, pays one premium, and then tries to raise money on the policy, the most he's likely to raise will be something less than the amount of the premium he's paid over. The policy, as a security, is worth only its surrender value; and if only a single premium has been paid, the surrender value is far less than the figure of the premium. But Johnnie Brandon wasn't Tom, Dick, or Harry. He had the expectation of coming into the Burling Thorn estate. So if anyone were approached and asked to lend money on Johnnie's insurance policy, they'd do it quick enough. If he died before coming into Burling Thorn, they could get their money back out of the policy payment; if he lived to inherit the estate, they could get repayment then easily enough. So Johnnie's insurance policy was quite a good security to back up any debts he incurred.

"Laxford's first attempt—to insure Johnnie in his wife's name —looks a pretty black business, if you assume that Laxford's plan was to murder the boy. But my own impression is that Laxford had no such notion. Most likely he intended to get some document out of Johnnie which would give Mrs Laxford a claim equivalent to the value of the insurance—something on the same lines as the assignment. That broke down, as you know from the insurance people's evidence. Laxford seems to have been too lazy to find out the legal position. He's like a lot of other criminals, very sharp on one side and a perfect bone-head in another direction. Then he tried a fresh line and got Johnnie to insure his own life and assign the policy to Mrs Laxford. Again he was too lazy to look up things beforehand, or he would have learned that Johnnie couldn't make a valid assignment till he came of age. Incidentally, to raise money for the first premium, he seems to have double-crossed the moneylender who was financing the Laxford ménage and got the money out of him by some cock-and-bull tale about buying Edgehill."

"He's a rank unscrupulous liar, on the face of it," Wendover interjected.

"Oh, quite," Sir Clinton agreed. "Well, he pays the premium, and then, somehow or other, he discovers that the boy can't make a valid assignment. If the boy dies before he comes of age, Laxford gets precisely nothing for his pains. And if the boy lives till he's twenty-one, Laxford has a shrewd idea that the rest of the Brandon family will make a violent effort to get their own way, as soon as it's possible to bar the entail. In the middle of a storm like that, it might be difficult to induce Johnnie to execute a legal assignment.

"So Laxford hits on a fresh plan, just as silly as the others he has tried already. He gets Hay down and dictates an *undated* assignment which Hay witnesses. The calculation probably was that, when Johnnie came of age, he could easily enough be induced to write the proper date on the paper—I mean the coming of age date. It could be represented as a mere formality; and Hay would be prepared to swear anything that was wanted about when the thing was signed.

"But that was only one of Hay's uses, as you know. To tighten his grip on the boy, Laxford had no scruples in using his wife; and it seems clear enough that the little game in the garden was staged to make Johnnie sign on the dotted line when he was asked to do so, even if the Brandons had begun to assert themselves.

"They came on the scene earlier than Laxford had expected. James Brandon turned up unexpectedly at Edgehill and nearly upset the apple-cart. However, they managed to pull off their little affair under his nose, after all; but unfortunately for everybody, James Brandon spotted the whole business.

"Now friend James's position was this. If the entail on the Burling Thorn estate was not barred, he got nothing. If the entail was barred by arrangement, he might get some small share in the plunder. But if Johnnie died before he was able to make a will or execute any legal instrument—why, James came into his own as next heir and could look forward to rolling in money as soon as his father died, an event which wouldn't keep him waiting long by the look of things. Friend James thinks more of money than most people, I should imagine; and that was an awkward set of alternatives to put before a man of his sort. You know what choice he finally made. It was the most natural one, considering his type of mind. Johnnie had had his chance, one must suppose; now it was friend James's turn. And what made it safer was this 'borough English' affair. It's so unusual, you see. Very few people would think of James as the next heir. If he'd shot his elder brother, people might have pricked up their ears. But a *younger* brother! Nothing in that to rouse the ordinary man's suspicions."

"Still, fratricide's a bit over the score," Wendover commented. "One would expect him to shrink from going that length."

"Why?" Sir Clinton retorted. "I didn't gather that he was fond of Johnnie to any marked extent. He showed no signs of it in any dealings I had with him. All that interested him was the money side, so far as I could see. Give him credit for not adding hypocrisy to his other misdeed, Squire. It's always something in his favour.

"To go on. He must have had the whole thing cut and dried before the morning of the shooting-party. He'd been over the ground the day before and had seen the he of the land. He pitched on the very place to suit his purposes. And that makes me think that he must have used that cut-cartridge game before, in ordinary shooting. His gun was a cylinder, and most likely he'd tried various dodges to reduce its scattering effect for sporting purposes. I don't think this can have been a mere first experiment in the method.

"Everything goes as he planned. He gets the beat he wants for his purpose. He shoots once or twice himself, to secure the empty cartridge case he needed. Then he conceals himself in the undergrowth at the bend in the Carron, waits till his brother comes along the ha-ha, and shoots him with the cut cartridge. The idea is, of course, to suggest a stumble and a gun-accident.

"Then comes the nerve-racking bit. He has to get hold of two things immediately: his brother's gun and the top part of the cartridge, if it hasn't fallen into the stream. He rushes round to the glade and naturally he has to play the part of a grief-stricken brother. I don't think anyone would envy his feelings as he knelt there; for he must have been in terror lest anyone picked up Johnnie's gun and found two live cartridges in the barrels. And yet he couldn't risk opening the breech himself amongst the crowd. Just imagine his state of mind when Dunne picked up the very thing he wanted to hide at any cost—the bit of the cartridge-case. He must have felt that the game was up, at that moment; for, of course, he'd feel sure that a single slip might give him away. And then, think of the wave of relief when Dunne pocketed that damning bit of evidence before anyone else paid any attention to it."

"Nasty minute or two for him, certainly," Wendover agreed unsympathetically. "And when he found that Dunne was a lunatic who wouldn't begin to think about the real use of the thing, he must have taken it as a direct intervention of Providence."

"Once he was out of that nasty corner," Sir Clinton went on, "the rest was child's play. He had only to pick up his brother's gun, lag a bit behind the others on the way to the house, take the live round out of Johnnie's gun and pocket it, replacing it by one of his own spent cartridges. And then he was clear. Nobody was likely to think of the trick of the cartridge-cutting. All he had to do was to give his evidence with a straight face and pretend that the whole affair was just an accident due to Johnnie's notoriously careless handling of firearms."

"He was on safe ground there," Wendover declared. "I could have gone into the box myself and sworn that the boy was a public danger with his gun."

"There's not much to amuse one in murder," Sir Clinton said with a slight change of tone, "but I can't help smiling at the way friend James's apple-cart was upset owing to Hinton picking up an entirely wrong trail. It's really funny."

"What do you mean by that?"

"Well, everything was going nicely for friend James, until the inspector failed to find any blood at the foot of the ha-ha. That started him in full cry after Laxford, on the ground that Laxford must have lied about the body being at the foot of the ha-ha. And so, in comes the word "MURDER" for the first time, and then a very rigorous investigation of the whole affair. And, all the time, Laxford's evidence was perfectly correct. It was just that affair of the bone blocking the vein that gave rise to all the trouble. But for that, friend James would have been in a happier position tonight."

He rose to his feet as he concluded his survey.

"Like the Snark, Squire, I own that I'm 'spent with the toils of the day.' I'm going to bed."

Wendover rose reluctantly from his chair.

"It's a bad business for the Brandons," he said regretfully. "One brother murdered and another one likely to be hanged."

"Oh, let's look on the bright side," Sir Clinton suggested, stifling a yawn. "Burling Thorn will fall into the hands of the only one of them who had the grit to work with a will for his living. That's always something in the way in a silver lining."

"The girl's got grit, too," Wendover mused. "It may give the family a start on a better road."

"A bit too late in the evening to start discussing eugenics, Squire. Good night."

Printed in Great Britain
by Amazon

82689858R00154